Praise for *Interlude*

"Mia's journey to save her sister threatened to break my heart, even as her relationship with Jax sought to mend it. Have a box of tissues ready. You won't want to miss this moving story of love and sacrifice."

—Kate Watson, author of *Seeking Mansfield*
and *Shoot the Moon*

"A heartfelt novel about the depth of a sister's love, the weight of choices, and the people who come into our lives and leave us forever changed."

—Katie A. Nelson, author of *The Duke of Bannerman Prep*

"A beautifully crafted tale of love, loss, and loyalty. Mia's feisty determination will quickly win over hearts, while the fast pace and surprise ending will keep readers turning the pages. *Interlude* is a pitch-perfect YA novel that will appeal to fans of John Green and Abbi Glines."

—Olivia Rivers, author of *Tone Deaf*

"Take one girl who will do anything to save her sick sister, add one rockstar on the run from his troubles, and one stormy family history, and you have Chantele Sedgwick's *Interlude*. Sweet, heartfelt, and full of music, it perfectly mixes family drama with a burgeoning romance and hits every note."

—Rebecca Christiansen, author of *Maybe in Paris*

"Throughout this complex adventure that starts off as a rescue and results in self-discovery, Mia must learn to trust in herself, her family, and new friends. Though the overlying theme of the story is relatively heavy, readers can connect through Mia's light-hearted narrative voice and relate to the tumbling emotions that the she feels throughout her journey. VERDICT This book, fitting into the same niche as John Green's *The Fault in Our Stars* and Jennifer Niven's *All the Bright Places*, will be a must-read for those fans."

—*School Library Journal*

"Swift, dialogue-driving pacing keeps pages turning . . . An emotionally satisfying read."

—*Kirkus Reviews*

"A sweet and innocent story, perfect for readers who love happy endings, especially when they seem out of reach."

—*Booklist*

Praise for *Switching Gears*

"An emotional tale of finding love after loss. *Switching Gears* boasts a cast of wonderfully flawed characters that grow their way into your heart."

—Kasie West, author of *The Fill-In Boyfriend* and *P.S. I Like You*

"Packed full of competitive spirit and restorative heart."
—Natalie Whipple, author of *House of Ivy & Sorrow* and *Transparent*

Praise for *Love, Lucas*

"Just as readers think they know how this story is going to end, a big plot twist changes the tale's course. . . . Fans of Sarah Dessen and realistic fiction with a poignant and sad slant will find this an enjoyable read."
—*School Library Journal*

"A deeply moving tale of unimaginable loss and the redemptive power of love. Sedgwick masterfully delves into the painful details of losing a loved one, breaking your heart even as her beautiful words stitch you back together. Romance and friendship, true growth and authentic healing, this story blew me away. It takes a special book to bring tears to my eyes *and* make me swoon."
—Rachel Harris, *New York Times* bestselling author of *The Fine Art of Pretending* and *The Natural History of Us*

"Chantele Sedgwick's *Love, Lucas,* is a beautiful story about finding hope, first loves, and learning to live again after the loss of a sibling. With a fantastic cast, and the gorgeous setting of the California coast, this book is one fabulous read."

"A beautiful, moving novel of loss and love. Sedgwick's elegant prose weave a heart-breaking tale that stays with you long after you have finished the last page."

"An emotional summer of love, hope, and healing! Love, Lucas is easy to adore with Sedgwick's real relationships, sweet romance, and tale of renewal."

"Chantele Sedgwick navigates the dark waters of grief with a deft hand and plenty of heart. *Love, Lucas* will drag readers under before bringing them back to the surface for a life-saving breath of hope."

THE
SUMMER OF
LOST THINGS

CHANTELE SEDGWICK

Sky Pony Press
New York

To Braeden
Who keeps fighting, even when the fight gets hard.

"Watch and pray, dear, never get tired of trying, and never think it is impossible to conquer your fault."
—Louisa May Alcott, *Little Women*

CHAPTER 1

*"Nothing is so painful to the human mind as a great
and sudden change."*
—Mary Shelley, *Frankenstein*

The second I step through the doorway to our new, yet old farmhouse, something in the air shifts. A thin wisp of dust rises from the hardwood floor, swirling around my feet for a moment before slowly settling back down. It's as if the house itself has been holding its breath, waiting for my arrival, and has exhaled in relief that it's no longer unoccupied.

I set the box I'm holding on the floor and take a step forward, staring up at the staircase in front of me. What was Mom thinking? We both knew this house was way too big for just the two of us. If Dad were here, he would have talked her into something smaller, more ... finished and updated. This place ... it's old and musty. It's not ... us.

Mom obviously thinks it is, though, and I shudder at the thought of the remodeling she's going to make me help with. She gets pretty ambitious when it comes to projects. Which, in my opinion, is not a good thing ninety percent of the time.

Someone comes through the door then, but I don't turn around. Just stare up the staircase, trying to make myself move. So much work. The walls in the living room to the left, for example, are covered in a hideous shade of yellow. I vowed when we were here a few weeks earlier getting Gran's funeral arrangements taken care of that I'd repaint them, stat. Only, the wall wasn't painted yellow. It's fuzzy. Yep. Fuzzy wallpaper. Like a baby chick.

"Why?" I whisper to myself, wondering what Gran was thinking when she put it up. It's the ugliest wallpaper I've ever seen, and I'm really not looking forward to tearing it down. Who knows what kinds of things are living in it. Since it's like a hundred years old now.

Even though this house and all that's in it belonged to my Gran, and my mom spent most of her teenage years here, I'm not afraid to say Gran had horrible taste.

I spy a picture of a creepy looking clown to my right.

Yep. Horrible. That clown gave me nightmares as a child, and I refuse to let it haunt me again. I walk over and take down the picture, trying not to look too closely at it, and turn it around before setting it on the floor. I lean it against the wall, though I wouldn't mind if it tipped over and shattered, honestly.

Gran always loved clowns. She said they made children happy. Like the one in the picture giving a balloon to a little kid. Clearly, she never saw *It*.

"Luce, could you . . . oh. That's a lot of dust," Mom says, setting two boxes next to mine. We watch the dust swirl and twirl before it settles like a blanket again.

"It's pretty bad, I have to agree," I say. "Maybe we need to fumigate this place?"

"Lucy," she says, shaking her head and rolling her eyes. "It's not *that* bad."

But it is. "It's only been a few weeks since we've been here and it's this dusty again? I think it's giving us a sign. It wants to be left alone."

She tucks her dark hair behind her ear. "It does not. This house is wonderful. Besides, your Grandma wanted to keep it in the family. None of my sisters wanted to move back here since they're settled in their own lives in different states. And since we're not in a stable situation and Dad isn't going to be here . . ." A pause.

Ever again, I want to say, but keep it to myself.

"I didn't really want to . . ." She sighs. "They gave me a really good deal on it. And I needed a good deal. We both did." She tugs on my braided hair, a sad smile on her face. "It will give us a chance to start over."

My phone dings and I glance at the text from my friend, Ashley King. My best friend I had to leave behind in Wyoming.

Ashley: Miss you already! You there yet? Call when you have a sec.

A pang of loneliness pricks my chest, but I ignore the text for now and slip my phone back in my pocket. "Still. We moved to the middle of nowhere."

Mom's mood changes in an instant, probably to try to make me feel better. "We did not! It will be so nice here. Just look at it." She glances around, trying to win me over

3

with her fake smile. Because it's totally fake. She doesn't want to be here just as much as I don't want to be here.

"I *am* looking at it."

I don't miss the tiny glare she sends, but then she has her smile pasted back on her face. "Isn't it gorgeous? Original wood floors, most of the furniture was already here, so we don't need to buy a lot of new." She touches a light fixture hanging on the wall and a knob falls off the bottom. She flinches and attempts to screw it back on but gives me a crooked smile before shoving it in her pocket. "It just needs a little love."

"Sure . . ." I gesture toward the yellow wallpaper. "How many baby chicks had to die to wallpaper this room?"

She rolls her eyes but looks at the wallpaper and cringes. "Okay, fine. Maybe it needs a *lot* of love. But just think about it: The beach is only an hour away. Oregon is full of hiking trails, waterfalls, beautiful trees. Pretty much anything nature-ish you'd want to see, you can. Perfect, if you ask me."

"I despise nature."

"Lucy, stop it."

"I'm just kidding." I try not to roll my eyes. "Why did they name this place Salem anyway? Are there witches here, too?"

She rolls her dark eyes. "Salem, Oregon, is a very nice and quiet city that has never dabbled in witch hunting." The corner of her mouth twitches, like she's holding back a laugh. "As far as I know anyway."

"Right . . ." The Salem Witch Trials actually fascinate me. They were a super sad part of history.

"Lucy," she says, shaking her head. "Come on, honey." She wraps an arm around me. "Think positive, okay? What happened to my positive girl?"

"She's in hiding," I mutter. "And I'm trying, okay?"

"Try harder."

"I will. I just miss home."

I hate that it's beautiful here. Because it is. I wasn't super attached to our old house, but I was attached to my old school and my friends. Moving out of state sucks. It's a strange feeling being in a place where I know absolutely no one. So unfamiliar, with no trace of our past anywhere. And Oregon? Who lives in Oregon? No one.

My phone dings again.

I ignore it. I know it's Ashley, but I have so much to do. Even though all I want to do is curl up in my new room and call her. Ashley's always been good at making me feel better.

"I miss home, too. But this is our new home now. And if you change your attitude, things will get better. Try. Please."

"I am! But it's hard when this whole house smells like old people. And dust." I don't really remember the house smelling so old. Maybe it's just because Gran was in a nursing home for the last year and a half of her life, so it took on a new smell. I remember smelling oranges here when our family would visit during the summers when I was younger. Citrus. Gran loved citrus.

We didn't visit often, since Gran would usually travel to see us instead. Mom wasn't a fan of traveling far. Or maybe she just didn't want to come back.

Yet, here we are.

"Hey, that's my mom you're talking about." She sniffs the air. "But, agreed." Mom glances around, taking in the ugly wallpaper and all. She always tries to be so brave around me, but her eyes well with unshed tears as she takes everything in. "I still can't believe she never changed anything. So many memories." She touches a painting of a horse and rider on the wall and runs her finger across the wooden frame.

I sigh as I grab her hand and decide to be nice, even though I really want to cry, too. She's overwhelmed, and I don't want to make things worse by having an emotional breakdown with her. I take in the dark circles under her eyes, the weight she's lost from so much sorrow and hurt. She needs to heal. And frankly, so do I. "That's what makes it so special. We'll make it our own somehow."

She gives my hand a squeeze. "We do need to change a few things. The outside shutters are falling apart, and I want to get rid of those hideous light fixtures."

"Those are the first things you mentioned? What about the baby chick wallpaper?" I remind her, chuckling.

"Yes. It's pretty bad, huh? I hope she won't mind us tearing that off to give it a new paint job. It really needs one."

"I'm sure she'd be happy with a change. Who would ever want to sit in that hideousness all day? I can't believe she did for all these years." I smile. "I didn't notice how ugly it was when I was little. But now that the house is yours, she'd want you to make it your own. I know it. Gran was like that. She loved making everyone else happy. So if it makes you happy, she'll be happy."

"I just don't want her ghost to move in and haunt us if we change something she didn't want changed."

I laugh, picturing Gran floating around with a grumpy look on her face and following Mom around the house. "Mom! She wouldn't haunt her daughter! I mean, if you deserved it I guess she could, but changing paint is not something she'll freak out about. I could see her haunting Aunt Mary more than you."

She chuckles, though I can tell it's a little forced. A smile is there, though, and that's all that matters. "I still can't believe all the dust. We should have taken better care of it. I just didn't have time." She rubs at her eyes. "There was just so much going on."

Don't I know it. Our home life has been a mess the past five years. All the fighting, the wondering when Dad was going to come home, or if he was even still alive when he'd disappear for days on end. Addiction is a horrible thing I'd never wish on anyone, but at least we know where he is now. Even if I'd rather not admit the fact that I now have a convicted felon for a father. I picture him sitting in prison and try to think of something else.

I grab her hand. "It's just lonely and needs a little love. Like us."

"We'll give it plenty of love." She sniffs and runs a finger under her eye, wiping a tear away before she thinks

I can see. "This place ..." Her expression darkens for a moment, but then she shakes her head and turns back to me with a fake smile on her face. "We'll get through this change together. Now, why don't you go upstairs and pick out a room and then come help me bring more stuff in. I should probably tell the movers where to put stuff."

"Okay." I grab my box and head up the stairs, wondering what memories Mom had been thinking of. By the look on her face, they weren't good ones.

There's a reason she didn't want to come back here. But being given a house that was paid off will make you do things you don't want to do. We can't afford much else right now, even with Mom's job.

Once I reach the top of the staircase, I turn and open the first door on the left.

Mom's old room.

I know she'll take the master bedroom at the end of the hall, so it feels right to take her old one.

As I open the door, I sigh. I knew I'd have to do a lot of redecorating in here but didn't realize how much until now. The only way to describe the room, besides the wooden floor and ceiling, is a pink flowery mess. The curtains are cream with dainty pink flowers, which match the two chairs and table covers and the pillows on the bed. The bedspread is fluffy and pink and sits perfectly made on an old bed with a wooden frame. Which is also covered in a thin coating of dust. The wallpaper plastered to the walls is full of little pink flowers, as well, and I fight the urge to rip it down at once.

It's the stuff of nightmares.

Like, the worst nightmare ever.

I wish someone would have taken care of her house. Updated it. Cleaned it. Everything was so neglected, and now we're stuck with all the repairs and remodeling.

There is one great thing about the room, though. One thing I don't have to change.

The bookshelves.

Four white ones all in a row covering an entire wall. There are a few books on the furthest one to the right. Mom's old ones. A few trinkets Grandpa brought from Puerto Rico when he immigrated to the United States. He gave them to Mom before he died, thought I wonder why she kept them here and didn't take them with her when she got married. Maybe Gran made her leave them here.

I set my box on the floor and turn to go get my books waiting in the truck outside.

Even if I feel lonelier than I've ever felt in my life, at least I have my books to keep me company.

CHAPTER 2

"Oh! I am delighted with the book! I should like to spend my whole life in reading it."
—Jane Austen, *Northanger Abbey*

It's been hours. Lugging all my stuff, especially the boxes of books, up the stairs took forever. Unpacking them took longer. Organizing them by author's last name took even longer. But now I sit on my newly furnished bed and stare at all the pretties, rubbing at my now aching arms.

Oh, how productive I feel. I pull out my phone and take a picture of my shelves and send them to Ashley. She appreciates books just as much as I do, and she'll adore these bookshelves. I send her a quick message telling her I'll call after dinner.

"Luce?" Mom pokes her head into the room and stares at the now full bookshelves. "Seriously? You organized your books before you unpacked your clothes?"

I roll my eyes. "Priorities, Mom. You know me better than that."

She gives me a small smile and shakes her head. "Dinner's almost ready."

"Okay."

She hovers in the doorway, watching. Anxious as she twists her hands together.

I smile at her. "I'll be down in a minute."

A nod and she leaves.

I sink to the floor and lean my head back against the bed. I know she's worried about me. About my moodiness. But right now? I don't really care.

I deal with things in my own way. And my own way right now is to keep busy and pretend my whole world hasn't been upended.

Truthfully, though, I think I'm just . . . numb.

I know bad things happen to good people, but why do they have to happen when you try to do everything right? We were the perfect family. Mom and Dad loved each other and they both loved me and we had everything. A home, friends, a happy life together. Why are things thrown into your life at the worst possible moment that end up ruining everything you've worked for?

With Dad, tiny things started his downfall. Then those tiny stupid choices spiraled out of control, and now he's gone, and Mom and I had to move to a whole different state to start over. We live in a house Mom didn't want to come back to, and now she's a single mother, trying to get by while raising me and, honestly, I have no idea who I even am anymore.

It's like someone picked me up and stuck me in the crappiest situation they could think of.

Not the crappiest, I guess. I know there are worse things. I do. I have Mom. I have my life. My friends are still there, even it they're far away. Things are just different. It's hard when people make bad choices and don't realize how much it will affect their families until it's too late.

I was happy. Comfortable. Now I'm the opposite. And I hate it.

All because of a stupid addiction that's not even mine.

Watching someone you love fight an addiction changes you. Even if it's just a small part of you. And not for the better. There's a piece of me missing that I know I'll be searching for the rest of my life. The piece unknowingly chipped away when Dad's life started to crumble.

When our lives unintentionally crumbled, as well.

Because of *his* choices.

I shake my head to refocus my thoughts and reach for the small pile of books on the bottom right of one of the bookshelves. I pick up an old copy of *Anne of Green Gables* that is shoved between the others and rub my fingers over the cover with a smile. It's worn and tattered from being read over and over.

Mom's old copy, it looks like, since her name is written in the righthand corner of the title page when I open it.

It was definitely loved. It looks like some of my favorite books.

Mom named me after Lucy Maud Montgomery, since she's her favorite author, so I feel like I have a special attachment to her and Anne. It's always fun seeing old pieces of Mom when she was a teenager. She obviously loved books, like I do, which I already knew since she has her own soon-to-be full bookshelves downstairs. Though, she didn't have quite the obsession as I do. I'd never leave my prized books alone for years like this.

I sigh and flip through the worn pages and stop when I reach a bookmark. It's actually a piece of folded paper. Setting down the book, I unfold the paper, which has yellowed from time, and read the inscription inside.

Ana and Susan's Summer Goals

1. Ride the horses at Kelly Stables
2. Go Swimming
3. Ice Cream at Joe's Ice Cream Emporium
4. Corn Dogs at 4th of July Celebration
5. Watch some fireworks on the 4th of July
6. Ride bikes over Cherry Creek Bridge
7. Climb a Tree
8. Find shapes in the clouds
9. Make homemade ice cream
10. Have a summer romance

A summer romance? With who? Dad? It couldn't be Dad. They met in college. I do wonder who it is, though . . .

All the items are crossed off. Even the romance one.

I read through it again. Did Mom really do the lame things on this list? It's interesting how different our lives are and what teenagers did for fun back then. I wonder if she was a teenager or a bit younger, actually. I may have to ask her about it.

I squint at the paper, noticing a number 11, but it's so light and looks like someone tried to erase it since black marks streak across the words. After several more seconds, I make them out.

Visit Susan's grave.

Susan's grave? As in, the Susan who wrote this list with Mom?

A chill settles over me and I swallow, hard.

What happened to this Susan?

"Lucy! Get down here before this gets cold!"

I jump, fold up the note, and stick it back in the book before setting it on my nightstand, then head downstairs for answers.

Mom sits at the dining room table and I cringe at the bright green walls. I'm not sure if they're better than the yellow living room walls or not. She drums her fingers on the table until I sit down.

"Gran sure liked her colors."

She ignores me. "May I pray now?" she asks.

I stare at the pan full of macaroni and cheese. Our easy go-to meal on busy nights. My stomach growls. "Sure. Sorry."

We fold our arms and close our eyes and she says a quick blessing on the food. When she's finished, she digs in, but I sit there, still wondering about that list. I pull the pan over to me and put a few scoops of noodles on my plate. I fill my glass up with milk and take a little sip, then set it down, grabbing a napkin to wipe off the few drops I accidentally dribbled on my pants.

"I would love to see you drink without spilling. Just once."

I chuckle. "Me too, actually."

She smiles and eats another bite of food. She seems like she's in a good mood, so I decide to ask her about the list in a round-about way.

"Mom, who's Susan?"

She stops chewing, her eyes wide. Then, just as quick, she shakes her head and swallows. "She's . . . uh . . . an old friend." She wipes her mouth with her napkin. "Where did you hear that name?"

I shrug. "I just saw it in one of your books upstairs."

"Oh. Well, I borrowed a book from her once. That's all."

"A book?"

"Yeah." She continues to eat but avoids my eyes. Instead, she pulls out her phone and stares at it before I call her out on having phones at the table.

"Mom. Phone."

She sighs. "I know. I thought it was ringing. Leave it to me to break my own rule about having phones at the table." She shoves it back in her pocket, gives me a small smile, and takes another bite.

She doesn't say anything else, which isn't like her. She's usually too chatty at dinner. Mom's never been one for secrets, but the uncomfortable look on her face when I said Susan's name is all the proof I need that something's weird and she doesn't want to talk about it.

I decide not to ask her about Susan again.

I don't mention her list either.

Maybe later.

CHAPTER 3

"You start a question, and it's like starting a stone. You sit quietly on the top of a hill; and away the stone goes, starting others . . ."
—Robert Louis Stevenson,
The Strange Case of Dr. Jekyll and Mr. Hyde

One good thing about Oregon is the weather. Even if we live in a place called Salem, it's not creepy. There isn't an ominous feeling of witchy-ness in the air. No. It's actually quite perfect. Not too hot, not too cold. And the air smells so clean. Which sort of reminds me of Wyoming, which is great, but makes me homesick.

Ashley's quiet on the other end of the phone, but I'm not really talking much either. It's not awkward, though. Being friends for three years makes things comfortable, yet sad that we're not together.

I hear her rummaging around on the other end of the line. "What are you doing?"

"Sorry, I tripped over some clothes and almost fell. I should probably clean my room."

"Sounds exciting. That's what I've been doing today."

She laughs. "You moved though. I haven't gone anywhere!"

"True."

"So, Dayson finally asked me out the other day. I posted a few pics online if you want to take a look."

"Really?" I smile. She's liked him forever and he's liked her. It was just a matter of time. "And I'll look when we get service. I can't use my data right now. Or you can just text them to me."

"Yeah, yeah. I know. I've been busy. Sorry."

"Did you already go on a date then?"

"Yeah. We went to a movie, though we didn't really watch most of it." She giggles, and I roll my eyes.

"Of course you didn't. I'm glad you finally went out, though."

"Right? He was so nervous when he asked me, too. Made him even cuter. Speaking of cute, have you met any cute boys?"

I swear that's all she cares about. "Ha. No. I haven't even left the house yet."

She laughs. "Just asking. You know you'll have to set me up with someone when I come visit."

"If I can find someone first," I say, rolling my eyes. "You know me."

She sighs. "Yes, unfortunately when it comes to guys, I do. It's so easy, though. All you have to do is say hi to one. Then fireworks, and bam. Date."

"Easy for you!"

"It was easy for you here!"

"That's because you were my wingman!"

She laughs. "True, true!"

"And why do you need me to set you up with someone when you're dating Dayson now?"

"I didn't say we were dating exclusively. We just went out. And kind of made out."

"Right." I roll my eyes again, glad she can't see me, then stare out into the trees as a breeze blows a few strands of my hair into my face.

Ashley says something to someone in the background, then groans. "Well, I'd better go. My parents are making me go to dinner with them."

"Making you?"

"You think I want to go sit through an entire dinner with just me and them? They'll probably be cuddling and making lovey dovey eyes at each other the whole time and I'll be the third wheel!"

I shudder. "Gross."

"Yeah. If you were here, you'd at least be with me and they'd behave themselves."

I laugh. "Well, have fun. Call me later."

"I will. Cheer up, okay? You'll make some friends. You'll be okay."

"I know. Thanks, Ash."

"You're welcome. Bye."

"Bye." I hang up and lean my head back, feeling a little better but worse at the same time.

As I sit on the rickety porch swing, hoping it doesn't break, I can't help but think of how boring this summer will be without Ashley here. There is absolutely nothing to do. I don't know anyone, besides Mom I guess, but I don't really want to hang out with her all summer, no offense to her, and school doesn't start for another two months. Not that I'm looking forward to *that* either.

Being the new kid at school? Ugh. Been there, done that. Don't want to do it again. Granted, I was only in fifth grade when we moved because of Dad's new job, but still. It's hard leaving people you already know and being thrown into a new school. There are expectations. Friends to make. You never know who to avoid, who to talk to.

I rub my hand over my face, exhausted already by my own thoughts.

Summer always seems to drag when there's nothing to do. Especially June. There's nothing to do in June. July at least has fireworks and things, and school starts in August, but June?

It's the boring summer month.

I twist my long dark braid around my finger and think of Mom's list I found yesterday. Maybe I should make my own list. One just for me. I'd make it a little more interesting, though.

Sudden hammering from inside the house jolts me out of my seat, and after I recover from the rapid thumping of my heart, I go inside.

"Luce?" Mom yells as I'm near the top of the staircase. "Where are you, honey?"

"Just heading to my room!"

She comes around the corner then, hammer in hand, and I peer down at her over the banister. "Where have you been?"

"On the porch talking to Ashley."

"Oh, good. Well, when you get a second, I picked out some paint samples at the store this morning. They're on the kitchen table. Have a look at them and we can start painting next week. I have a whole remodel/renovation schedule printed out, too. Since there's not much for you to do this summer, I'm gonna keep you busy, busy, busy." She gives me a thumbs up, which I don't give back, and disappears into the other room.

I groan, thinking of all the work we have to do here. Also, I didn't even hear her leave this morning to get said paint samples. She's an early riser, though, while I enjoy my sleep, like Dad.

Thinking of him makes my thoughts grow dark, so I shake my head and focus on the hammering again. Maybe helping her will take my mind off things. I walk downstairs and see Mom bent over a pile of wood in the kitchen.

"Do you need any help, Mom?"

She looks up, nails in her mouth. She takes them out and smiles. "No. Not right now. Later. Why don't you go outside and get some fresh air?"

"I just told you I was outside."

"Oh. Right. Well, maybe I can drive you into town later and we can look for applications for you to get a job. Then you can make some new friends before school starts. Earn a little money."

"Whatever you want, Mom." That's all I want to do. Get a job so I can't do anything fun over the summer. Sure, I'd like to make some money, but I'd like to actually settle in our new life first. I wonder why she wants me to work now? She's never mentioned it before. I've had babysitting jobs before and worked part time at the library when we lived in Wyoming, but I don't really know the area well yet.

I do wonder where the library is. Maybe they need a part-time person? I'd love to shelve books.

Mom starts hammering again, and honestly, I'm really not sure what she's working on, so I turn and head back upstairs to my room.

Anne of Green Gables is still sitting on my nightstand. I hurry over and flip it open, pulling the list from inside.

I study it. The curves of Mom's handwriting are so similar to mine, it's like I wrote it, though my handwriting is just a little bit loopier.

My eyes skim over her words and I make a decision. Making a list will save my sanity. I can maybe do a few things on her list, but I have no idea where anything is, since it's been, what? Twenty years or so since mom lived here? Probably more. I'm sure a lot has changed over the years, but she definitely knows more than I do about this place. I know where the gas station is and Walmart, but that's about it.

The biggest thing I'm curious about, though, is Susan. I'll definitely be figuring out why Mom won't talk about her. And what happened to her, since she helped write the list and then, I'm pretty sure, died. Mom was supposed to visit her grave and never crossed it off, it looks like. I wonder how she died? Was Mom involved? Is that why she won't talk about her?

Nothing like starting the summer off with a bit of a mystery.

I sit down on my bed a few minutes later, notebook and pencil in hand. My plan was jumping on the computer and typing out a list, but when I thought about it, I remembered it wasn't hooked up to the printer yet and I don't want to try to figure it out by myself.

So I'll do it the old-fashioned way.

I tap the pencil on my chin as I stare at the crisp clean paper, wondering what the heck I'm supposed to write down. Oregon is new to me and I'm not sure what I can even do alone. I'm not normally one for being spontaneous or . . . brave even. I like doing my own things. I like having a schedule. Repetition. Maybe it's time to change that. I need a little more adventure in my life. Anything to keep my mind off our new circumstances and the one person I'd rather forget.

Dad.

I smooth out the paper, even though it's not wrinkled in the least, and put pencil to page. I decided on a pencil just in case I need to erase.

I'd much rather use a pen.

Lucy's Summer Bucket List
1. Read twenty-five books.

I start easy, knowing it will be one I can actually complete. Reading is my jam.

2. Go swimming at the beach.

Tapping my pencil on my chin again, I frown. Boring. I need to make it challenging. Something worth doing. I've been to California's beaches before, so something a little more daring would be best. I need to do something crazy. But not too crazy.

2. Go swimming at the beach. At night.

I nod, liking that it's different, a bit daring and doable, since Mom said the beach is pretty close. I chuckle to myself. Swimming at night is daring? I'm such a wimp. I should put diving with sharks or something, but then I think of my cousin Oakley's fiancé, Carson, who lost a leg to a shark, and rethink that idea. I keep the beach thing, but no shark diving.

Thinking of Oakley, I pull out my phone and send her a text. We've always been close, besides the time right after her brother Lucas died. She had a really hard time with that and needed time to heal. Dad talked to her dad a lot, asking how she was for me, since they're brothers and all. After a month or so, she was doing a little better and finally started talking to me again. It's been a few days since I've heard from her, so she's probably wondering if we made it to Oregon. The text is short and sweet, a *We're all moved in to our new house, call me when you can* text.

She's busy with work during the day, and wedding planning at night, so I don't expect a text back immediately. I focus on my list again.

3. Learn a new skill.

I'm not sure what skill exactly, but it gives me some wiggle room. Cooking maybe? Painting? The scenery is beautiful here, but I've never picked up a paintbrush in my life. I can draw, and actually love it, but since Dad went to prison, I refuse to draw anymore. I don't want to be like him in any way. He's an artist and was planning on teaching me how to paint. I was really looking forward to it.

Not anymore.

Disappointment rises in my chest, and I fight the urge to get out my sketchbook. I really miss drawing.

I glance at the trusty old desk Mom helped me put together last night before she went to bed. It's pretty ugly, white paint peeling off, and I hate the fact that it takes up half of one wall, but the good thing? A ton of drawers. I couldn't sleep, so I ended up putting all my art supplies in my desk drawers instead of hiding them in a box in my closet. Which I think is a step in the right direction. I don't have any desire to draw right now, but maybe I'll have to urge to pick up that sketchbook again. Just knowing it's there gives me a bit of comfort. It's a piece of me I may be able to get back once I heal. Maybe.

Shaking my head at my train of thought, I focus on the next item.

4. Meet someone new.

A friend would be nice. Maybe. I don't know how to twist it into something more challenging, since it's already challenging enough, so I leave it alone. The ideas come easy now. Most are doable and safe. I like safe, since I'm not a huge thrill-seeker. If this were Ashley's list, it would look totally different. I smile at the thought, then write one just for her.

5. Do something crazy. Something I'd never normally do.

Perfect. With that number five, she'll be part of my summer, too. I keep writing, smiling at my challenges.

6. Find an awesome and challenging hike.

7. Try a new look. Dye my hair? Cut it? Something daring.

8. Attend an outdoor concert.

I adore music. Especially live bands.

I have no idea what else to write. I pull Mom's old list back out of the *Anne of Green Gables* book to get more ideas. I roll my eyes and write down the next one, since it will be a huge feat to actually have a chance at crossing it off.

9. Have a summer romance. (There must be kissing for it to count.)

Right. Pretty much a long shot, but I had to write something. The last one I already know. Mom's list helps with this one, too.

10. Find out who Susan is and visit her grave.

I set the pencil down and stare at my new list. They mostly seem doable, besides the summer romance, but hey, a girl can dream.

Since Mom had eleven things, I hesitate before I write one last item down, which I know will probably be next to impossible.

11. Forgive Dad

I don't know if it's possible. I don't know if I'm ready. The pain is too raw. I could write to him, but I have nothing good to say to him right now. So I ignore that item for now. It hurts to think about him. I try my best to forget I wrote it at all.

But I know it's there.

And I know it will keep bugging me until I actually do it.

CHAPTER 4

"My life is a perfect graveyard of buried hopes."
—L.M. Montgomery, *Anne of Green Gables*

After my list is written out, I open another box to unpack.
After putting all my clothes in my dresser and hanging up
my dresses and shirts in the closet, I decide I need to do
something unproductive to get my mind off things.

"I'm going for a walk!" I yell as I hurry down the stairs.
I have no idea where I'm going, but I need to get out of
the house for a while.

Clear my head.

"Wait, what?" Mom comes around the corner holding
a stack of papers. "Where are you going?"

"Just around."

She hesitates a moment, then nods slowly. "Okay. Don't
go far, though. You don't know your way around yet." She
glances out the window, looking worried.

"Mom, I'm not five. I think I can handle a little walk."
She looks up at me as she sits down on the couch, the baby
chick wallpaper surrounding her in all its glory. I try to
shield my eyes, but it's too bright. Too soul sucking.

"Still. New place, new people, new things that could get you into trouble."

I roll my eyes. "Seriously? Since when have I been a troublemaker?"

"You could turn into one at any time. I'm counting down the days until it happens."

"Right." I sigh as she sets the stack of papers down, tucks a pencil behind her ear, then starts typing something on her laptop. "I'm just going for a walk. I'm not going to get lost in the driveway."

She looks up again, the corner of her mouth twitching. "It's a pretty big driveway."

I chuckle and shake my head. "You're right. But I have my phone. I'll text you if I get lost between here and the mailbox."

"Good. Be careful," she says, her voice not too worried but serious just the same. "Please only be like ten minutes or so."

"Mom, you're the one who wanted me to get out and see the town. Get a job."

"I know, but getting a job is different. You go to the same place every day so I know where you are. Going for a 'walk,'" she says, while making air quotes with her fingers, "does not make me feel like you're safe."

"You said this place was safe."

"It is."

"Then stop worrying."

"I'm your mother. It's my most important job to worry about my almost rebel child."

"All this for going on a walk? Seriously, Mom . . ." I groan, shaking my head as I head toward the door. "Stop being weird."

She laughs behind me. "It's my job to be weird, too. But in all seriousness, be careful, okay? Seriously. Text me if you get lost."

I open the front door. "I will!" I yell, exasperated.

The cool misty air hits me when I walk outside and I breathe in. It smells so fresh. Not stuffy or full of pollution, but clean. Like the air itself has been scrubbed and infused with every scent nature has to offer.

I adore it.

It reminds me of home.

I've never lived in a big city, and I'm actually happy about it. I've always had a nice fenced-in backyard, grass, trees, flowers. Not a high-rise apartment. I've been very lucky to have an actual yard growing up.

I love walking, too. We used to go on walks a lot. And when the snow would get deep, Dad would dig a trench to get to the mailbox. He'd also snow blow the driveway and I'd use all that extra snow to build slides. We'd build snow forts and have snowball fights, too. I frown. I have no idea if it snows here.

So far, though, this place is nice enough.

I do miss the smell of cows, though. We lived by a farm in Wyoming and I could always smell it on the wind. What a thing to miss. The smell of cows.

But it was home.

I bet I'm the only person in the world that would miss that smell.

Birds are singing as I start down the driveway, trees covered in moss reaching toward the sky on both sides. There's an old beat up mailbox at the edge of the street, our house numbers barely visible from the old paint.

I may need to mention that to Mom. Also, I think the trees could be trimmed up a bit so they don't poke someone's eye out when they come to see us. If anyone ever comes to see us. I'm getting ahead of myself. No one even knows us here. And Mom has too many other projects to focus on for now.

Loneliness creeps in as I think of home again. Lots of green, lots of trees. The mountains.

I turn left. The thing about this place? There's a whole lot of land and houses that aren't stuck right next to each other. That also reminds me of Wyoming, though the trees are a bit different here and the sky isn't as blue. Probably because it's overcast today, but still.

A car drives by and the driver, an old lady with gray curly hair, waves. I smile, and awkwardly lift my hand a little in return, then trip over a rock for good measure.

Nice.

A shout brings me up short and I turn to see two people on horses, racing across the pasture next door. I didn't even know it was here, since the trees surrounding our house are so thick. There's a white fence around the property, with horses grazing here and there. Trees litter the backyard of the farm house in the distance, but the pasture is green, clean, and cut short for horses to graze in. I lean against the fence to watch the riders, wondering if Mom ever learned how to ride a horse.

"Hey, no fair!" the same voice yells. It belongs to a girl who races her horse toward the huge stable in the distance, tearing after the rider in the lead.

They're young, I think. Maybe close to my age. I wonder if we'll go to the same high school. I wonder if they have a big group of friends they hang out with every weekend.

How it would be to have friends here.

I can sit and tell myself how much I don't need friends, but I know it's a lie. I love people. I love being around them, talking to them, listening to them. People make me happy. Almost as much as books do.

I miss Ashley.

As I watch them race across the grass, I hear a whinny from my right. A black horse walks toward me and I stumble away from the fence, lose my balance, and land squarely on my butt.

"Thanks a lot," I mutter to the horse. I've never been calm around animals. Especially giant ones like horses. Horses are so unpredictable. Even when you're riding them, they could buck you off like you were nothing if they wanted to.

It whinnies again, nodding its head up and down, staring at me with its big brown eyes, like it's waiting for me to say something else. I stare back. He's really beautiful. All black, save for a white patch on his forehead and white patches around his hooves. And yes, he's a *he*. Even if I don't know a lot about horses, I do know how to tell *that*.

He's still watching me as he leans his head over the fence, nickering. "What?" I ask, standing. I pat the dirt off my pants and frown. "You think you're funny?"

He stares at me, waiting. Like he knows what I'm saying.

"You don't seem too mean . . . can I pet you?" I don't know why I'm talking to a horse, but it's not like I have anyone else to talk to. I take a step forward and slowly lift my hand. The horse doesn't move, so I reach forward, placing my hand on his nose. His skin is like velvet, soft and smooth as I run my hand down his skin, gentle and slow.

"I have no idea what your name is, but you're pretty sweet."

The horse shakes out his mane, then stills again, and I resume petting him. The white spot on his forehead kind of looks like a star. I like it.

"You're a good boy, aren't you? I'll bet you just run around and eat grass all day without a care in the world, huh?"

"Unfortunately, he probably won't answer."

I jump and back away from the fence as the horse whinnies again and paws the ground with his hoof. He moves toward the low voice that spoke.

A guy with dark hair stands a few feet away, on my side of the fence. I have no idea how I didn't hear him coming. He's like a ninja or something, though not dressed like one, that's for sure.

"What the . . ." I say as I stare at him. He's about my age, but about a foot taller, and he's wearing a cowboy hat, jeans, and a button-up shirt. His eyes are dark, with nice eyebrows and a strong jaw. His skin is tanned and he's pretty skinny, though I can see the outline of muscles in his arms without him even flexing. He looks like he works outside a lot.

Like, a lot.

I want to defend my horse speaking, but nothing comes out. I'm all pink cheeks, I'm sure. All I can do is stare and stand there super awkwardly, no clue what to say. Because I was just talking to the horse.

He heard me talking to the horse.

I want to run away now.

"Sorry," he says, reaching out to pet the horse. "Didn't mean to scare you." The corner of his mouth turns up like he's trying not to laugh at me. "This horse usually doesn't take well to new faces, yet he seems to like you."

It takes me a moment to calm my racing heart, and then I shoot him a smile as I reach out to pet the horse again. "You scared the heck out of me. Do you always sneak up on people when they're trying to have a conversation with someone?"

He looks at me like I'm insane. "You mean, do I make it a habit to eavesdrop on horse/human conversations?"

I fold my arms, challenging him with narrowed eyes. "Yes. You seem pretty good at it."

He looks slightly uncomfortable. "Well, no. But I am curious about something."

I wait. "What?"

"I just wanted to know if Sherlock talked back. Now *that* would be interesting."

I stare at him. Even if I unnerved him by pretty much chewing him out, he still stands there, watching me. I can tell he's on the shy side by the way he rubs his hands together, like he's nervous. He seems nice, though. I need nice. I don't answer his question. Instead, I change the subject. "Sherlock, huh? That's a nice name. Very bookish. I appreciate that."

"Books, huh?" He raises an eyebrow and cracks a bigger smile. "You like to read then?"

"Who doesn't?"

He chuckles. "I can think of a few people who don't. One, in particular."

I let out an exaggerated gasp and put a hand to my chest. "Who doesn't like reading? Don't tell me it's you or we may not be able to be friends."

The corner of his mouth twitches. "Maybe. I'd rather do something productive with my time."

My eyes widen, then I frown again. Oh, no he did not. "Reading is productive! Do you know how much information and stories are contained in books? You do go to school, right?"

"Of course I do." He raises an eyebrow at my outburst. "Do tell me why reading is productive, though. Besides studying for a test."

"You mean, you don't read for fun?"

He shrugs a shoulder. "Reading is work."

"I don't even know what to say to that."

"It's time consuming. I don't have a lot of time. So, argue for the sake of your books. Prove me wrong."

"Lot's of reasons. One, you're gaining knowledge. Two, you can learn so many things from reading. Different stories, characters, languages. You can learn how to do things like," I gesture toward his horse, "ride a horse, for example."

"I learned the old-fashioned way. Trial and error."

"Boring."

He laughs. "I'm kidding. My uncle taught me how to ride a horse when I was three."

"Three?" I stare at him, my mouth open. Then I realize what I'm doing and close it, shaking my head. "Anyway.

Books are one of the best creations on Earth. They're my very favorite things. You can escape into them. Leave the real annoying and horrible world behind for a while."

"The world isn't that bad."

I ignore that. "Books are magic. The stories, the smell of them, the feel of a new hardcover in my hands. It's ... magical. Like I said. They're magic." I know I probably have a goofy dreamy look on my face, but I don't care. They're my whole world.

He cringes. "The smell of them?"

"Don't tell me you've never smelled a book."

He chuckles. "Can't say that I have."

"Well, you're missing out then. They smell much better than a horse."

He laughs again and, as if on cue, Sherlock lifts his tail, leaving him a present on the ground. "I believe that."

The sound of hoofbeats come our way, and I glance up as the girl seated on a chestnut horse stops near Sherlock. Sherlock doesn't turn around or seem to care she's there.

The girl looks about my age, the one who was riding earlier, as does the guy still standing next to me. Her brown eyes appraise me and a smile graces her dark, pretty face.

"Seriously, I've been looking for you for ages," she says, giving the guy a strange look before eying me. "Am I interrupting something?"

I say no at the same time the guy says yes.

I clear my throat as his cheeks turn pink.

She raises an eyebrow as she glances from me to the cowboy. I reach out to pet Sherlock again, trying to break

37

the new weird tension. "Oh!" she says, surprised. "He likes you. Sherlock doesn't like anyone."

"That's what I said," the guy says.

"Well, he seems sweet." I stroke his nose again. "He's a very good listener."

She glances at the guy again as he lets out a snort at my comment then frowns at him. "So, am I supposed to just sit here, or are you gonna introduce us, Jack?"

Jack. A simple, nice, older name. Like mine.

Jack shrugs. "Not sure yet."

She turns back to me. I'm still petting the horse. "He's pretty picky with people. Usually stays far away from new faces."

I'm not sure if she's talking about Sherlock or Jack.

She slides off her horse. "I'm Mira. Mira Kelly. Jack's my cousin, if he hasn't already introduced himself."

She shoots him a look and he only shrugs again. "Looks like he hasn't." She rolls her eyes. "Boys."

"Hey! I was getting around to it," he says, but she ignores him.

"Jack and I work at the stables here, and we both live a few houses over. He lives across the street from me. Anyway. It's nice to meet you."

She holds out a hand and I shake it awkwardly.

"Nice to meet you, too."

"You're new, right? Just moved in? I saw your car and a moving van turn down your driveway yesterday. That's not a common sight since that house has been vacant for so long."

"Yeah, we're new. Well, I am. I just moved here with my mom, but it was her mom's, or, I guess my grandma's old house and she left it to us. My mom grew up here. It's . . . Nice, I guess."

"Your grandma? Oh, I adored your grandma. I knew her pretty well. She was a sweet lady."

This surprises me. "You knew her?"

"Yep. She was good friends with our Granny. And I've always loved that house," Mira says, her face thoughtful. "Beautiful on the outside at least."

"Yeah, I agree. My gran had some weird tastes."

"The yellow carpet on the walls?" She grins.

I laugh. "Baby chick wallpaper?"

She laughs as well. "It really is!"

"Besides the paint and wallpaper, though, it's nice. We're going to paint everything in the next few weeks. And do lots of other stuff. More than I want to do anyway. My mom's excited, which is normal. She likes challenges." I have no idea why I'm telling her this. But I can't make my mouth stop moving.

"Totally get it. You should have seen my house when we moved in a few years ago. It was a disaster." She glances at Jack, who studies me with a curious expression. "How old are you anyway?"

"Seventeen."

"Cool. So is Jack. That means you'll be in the same grade when school starts. I'll be a lowly junior." She glances at Jack. "You'd better be nice to her, with her being the new girl and all."

"Only if she's nice to me," he says, shooting me a sly smile.

I raise an eyebrow.

Mira turns her attention back to me, her long braids turning with her. "Only child then? Or do you have siblings?"

I shake my head. "Just me."

"Lucky." She lets out a sigh.

I smile. "I actually wish I had some. I've never loved being an only child. It gets a little boring sometimes."

"Well, sometimes it's good not to have siblings to worry about." She glances at Jack, who just shrugs. "If you get bored, you can hang out with us. If you want, I mean. I know what it's like to be a bit lonely. And we don't bite. Promise."

"Really? Jack seemed a little hostile when we first met." I give him a sly smile of my own.

Mira turns on her cousin. "What did you do to her exactly?"

He raises his hands in defense. "Nothing! She was talking to the horse and I accidentally caught her." He cocks his head to the side. "It was a pretty interesting conversation, though. In my opinion."

She smiles. "I apologize for you meeting him first. He's always been a bit awkward around the ladies."

"Mira," he starts, his ears turning pink.

She waves him away. "Seriously. He is."

I laugh at his expression. He looks embarrassed and furious at the same time.

"Jack's a good guy but not as fun as me."

He rolls his eyes at her before smiling at me. "Actually, I'm the funnest. Obviously."

"Funnest is not a word," Mira says. "How many times must we go over this?"

Jack rolls his eyes again. "Everyone says it."

"Doesn't matter. It sounds like you don't know how to speak proper English when you say it."

"I'd have to agree," I say, teasing.

He just shakes his head and kicks his toe into the dirt at his feet, muttering something that sounds suspiciously like *English professor wannabes* under his breath.

"I like you already," Mira says.

"Thanks," I say, my cheeks heating. I don't know why I'm embarrassed. She's just being nice. But she's a person. A real person who is having a real conversation with me. Maybe we can be friends.

"Well, I need to get back." She looks at Jack. "You coming?"

He shrugs. "Yeah. I'll be there in a sec."

Mira climbs back on her horse, but before she leaves, she looks at me again. "Do you want to hang out or something tomorrow? I have a few errands to run if you want to come with. Jack can even come along." She gives him the side eye. "I guess." She chuckles and shoots him a smile. He sighs and shakes his head. "What's your name, anyway? I totally should have asked you that first. Sorry about that."

"Oh, don't apologize. You're just fine. I'm Lucy. Lucy Nelson."

"Oh! My first dog was named Lucy. Nice name," Mira says.

I crack a smile at that and put a hand to my chest. "I feel so honored."

Jack chuckles. "Nice, Mira."

She just shrugs.

Jack meets my eyes then. "Lucy's a great name." He grins.

"Thanks, I think." I grin back.

Mira clears her throat and we both look up at her. "Well, I'll see you tomorrow then," she says, eyeing Jack again, a slight frown on her face. "Sometime in the morning alright for you?"

"Sounds great. It was nice to meet you, Mira."

"You too," she says, smiling. She turns her horse around and heads back across the field.

I watch her go, my mouth slightly open. "I don't know how people ride horses like that."

"Like what?"

"Like making them run with you on them. I'd be way back here lying in the dirt if that were me."

Jack chuckles. "It's not too bad. Once you learn how to properly ride a horse, it comes easy. Like riding a bike."

"Sure ..." I say, the sarcasm thick.

He stands there, awkwardly for a moment, then looks away. "Well, I'd better get back. My uncle's probably wondering where I am."

"Okay."

"It was nice to meet you, Lucy Nelson."

"You too, Jack ..." I have no idea what his last name is.

"Kelly."

42

My eyes widen. "As in, the *Newsies*, Jack Kelly?"

He laughs. "Smart girl. I'm obviously no Christian Bale, but yes. Jack Kelly. My Mom was obsessed with that show when she was young and decided to name me after her movie crush, since she married a Kelly and all. So here I am. Jack Kelly. Minus the newsie hat."

"No way! That's awesome! I'm named after my mom's favorite book's author, Lucy Maud Montgomery."

"So, it's official. We both have weird parents," he says.

"Yes, we do," I say, chuckling.

Jack shoves his hands in his pockets. "Well, uh . . . Anyway. I'll see you. Later. Sometime."

"You too," I say.

He pulls a hand out of his pocket, tips his hat at me, and walks toward the stables.

I watch him go and pet Sherlock again. They were both so nice. Maybe I really can make some new friends. And hopefully my summer won't be so boring after all. Maybe I can get them to help me with my list.

"Thanks for the chat, buddy. You're a great listener, you know that?"

Sherlock whinnies in response.

CHAPTER 5

"We must go on, because we can't turn back."
—Robert Louis Stevenson, *Treasure Island*

As soon as I through the door, Mom begs me to pick a house project before I do anything else. I decide on looking at paint samples and helping her pick what colors we want to paint each room.

"I'd like this blue for mine," I say, still shivering at the thought of my pink room. It's hideous, and I'll stand by that fact forever.

"You're getting rid of the pink?"

"Mom, it's pink wallpaper. I can't deal."

"But it's so cute! So girly!" She sees the look on my face and sighs. "Fine. I guess it's a little outdated."

"A little?" I smile at her tiny grin.

"Okay, fine. A lot. Sometimes it's hard to change things when you're used to them being the way they've always been. Even if it's ugly wallpaper."

"Yeah, I know." Changes make me think about Dad. About our new life without him. It's really hard. And strange. They've been divorced for about six months now, and he wasn't around much before that, but still. It's weird.

Weird that I won't see him like most divorced families where the kid gets shuffled from parent to parent. They don't let parents raise children in prison.

Which is a good thing.

I wonder if Mom will ever date again. If I'll get a step-family someday.

So many "ifs."

"I'll go pick up some blue paint tonight if you'd like," she says.

"Yes, I'd like that."

"Oh. I almost forgot. This came for you in the mail today." She hands me a letter.

"Who would be writing me letters already?"

She doesn't answer, just watches me as I take it. The familiar handwriting makes my stomach hurt. Dad's handwriting. "You should read it," she whispers.

I stare at it for a moment, so many emotions rushing through me. Panic, anger, frustration, sadness. The anger wins. There is no way I'm going to read this. "No."

I try to give it back to her, but she pats my hand instead. "He wrote to you. Not me. You. He's trying to fix things, honey. He still loves you. Whatever is in that letter is good, not bad."

I'm shaking my head before she even finishes. "Did he *try* to fix things before he went to prison? Did he *try* to work things out with you? Did he *try* to stop doing drugs? No. He didn't. That's why he is where he is and we're where we are. Alone." Since she won't take it, I drop the letter on the floor and fold my arms. I don't want anything to do with it. Not right now.

"People make mistakes, honey."

"Not that big. I can't name one person I know with a parent in prison. Not one. This is not a normal thing that happens to families. And it shouldn't have happened to ours."

"Every family has baggage. Sometimes you just can't see it because they hide it so well."

I shake my head. She doesn't understand. "It doesn't matter. It's not the same. Our baggage is like a freaking mountain for everyone to see."

"No one even knows around here."

"I'm sure someone does. And if they don't, they'll find out somehow."

"You shouldn't worry about that. No one will judge you for it. There are worse things, Lucy. You know that."

I laugh, but it's not funny at all. And I know there are worse things. What if I didn't have Mom? What if we were homeless? What if one of us had cancer? But still. This is huge, too. I should be grateful for so many things, but the anger keeps building and that's all I can see. At least for the moment. "Mom. Do you have any idea what people are like these days? People judge each other over what color socks they wear! That's how ridiculous people are!"

"Not everyone."

"Most. You post one thing on social media and people pick it apart. Even if it's a good thing!"

"Then stay off the computer."

"I do! Our computer's not even hooked up yet!" I have a few sites I normally visit but nothing excessive.

Mom picks the letter up and sets it on the table in front of me. "Please read it. It might help you heal."

I lean away from it. "I don't want to hear what he has to say. I don't want to have any part of him in my life. I'm done. I was done when he walked out our door and never came back."

"He's your father. He'll always be a part of you whether you like it or not."

My hands clench into fists. She's right, but I don't want to admit the fact. I can make him go away, though. I don't have to accept it. "He's a drug addict and a murderer. Why would I want any part of that?"

The pain on her face is raw and I take a deep breath, knowing the depth of her emotions are mirrored in my own expression. "It was an accident, Lucy," she whispers. "You know that. We've talked about this a thousand times. He didn't mean to do anything wrong. They were both just in the wrong place at the wrong time."

"It wouldn't have happened if he wouldn't have been on drugs. He'd still be here with us. Our family wouldn't be so broken!" I don't mean to yell, but it just comes out. My body is shaking and I'm breathing hard, trying to keep my emotions in check and failing. I fight the tears clouding my eyes. I've lost too many nights of sleep and wasted too many tears on him because of his mistakes. Not *my* mistakes. Not Mom's. Just *his*.

Not anymore.

She sighs and rubs the back of her neck. She doesn't berate me. Doesn't do anything. She's used to fixing things for people, being a certified life coach and all, but not today. Instead of lecturing me or making me share my feelings, she just stands there for a moment, taking measured breaths. Possibly to keep herself from crying. She doesn't like crying in front of me.

And I hate seeing her cry.

I feel bad I overreacted. Again. But it's so hard. I don't know how she can be so calm about this. He was her *husband*. How can she forgive him so easily? How can she forget all the things he did to us? To her? It's not fair and it doesn't make sense. He took her happiness away. I know she tries to put on a brave, happy face, but I still hear her crying at night. Though she'd never admit she does.

I would do anything to go back to the days when Dad would come home from work, drop everything and wrap me in a hug, then talk to me about friends, school, anything. To watch him hurry over and kiss his wife, asking about her day. To hear him tell everyone to jump in the car because he was taking us for ice cream. Just so we could talk and spend time together. Laugh together. He was a good dad.

Before.

"Mom . . ." I start, the guilt creeping in as I stare at her stiff, yet defeated posture.

"I'm sorry, I just—"

She shakes her head and clears her throat, cutting me off. "It doesn't matter. Did you have fun on your walk earlier? Where did you go? Not too far, right?"

I twitch at the change of subject, then relax, grateful we're talking about something else now. I can't focus on Dad very long. But we need to talk about it. I know that. I'm just too angry to do it without freaking out. "Yeah. I actually met a few people."

She raises an eyebrow. "Really?"

"Yeah. Two kids around my age. They seemed nice. They want to hang out tomorrow. Which is weird, since I just barely met them. But I'm kind of excited to go with them."

"I thought we were going to repaint the kitchen tomorrow?"

"Well, I can help with that, but I'd really like to make some friends, too, Mom."

"You can make friends with coworkers when you get a job."

"Mom. Sometimes coworkers are like sixty-year-old ladies. I have nothing against old ladies, but I'd like to have some friends my age. And they even go to my new school. We're just running a few errands around town. Nothing crazy."

"Well, if you'll be close, I guess it's okay. Just make sure you take your phone with you."

"Don't worry. I'll have it with me."

"So, what were their names? Where are they from?"

"The girl's named Mira Kelly. The boy is Jack Kelly. They're cousins, I guess."

Mom drops the paint sample she's holding and stares at me. "What?"

"They're . . . cousins?" I say slowly.

"No, the name. What was the name again?"

"Oh. Jack Kelly. Like the newsie." I smile. "Isn't that hilarious?" I still think it's funny.

She stares at me a moment, then picks up the paint sample again, seeming very interested in it. "Kelly, is it? From next door?"

"Yeah?" I frown. Why is she being so weird? "They have horses and stuff. A lot of land. A whole ranch or something it looks like. So, kind of next door? It's quite a walk."

"Not really a ranch. Kelly Stables. They've been there for years. They do rodeos, board horses, and teach horseback riding lessons. Stuff like that." She stares at the wall, her eyes misty.

"Mom, what's wrong? Are you okay?"

She doesn't answer for a moment, and just as I'm about to ask her again, she shakes her head. "Nothing." She forces a smile. "I'm fine. Really. Just . . . have fun tomorrow. And be careful. Don't do anything I wouldn't do and please don't be gone long. I really need your help around here." She grabs the paint samples I picked. "I'm going to go to the store to buy some paint. Can you make us some lunch?" She gives me a quick hug, then hurries into the other room, I assume to get ready.

Weird.

Maybe she knows the Kelly family? She did live here a long time ago. But why would she be weird about them now? Maybe they have something to do with the reason she didn't want to move back here? Or maybe they have something to do with Susan?

I drum my fingers on the table, frowning. I'm going to have to do some digging to find out what's going on. Because judging from her weird reaction, something is definitely going on.

A text message pulls me out of my thoughts. I glance at my phone and smile.

> Oakley: I'm so happy you made it to your new house! I can't wait to come see it. Have you gotten settled then? Does it need a lot of work? I need details!

> Me: Lots of work, but doable. I'll have to send you a pic of the wallpaper. It's hideous.

> Oakley: Can't wait! Also, a heads up. A wedding invitation should be on the way to your house. Watch for it. ☺

> Me: I'm so happy for you. I can't wait to see it! And you! It's been way too long. I still can't believe you're getting married. You're only a year older than I am! What??

> Oakley: It's pretty crazy. But when it's right, it's right! Right? lol

> Me: Of course. I can't wait to meet him.

> Oakley: Pics don't do him justice. IMO. I've gotta go, but we'll talk later, yes?

Me: Of course!

Oakley: You're doing okay, right, Lucy?

I hesitate. Am I doing okay? Not really. But I'm not about to tell her that.

Me: I'm fine.

Oakley: Lies. But I get it. Love you.

Me: Love you too.

I slide my phone back in my pocket, missing pretty much everything and everyone.

Instead of letting myself sulk, I focus on finding something to make for lunch. I pull some peanut butter and bread from the cupboard and grab some jam from the fridge. Hopefully Mom's okay with sandwiches, because I have no motivation to make anything else.

And who doesn't like peanut butter sandwiches? They're at least one constant thing in my life and have never let me down.

CHAPTER 6

"If you tell the truth you do not need a good memory!"
—Mark Twain, *The Adventures of Huckleberry Finn*

Mira and Jack show up ten minutes *before* eight the next morning. She didn't tell me it was going to be *early* morning errands. I could have used those last ten minutes to finish getting ready.

"Hey," I say as I come down the stairs, my hair thrown back in the fastest ponytail I've ever done. Mom's already talking to Mira near the door, and Jack stands quietly at the bottom of the stairs.

"Hey," Jack says. "Nice to see you again. Have any chats with Sherlock lately?"

"Maybe later for sure. What did I miss?"

He glances at Mira. "Your Mom and my cousin seem to be hitting it off."

"I don't know if that's a good or bad thing," I say.

He laughs.

I turn my attention to their conversation.

"I do know your family," Mom says. "We grew up together. I knew some of your uncles from school."

"Really?" Mira asks. "Did you know my dad?"

"Which one is your dad?"

"Brendan."

"He was a few years older than me, but yes, I remember him."

"Awesome! Maybe we could have some kind of reunion with everyone. I'm sure the family would love to see you."

"Maybe." Mom smiles, but it looks forced.

There's an awkward silence for a moment, and I feel like Mom's about to bolt, so I clear my throat. "So, you guys ready?"

"Yep," Mira says. She starts toward the door, and I glance back at Mom, who gives me a small grateful smile.

"Have fun," she says. "Be safe, Luce."

"I will."

"We'll take good care of her, Ms. Nelson!" Mira yells.

I catch a glance of Jack's face and he smiles but shakes his head at her.

He's quiet as we walk back to the car. He seems shy again. Maybe he is all the time.

He didn't have any trouble talking to me at the fence yesterday. Or making fun of me when I was talking to Sherlock.

I decide to pay attention to see if I can figure him out.

"Are you always early when you're picking up random strangers to show around town?" I ask as Mira leads me to her car.

"My mom always told me it's better to be early than late. And if I'm going to be late, it's better not to show up at all.

So, I'm always early. To school, church. Everything. Even when I'd really rather sleep in a bit more." She stretches her arms over her head. "So. Tired. I hate mornings, really."

"That's a good habit to have, though. Being early."

I notice the "Mom always *told* me" instead of "tells me." I wonder if she passed away or something. I'm too nervous to ask, though. I barely know her to ask her something so personal.

"If it were up to me, I'd still be asleep," Jack says. "It's Saturday. Weekends mean sleep."

Mira elbows him. "Don't listen to him. He's up at five every morning helping our uncle at the stables."

Jack doesn't deny it. Just smiles and shrugs.

"Impressive," I say. "I don't do mornings. Normally."

"Yet, here you are," he says.

I stop and look at him, wondering how to reply.

"Hop in," Mira says, startling us both as she climbs in the driver's seat of a little beat up silver car. I have no idea what kind of car it is, but I love it. It has personality with all its dents and dings.

"In the back, Jack!" Mira says.

I chuckle at the rhyme, but Mira doesn't seem to notice.

"Ladies get the front," she continues.

Jack shakes his head but doesn't argue. He just climbs in the back. I get in the passenger seat and buckle as she starts the car.

It's a little awkward. We barely know each other. I'm sure they're as curious about me as I am about them. The silence overwhelms the car as Mira pulls out of the driveway.

"I need to pick up some milk for my dad first, so the grocery store will be our first stop."

"Sounds great."

One thing I learn during our drive through town is that Mira never stops talking. She knows everything there is to know about everything and everyone. And I mean everything. "There's our high school. West Salem. We're kind of in our own little corner. There's Salem, and West Salem, which is still technically Salem, just west. I think it's weird. Why not just call it all Salem in the first place? Because it is." She shakes her head. "I don't know why they won't let me name cities. There would be none of this west and east nonsense."

"I have a feeling you'd do the world justice," I say.

She laughs. "Thanks."

I chuckle at her random thoughts. She's pretty funny, and it's nice to hang out with someone with a sense of humor. Jack, on the other hand, says nothing. He's quiet in the back seat, just listening. Or pondering. Or something. It's a bit unnerving.

"So," I say, when there's a long break in the conversation. I don't do well with awkward silences. "You two are cousins then?" I already know this, but I can't think of anything else to say.

Mira laughs. "Yep. Don't we look so much alike?"

"Like twins."

She laughs.

"But really. No. Nope. I wouldn't have ever guessed you're cousins."

"Obviously," she says, flipping her long braids over her shoulder.

"So, how are you related?"

"Our dads our brothers. They have a big family. Five boys and two girls."

"Oh. That would be nice."

"Meh. Sometimes. My dad met my mom at college. We lived in Nevada for a while, then after my mom died, Dad moved my brother and me back here. Back to his family."

"Older or younger brother?"

"Older." She frowns, then shakes her head. "But enough about him." She doesn't elaborate.

Interesting.

"I'm sorry about your mom."

She just shakes her head again. "Don't be sorry. It's been a long time. Almost four years. I was twelve. Everyone says I look like her. Besides my blue eyes. I got those from my dad. Older people always say I look like Vanessa Williams. Because of my eyes."

"Who?"

"She's an older singer. Close to my dad's age. And we do resemble each other, I guess. She's a superstar, so that's a plus. Maybe I can get a record deal too!"

I laugh at that.

Jack pipes in then. "She resembles Vanessa Williams, I guess, but I think she looks exactly like her mom."

Her mom must have been gorgeous. Her dark skin is flawless and such a rich brown. It's beautiful. And her hair is so long. I wish I could pull off braids like that. I want to ask how her mom died, but it doesn't feel right. I don't know her well, so I decide to ask her another day. Maybe when we know each other better.

"Jack's parents are nice. His mom always makes the best meals. We eat over there. A lot."

"She's pretty great," Jack says. "Dad works a lot, though. We don't see him often."

We at least have that in common. Besides the working part.

"Tell us about your family, Lucy. You live with just your mom?"

"Yep. Just me and Mom."

"She seems nice."

"She is. She can be a bit . . . eccentric, I guess. Depending on her moods."

"Well, if you look at your grandma's house, I wonder where she gets it from."

I nod. "True." It's quiet for a moment, so I break the silence again. "Your family seems really close."

She nods. "We are. There are a lot of us cousins, but Jack and I are the same age, so we usually hang out together."

"I have one cousin who's close to my age. She lives in California though and is studying marine biology. I haven't seen her in about two years." I pause, thinking of Oakley's texts yesterday. I didn't realize how much I missed her. "We were really close when we were younger. She's getting married in August, and we're going to drive down to be there for the wedding."

"That's cool. So, what about your dad? Where does he fit in?"

The question is innocent enough, but panic wells up in my chest. "My dad?" I try not to seem nervous, but my voice catches anyway.

She gives me a weird look. "Well, yeah. You have one, don't you? Is he out of the picture then? Since he obviously doesn't live with you."

"Yeah. Um . . . he . . ." I hesitate. What do I say? My mouth speaks faster than my brain works and it just comes tumbling out. "My dad died. A long time ago." The lie comes easy. I ignore the butterflies in my stomach and my conscience yelling at me, calling me a big fat liar.

I'm a big fat liar.

"Oh. I'm so sorry," Mira says. "What from?"

"Cancer," I blurt. "Osteosarcoma in his leg. Then it spread everywhere else. There was nothing they could do. It was really hard on all of us, but such is life. Life is hard."

I want to stop talking. I want to take it back.

"Cancer's rough," Mira says.

"Yeah. It is. It's the worst, really." I think of my cousin Lucas, who actually died of osteosarcoma. He'd be so disappointed in me right now for telling his true story as my dad's fake one.

"My mom died and so did your dad," Mira says. "Pretty crappy thing to have in common."

"Yeah. It is." Guilt fills me and I want to take everything back, but it's too late. I can't do it. Besides, who wants to tell a new friend her dad's in prison? And that's a big reason we moved here? To start over and get away from where everything started.

If we wouldn't have moved to Wyoming for Dad's new job, he never would have met his dealers. He never would have gotten way too stressed at work and turned to prescription pills to dull his senses. The changes came gradually after that. The no sleeping, the dark circles under his eyes and the way his hands shook when he needed more pills. When the pills weren't enough, he somehow found his way to heroin. He'd wear long sleeves in the summer and stay up all night, staring at the TV, but not really watching. He was still Dad, but he wasn't. Not really.

Mom tried everything to help him, but things just got worse. When we found out he was on meth, everything changed. He became paranoid and angry. Only caring about his next fix. Watching him spiral out of control was unbearable and eventually, our family was torn apart.

If we would have stayed in Idaho, we'd still be together.

I look out the window and let out a slow breath. If I told them the truth, they'd look at me like I was a freak. Or they'd pity me. I want no one's pity. So the lie sticks.

I feel sick.

"You've been to California before, then?" Mira says, gratefully changing the subject.

I nod. "Yep. We went to Disneyland a few years ago. We went to the beach for a few days, too."

"Have you seen our beaches yet?" Jack asks, making me jump. I forgot he was even back there.

Listening to everything.

The lie.

"No, not yet."

"We'll have to take you. And we'll have to take you cliff jumping, too. There are a bunch of spots in Oregon." His voice has an energy that hasn't been there before. He must really love cliff jumping. Or extreme sports.

"Cliff jumping?" My heart races. That sounds pretty dangerous. And exciting.

"Yeah! It's awesome. If you like thrills, I guess."

"I'd love to go." And I would. Deep down, though, I'm terrified of the prospect.

He laughs. "You don't sound too convinced."

I put a little pep into my voice. "I really would. It sounds crazy."

"It's an adrenaline rush, that's for sure. You have to be careful, sure, but—"

"Don't scare her already, Jack! Then she won't want to hang out with us," Mira says, turning onto a bridge. There's gorgeous blue water on both sides.

"What is this river called?" I ask.

"Willamette River. Beautiful, huh?"

It really is.

"Thanks for letting me come with you today. You have no idea how happy I am to actually be doing something."

Mira pats my hand. "You're welcome. I've been the new kid before. It's not easy. Or fun."

No, it's not. But hopefully things are starting to look up. Even if I just lied about my life.

But I don't know how to fix that without ruining everything I've already started.

So the lie sticks.

For now.

CHAPTER 7

"I have taken to living by my wits."
—Arthur Conan Doyle, *The Adventures of Sherlock Holmes*

"We should show Lucy the stables," Mira says. "What time do you have to get home?"

"Just before dinner. My mom likes to eat together. Family time." I shrug. I know I should actually be home sooner, since Mom really wants me to work on the house, but I don't want to leave just yet.

So, basically, I just lied again.

What is wrong with me?

"I like your mom," she says.

Ten minutes later, Mira pulls down the road before my house. I've seen the land the horses run around on but haven't been up close to the stables or barn, or whatever it is. We pass a house on the right. It resembles my house. Old, farmhouse, white paint, green shutters. It looks like the owners have done a lot of work to it, though. I think about some of the paint-chipped shutters dangling from our windows.

We have a lot of work to do.

"That's our grandma's place," Mira says. "She was good friends with your grandma, actually. They would have a glass of lemonade every Monday night and sit on the porch and chat. They'd always give us cookies." She frowns. "I really want some cookies now."

My stomach growls on cue. "Me too, actually."

"Jack makes some amazing chocolate chip cookies."

I glance back at him and he looks like he's sunk halfway into his seat. "You bake?"

"Sometimes." He doesn't say anything else, just looks embarrassed.

"Oh, don't be so modest, Jack." She leans closer to me, half whispering, "Seriously. They're like the best chocolate chip cookies I've ever had."

"Really," I say. "I'll have to try these famous cookies." I glance back at him and instead of continuing to look embarrassed, he smiles.

"Maybe."

"That house is Jack's," Mira says, gesturing toward the left. The house sits back in the trees, yet is still visible from the road. It's about the same size as the other one we passed.

"Mine's right across the street. She points to a pinkish house, then turns left into a parking lot. A building that says KELLY STABLES on the front stands tall ahead of us. The wood is painted a dark red and the doors to the stables are a shiny black. There's another building next to it on the right that looks exactly like the first one, then one on the other side of that, but it's a bit smaller and a faded brown.

"Wow," I say. "This is a nice place."

I get out of the car and look over the land to spot my own house across the field. Neighbors, but not right next door. If you want to walk an acre or two, or three, then sure.

"Welcome to Kelly Stables," Mira says. "Home of a whole lotta horses. People board there horses here, so we have a lot of stalls. Uncle Mike has a big staff and Jack and I work for him, too, along with a few friends and more cousins." She shrugs. "It's a family thing."

"You'll like it here," Jack says. "To me, it's home. Maybe you'll feel at home, as well. I mean, once you get to know the horses and things." His ears turn red and he looks away.

I smile at him. He gets embarrassed easy. "I do like animals. Unless they're trying to eat me."

"Do animals try to eat you often?"

I chuckle. "No. I try to avoid those kinds."

"Well, you've already met Sherlock, and he's one of our most spirited horses. You can have a chat with him later if you want."

"Looking forward to it."

"Me too, actually." He grins. "Anyway, most of the other horses are mellow compared to him."

"Good to know."

"Uncle Mike!" Mira yells, waving and running toward a man leaning against a fence watching some kids riding horses.

"You've gotta watch out for Mira. She'll come and go faster than you can blink. She has so much energy." Jack shakes his head. "I have no idea how she does it."

"I've noticed," I say with a laugh. "I like her."

"Most people do." He lifts a hand, hesitating a moment before setting it on my shoulder. "Shall we give you a tour?"

"I'd like that."

My cheeks heat as he drops his hand and leads me toward the barn, where Mira and her uncle are now headed.

It's not like Jack is the best-looking guy I've seen, but he's a quiet cute. A kind cute. He's not cocky or annoying like most of the boys I've gone out with. Not that I'm going to go out with Jack, I barely know him, but I like him. As a friend.

In Wyoming, I dated more outgoing guys. Because Ashley did. And she usually introduced me to them. When she'd want to hang out with a guy, she'd bring me along and always have a guy for me to hang out with, too. I did have fun, but it was draining sometimes, being with so many extroverts when I'm more of an introvert. I may not really know what kind of guy I like, now that I think about it.

Jack stops when we meet Mira. "Uncle Mike, this is Lucy Nelson. She just moved here."

He's tall. Quite handsome for someone who could be my dad's age. He resembles Jack, actually. There's a quiet kindness behind his eyes as he searches my face. "Lucy, is it?" He reaches out and takes my hand, giving it a shake.

"Yeah. Lucy Nelson." I cringe. He has an iron grip.

"Wait a second," he says, pausing mid-shake. "You're Ana's daughter."

"Yeah," I say slowly. "How did you know that?"

He's still staring, his mouth slightly open. "You look just like her." He must realize what he's doing because he closes his mouth and shakes his head. "Sorry. That was . . . sorry. I wasn't expecting to . . ." He clears his throat. "I knew your mom. A long time ago."

"Really?" I smile, excited to maybe here some stories from her past. She doesn't talk about her life here much. I'm not sure why. "How did you know her?"

"I knew her quite well in high school. And after." His expression surprises me. It's . . . sad. "How is she? I haven't seen her for years."

"She's doing well enough."

"Still married and happy?"

I shake my head. "No." I don't elaborate. I don't want to lie to him, too. I will if he asks what happened to my dad, but I pray he doesn't. "About the married part. She's happy, though. If you knew her, you know how happy she is. All the time." I chuckle. "It gets annoying sometimes when I'm in a bad mood." Especially when I'm in a bad mood and want to be left alone.

"Huh." He shakes his head, then drops my hand. "And yes, I do know that. She was like sunshine to anyone who knew her." He smiles. "Well, it's nice to meet you, Lucy. Tell you mom hello for me, okay? If you want."

"You too. And I will."

There's an awkward silence as he folds his arms, still staring at me, and then Mira laughs. "Well, this is interesting. We'll delve deeper into the mystery of you and Lucy's mom later, I suppose. But for now, we're gonna show Lucy the horses."

"Have fun," he says. Then he walks quickly away and disappears around the corner of the stable.

Mira leads us into the stable.

"That was weird," Jack says. "I've never seen Mike so … well, weird. I wonder how well he actually knew your mom. Did they date or something?"

"I have no idea," I say. "She's never mentioned a Mike. But she doesn't really talk about her childhood much. Just that she loved Oregon when she lived here. But when I ask her other questions, she barely gives me any information about it."

"Uncle Mike has never mentioned an Ana either …" Mira says, frowning. "He's never really dated anyone. Not that I know of, at least. He's just always been Uncle Mike without a Mrs."

The plot thickens. I need to do some digging. Ask her some questions. Maybe I can get Mira to ask her uncle some questions too. The way he looked at me, it was like he was seeing my mom. There was complete surprise, and some sadness, there. They have a history, I just know it.

"I think we have ourselves a mystery," Jack says, a gleam in his eye.

"Right?" I think of my summer list mystery, as well. Visit Susan's grave. I wonder if she's the reason Mom won't talk about her childhood. Something happened to her, obviously. But what? Maybe I'll ask Jack about her. Maybe I'll even show him my list.

What am I thinking? Of course I won't show him my list!

"Why are you two walking so slow?" Mira asks, hands on her hips. "Hurry up!" She turns, and Jack and I glance at one another before following.

The stables smell like hay and, obviously, horses. But a good, clean smell. Like the stables are well taken care of.

There are about twenty stalls inside, but only a handful of horses poke their heads over their stable doors.

"Ashton!" Mira shouts, spotting a boy around our age at the other end of the stable. He's taking a horse out to the pasture but stops when he sees her, a huge smile on his face.

"A friend of hers?" I ask Jack.

"More than a friend, I think. He likes her and she likes him, but they're both too stubborn to do anything about it."

"Huh."

I look around at the horses, which are staring at me as I walk by. I recognize the one I petted yesterday. Sherlock. He whinnies when I walk over to him. I hesitate only for a second before stroking his nose.

"You remember me, don't you, boy?" He nuzzles my hand.

"He still likes you," Jack says, appearing at my side.

"Not sure why," I say, as Sherlock shakes out his mane, forcing me to back up a bit.

"You're kind. And you have a calmness about you. Animals can sense when people are stressed out or scared."

"I'm not gonna lie. Horses do scare me. And I really don't feel calm at all. There's always something going on in my head."

71

"Me too." He lets out a breath. "Most horses are gentle. Be kind to them and they'll know you're a friend, not an enemy."

"I've never really been around animals. We had a cat once, but one day he decided he didn't want to be our cat anymore and we never saw him again."

Jack shivers. "I'm not a cat fan."

"Me either. I swear they're going to take over the world one day. They're so mischievous. And calculating."

He laughs, a real, deep laugh.

He has a nice laugh.

"Lucy, this is Ashton," Mira says, pulling the boy over to meet us. He's tall, though not as tall as Jack, and has light hair. He's handsome. *Very* handsome with blue, blue eyes.

He shakes my hand. "Nice to meet you."

"You too."

Mira puts her hand on his arm. "Ashton helps teach kids how to ride horses. He has a few classes. It's fun to watch, especially when the kids are being difficult."

He bumps her shoulder. "They're mostly pretty good."

"What about Emily?"

He groans. "Besides her."

"She has a crush on him. And it's hilarious!"

Ashton shakes his head. "She's six. And she calls me her boyfriend."

We all laugh.

I glance at my phone and check the time. It's nearly dinner time. "I'd better get going. My mom's going to be waiting."

"I can take you," Mira says.

"Oh, it's fine. I can walk. I like walking and it's not too far."

"I'll walk you back," Jack says, surprising everyone, especially me.

Mira raises an eyebrow at him but doesn't say anything.

"Oh, okay. Thanks." I give him a smile.

"We'll see you tomorrow then?" Mira asks.

"I hope so. I'll be around."

She jumps at me, wrapping me in a hug. "It was so nice to get to know you a little better. We're going to be great friends."

"I think we are." I hug her back and then she lets go.

"See you later," Ashton says.

"Bye."

Jack and I walk out the stable doors and start across the field toward my house. He has his hands in his pockets as he walks, his eyes cast down. I never thought I'd be friends with a cowboy. Even though Wyoming was pretty much full of them.

"Do you have any siblings?" I ask, breaking the silence. It's not awkward silence, but silence all the same.

"Two. Both married. One lives in Portland, the other in Seattle."

"You're the baby then."

"Yep. So, an only child right now, I guess." He smiles crookedly.

"I know how that is."

"You don't have a secret sibling that you haven't mentioned?"

"I wish, but no. I really am an only child. My mom almost died having me and the doctors told her if she had any more, she probably wouldn't make it past delivery. So, here I am. Just me. It's fine most of the time, but sometimes it gets lonely."

"I'll bet."

"That's why I read so many books. They're like my family."

He shakes his head, a grin on his face. "Books again."

"Books, always. There are books for everything. If you're feeling sad, there are happy ones. Lonely and need a good laugh? Funny ones. Angry and need to calm down? A nice fat fantasy to make you think or disappear from the world. Want to cry? There are sad ones. See? Something for everyone."

"All that emotion makes me twitch."

"Emotion is what makes a book stick. If you feel for the character and the words can pull you in so much that you feel what they're feeling? Gold, I tell you. My favorite books are the ones that either make me laugh out loud or cry."

"I believe you, but I'm still not convinced."

"I like a challenge. Truly." I glance at him and the corner of his mouth turns up into half a smile. "I will win you over with my book-loving self."

My eyes widen and I look away. Why do I keep talking? I always end up embarrassing myself. I'm sure he thinks I'm hitting on him now.

Nice, Lucy. Nice.

"Sorry. I'm being weird, aren't I." It's not a question. "I do like movies, too. Movies are second best."

"Me too," he says. I can hear the smile in his voice. "We should watch one together sometime."

I glance up at him. "I'd like that."

We continue in silence for a while. We're getting closer to my backyard, so I slow my walk a little. Jack's really easy to talk to when he wants to talk. He was so quiet most of the day, I wasn't sure he had it in him.

"Do you have any nieces and nephews?" I ask.

His expression brightens. "I have two nieces. Alexa and Britta. They are ..." He chuckles and shakes his head. "A handful. But they're so much fun. I love being an uncle. I wish I got to see them more, but my sister doesn't come down very often. The one in Seattle. Alexa's four and Britta's two. My other sister is pregnant right now and is having a boy, so that should be fun."

"That's awesome. I'd love to have nieces and nephews. That's one thing I'll never have."

He looks at me sympathetically. "You might have some when you get married."

"True. I never thought about that."

"If you marry someone who has siblings, they'll be your siblings, too."

"I hope so. I always wanted a big family. So did my mom." I shrug. "It's okay, though. We have each other. And I have a few cousins, as well, though I don't see them often."

"I wish I didn't see some of mine so often," he says, laughing.

I think of Mira. "Your life would be so boring without her."

"I know."

I keep talking. He's easy to talk to. "Do you have a lot of friends? Or do you hang out with your cousins mostly?"

"Mira has the friends. I have a few close ones. I'm more focused on other things, though. School. Horses."

"You're a senior. Like me. The rulers of the school."

"I guess." He pulls a leaf off a tree and spins the leaf in between his hands. "Which means I need to take a bunch of college classes this year and I need to start looking at colleges, too."

"Me too."

He bumps my shoulder, surprising me. "Think you'll survive your last year of high school at a new school?"

"Maybe. It's the worst year to move, I know. But we had to, so that's that."

"I hope you like it here."

"Me too. If I don't, at least I can go have a good chat with a certain horse when I'm bored. He's such a good listener."

"Sherlock usually just ignores everyone, so I'm glad you found someone to tell your deepest secrets to."

"As long as he doesn't talk back, I'll keep talking to him."

He laughs as I stop walking when we reach my yard. I clasp my hands together, nervous to say goodbye. Which is stupid. It's not like we're on a date or something.

"Well, thanks for walking me back," I say, wishing I had something else to say, but my mind is now blank.

"You're welcome." He hesitates. "I'll ... uh ... see you around?"

"I hope so." I smile, a blush creeping to my cheeks. *Why, Lucy? Why? Stop making things so weird!*

He shoots me another crooked smile before he turns and walks back the way he came.

I watch him go for a moment, then realize I'm staring at his really nice butt ... which I can't believe I didn't notice earlier. As I head inside, I wonder why I'm so drawn to him. My last boyfriend was so different.

We had met in History, and he was always so fun to talk to. He was on the loud, class-clown side of the spectrum, and I was shy, but we had the same weird sense of humor and he was friends with Ashley, too, so she helped things along. I think the reason I went out with him in the first place was because he was hilarious, though, not because of Ashley's coaxing. He liked the idea of me, but we didn't last long because he was too wild and I wasn't wild enough. He and his friends would ride shopping carts down a hill and get flung into a pond for fun. While I, of course, would stand by and watch, because, hello broken arm or broken neck! And who knows what was living in that pond. I'm surprised he didn't get a disease from the disgusting green water.

He also got dared to strip down to his socks and streak through the school one morning before the bell rang to go to class. Of course he did it. Then he was tackled to the ground by the assistant principal and suspended.

I, unfortunately, along with a hundred other students, saw the whole thing.

Idiot.

We had already broken up before that specific incident, though. Thank goodness.

If there's one thing I'm not good at, it's doing "scary" things. I'm a total wimp. But I'm okay with that. I know my boundaries and what I will and won't do. There's nothing wrong with that. It took me a long time to realize that fact.

But Jack doesn't seem like a wild kind of guy. He's clearly quiet. Doesn't show off at all. I already know he's a hard worker and he cares about school. He seems like a great friend. Really easy to talk to. And all this I know after only two days.

I hope I get to know him even better.

CHAPTER 8

"Ah, lips that say one thing, while the heart thinks another."
—Alexandre Dumas, *The Count of Monte Cristo*

Mom's sitting at the kitchen counter, waiting for me when I go inside. She's on her laptop, probably answering emails or something for work. "Um, where have you been?"

"Sorry. We got carried away talking and I lost track of time. We were just over at the stables."

"Oh." She's thoughtful for a moment. "Did you have fun?"

"I did. They're really nice." I gesture at her computer. "Printer hooked up yet? Wi-Fi on?"

"Yep. A guy came today and set it all up. Now you can be a normal teenager again and stare at your phone all day while ignoring the world."

I roll my eyes. "You're just as bad as I am."

"Right."

I pull out my phone. "No, truth." I smile at her annoyed expression. "Username and password?"

"Same as always."

"Good." I type the information in and smile. Back in the real world.

"Thanks, Mom."

"You're welcome."

I scroll through a few social media feeds, seeing Ashley smiling with her date, Dayson, in several photos, our group of friends hanging out at her house in another. They look like they normally do. Happy, having fun. In one picture, Ashley has her arm around two girls from our group, Breanne and Michelle. The caption at the bottom says "I love my besties." I put my phone away, my mood not as bright.

"I'm going upstairs," I say, wondering what Ashley is doing right now. Something fun I'm sure. I frown. Probably hanging out with her *besties*.

Mom looks at her laptop for a second, then shuts it and focuses on me. "Hang on. Where did you go today? Was it just you three?"

"Yeah. I met a few other people, but most of the time it was just us three." I shrug. "And we went everywhere, I think. They showed me where the high school was, the library, we went to a few stores. We went across the bridge that goes over Willamette River and then came back. Really pretty over there. They do fireworks on the Fourth of July at the Riverfront City Park. I'd like to go to that."

Mom's eyes light up. "Oh, that would be fun! We should make it a girls' night! They always have fun activities on the Fourth around here. We haven't had a girls' night in forever."

I stare at her, not really wanting to crush her dreams of a girls' night, but I really don't want to hang out with my mom on the Fourth of July. I'd like to maybe hang out with my new friends. I sigh and nod anyway. "Yeah, that does sound fun. I love fireworks." Maybe they'll have a live band. I could cross that off my list. "So, what do we need to work on today?"

She sets her laptop next to her. "Oh, everything. I've had lots of client emails I've had to answer and catch up on, so it's been a work-in-pajamas kind of day. I really need to get started on the house. If you would have been here when you said you were going to be here, we could have gotten more done." She shoots me a glare.

"Sorry. Again."

"Lucy, I'm glad you've found some friends, but I still need you around here, okay? And I don't want you running off and not telling me where you're going."

"Okay."

She sighs. "Look. Why don't you start taking down the wallpaper in your room?"

"Sounds exciting." I smile, making sure she knows I'm joking.

"Hey, working isn't supposed to be fun all the time. At least start on it. I got paint for the bathroom down here, so I'll start on that."

"Do you have a spray bottle?"

She points to a box on the counter. "You may want a wet rag, too, just to soak the wallpaper so it comes off easier."

"Wallpaper's the worst, Mom. Ugh."

"It'll be good for you to work. And while the wallpaper is soaking, take out the stuff you don't want in your room, like all the pink that you love so much," she grins. "Then we can get new window coverings, fix up those bookshelves, whatever, this weekend maybe. You can take those baby ballet pictures off the walls too."

"Yeah . . . already done that. Almost the first thing I did, actually."

She rolls her eyes. "Of course you did."

"Hey, I'm seventeen. Not seven."

"Noted. Oh, and dinner will be ready in about an hour. I was a little late getting things in the slowcooker."

"Sounds good. Thanks, Mom." I head upstairs, spray bottle and wet rag in hand.

As soon as I open the door, I freeze, my fingers wrapped around the doorknob. My stomach drops and I let out the breath I'm holding.

Dad's letter.

It's sitting on my desk.

That's why she wanted me to come upstairs.

It's interesting what a simple piece of paper can do to your brain. Even without reading it, a simple letter causes so many emotions to stir. This time, though, it's anger that presents itself. As it does whenever I think of him lately.

I storm over to the desk, grab the letter, open my desk drawer, and shove it inside, then hesitate. There's another letter in there. It's addressed to me in flowing handwriting and has been there for months. I can barely look at it; it's from the family of the daughter whose life Dad took. Hers and her new husband's.

Alexis and Kevin Walker.

I'll never forget those names.

Mom got a letter from Alexis's mother too and said it was worth a read, but I can't bring myself to read it. I don't know why I keep it, knowing I'll only read words of hurt, sorrow, and blame for ruining her family's life. I can't handle it. I can't think about it. My eyes well with tears and I slam the drawer shut.

I'm sure the slam could be heard downstairs. I don't hear Mom at all, though, and don't want to confront her about Dad's letter right now. All I want is to be left alone. No more letters. I swallow. No more lies either. Especially coming from my own mouth.

I still can't believe I did that. Lied to Jack and Mira and told them Dad had died. I guess I panicked, but still. What was I thinking? Which brings me to the reason I lied in the first place.

Him.

If he would have cleaned up his life, I wouldn't have had to lie about him. If he would have cared about his family more than his drugs, he'd be here now, teaching me how to paint, looking at my drawings. Loving me.

We did so much together. He'd come to my art shows when I was in middle school, take me to grab a burger when I'd have bad days and Mom was working. Then once day he stopped coming to my shows. Stopped taking me to do things. Started yelling and snapping over the tiniest things. He finally just stopped caring. He didn't want me anymore. He didn't care about anything but himself.

So why doesn't anyone get it? Why can't Mom leave me alone about it? I don't want to know how he's doing. I don't want to know what he has to say. I don't want to read his letter.

I. Don't. Care.

Because he doesn't care about me.

Still stewing, I pull out my summer list and study it instead, trying to block out the negative emotions fighting to get out.

Meet someone new.

I think of my new friends. Hoping they won't ditch me because I'm weird or awkward. Because they could, once they really get to know me. I try to think positively though and smile as I put pencil to paper and draw a line over the words. Besides, it's always so satisfying crossing things off a list.

I scan the rest, wondering what things I can work on next. Maybe learn a new skill? Or look for challenging hikes? I'm sure there are a lot in this area.

I loved hiking in Wyoming. Ashley and I went all the time with our group of friends. When Dad was normal, we went as a family a lot and took picnics with us. The more challenging the hike, the better. It was always so fulfilling when we'd reach the waterfall or the top of the hill and see what we'd accomplished.

There's Dad creeping in again.

I put the list down and settle on reading instead to take my mind off things. Working on reading twenty-five books is doable at the moment. I pick up my copy of *Jane Eyre*. It's a little thick, but like that will deter me. I can get through it in a day or two. I set it on the bed and look around my room, wondering if I should get started on reorganizing and making things better. Like I just told Mom I'd do.

My eyes fall on the pink window coverings. I walk over and start taking them down, just to make Mom happy. And me, as well. They're hideous. Not as bad as the yellow wallpaper downstairs, though. Nothing will ever top that monstrosity.

The room is brighter once I'm finished, since the sunlight can actually shine through from outside and light up the room. Satisfied, I grab the spray bottle and start on the pink wallpaper.

Hopefully it will distract me for a while.

CHAPTER 9

"But remember that the pain of parting from friends will be felt by everybody at times, whatever be their education or state. Know your own happiness. You want nothing but patience; or give it a more fascinating name: call it hope."
—Jane Austen, *Sense and Sensibility*

Sundays are always good for my soul. I wake up to church music floating upstairs from the living room and a peace fills my heart as I slide out of bed.

I thought a lot about things last night when I couldn't sleep and ended up staring at the ceiling for hours. I'm tired of feeling this way. I need to let my anger go. I need to tell Jack and Mira the truth. There are worse things than having a dad in prison. I still have so many things to be thankful for. It may take a while, but I'm determined to let this go. I don't want to keep feeling like I did last night. So angry.

I kneel down next to my bed and say my morning prayers. Once I'm done, I put on my slippers and go downstairs for some breakfast. I can smell . . . waffles, maybe?

My arms hurt from ripping off wallpaper and rubbing the glue off the wall with the rag last night. Hopefully we can paint tomorrow. I roll my shoulders and stretch out my muscles as I reach the bottom of the stairs.

Mom's already in a dress and ready for church when I reach the kitchen. She's humming along with a beautiful hymn as she sets pancakes out on the table for me.

"What's this for?" I ask, pulling up a seat and sitting at the counter.

Mom's not really one to make a hot breakfast.

"It's a new day and we're gonna make the best of it." She pushes the bottle of maple syrup toward me and I pour it on my pancakes.

"Thanks, Mom," I say between bites. "You're the best."

"I know." She grins and puts a few dishes in the dishwasher. "Church starts at eleven, so hurry up and get ready."

I look at the clock. "It's only nine."

"Exactly."

"Mom, you take way longer than me to get ready. You know this."

"Lies," she says. Then she shrugs. "Yeah, you're probably right."

She's wearing a long dress covered in bright colors and flowers. Her hair is up on her head in a cute bun. She even has makeup on; since the divorce, she hasn't really worn any. "Mom, you look really nice today."

"Thanks," she says. "Now, go get ready."

I groan and slide off my chair, but I smile at how happy Mom seems. She's always pretending to be happy, but she looks genuinely happy today. She does love going to church, though. That may be why.

Our first week at church is actually quite nice. Everyone is so kind and welcoming. After the first hour of services is over and the speakers have returned to their seats, we sing a hymn before the closing prayer. I glance around, surprised to see Jack at the back of the congregation, sitting by the door of the chapel. He meets my eyes and smiles. I smile back.

I had no idea he went to our church. That makes me happy. I see Mira, as well, right next to him. As usual. I wish Oakley lived closer. I miss having my cousin with me all the time.

After the prayer, everyone starts going to their Sunday School classes. A group of people are gathered around Mom talking, telling her how happy they are to see her again. A lot of them know her from when she was a teenager.

At first, it looks like she's totally fine and happy to see people. But when I get a closer look, I can see she's shaking.

I make my way through the crowd toward her. "Mom?" I ask, touching her shoulder. "You okay?"

The crowd then swarms me, telling me how much I look like Mom and asking why we moved back to Oregon, where's Mom's husband, etc. I spot Jack coming toward me with what looks like his parents, Mira, and two other men. One of them is their Uncle Mike. Mom glances over at the same time I do and freezes.

Mike looks up, meets Mom's eyes, and stops in his tracks.

Mom's hand wraps around my arm and she pulls me out of the pew and down the aisle. "You ready?" she asks, her smile tight. "I think we're gonna head home. It's been a long morning."

"We're not going to class?"

"No. Is that okay?"

"Uh . . . yeah, I guess." I wanted to go talk to Jack and Mira, but she's pretty much pushing me toward the door.

I give him and Mira a shrug of my shoulders and wave. They wave back.

Mike's still staring at Mom.

Mom's still freaking out and opens the door to go outside to the parking lot. She pulls me along with her, her hand digging into my arm, and we get to the car. Once we're inside, she pulls out of the parking lot faster than she probably should have.

She's breathing hard, sweat pooled on her forehead.

"Are you okay?" I ask.

She jerks when I speak, like I've scared her.

"I'm fine. I just . . . need to go home."

I stare at her, her knuckles turning white as she grips the steering wheel. Is she having a panic attack? "Are you sure you're—"

"I'm fine," she snaps.

She doesn't apologize or even look at me. Just drives, her hands still clenched tight around the steering wheel.

I sit back in my seat and wait out the silence of our drive home.

I don't ask her if she's okay again.

CHAPTER 10

"A wonderful fact to reflect upon, that every human creature is constituted to be that profound secret and mystery to every other."
—Charles Dickens, *A Tale of Two Cities*

The doorbell rings bright and early the next morning. I'm in my room, dressed in old paint clothes with the furniture all pulled the center of the floor. Books are scattered all over my bed and floor. The wooden floor isn't covered with plastic or anything since Mom wants to replace it or restore it or something, but basically the room's a disaster.

Mom and I have been painting for an hour already, since I woke up early after having a really restless night. Three walls are covered in one coat of light blue paint so far. We'll have to do a few more coats to make it look nice.

The no-sleep thing was rough. I couldn't stop thinking about Mom's freak-out at church. When she saw Mike ... He told me he knew her, but how well? They acted like they were seeing ghosts or something. I'm wondering if they dated. Yes, that's the only logical explanation. They dated and had a bad breakup or something. Maybe? Why would she still be weird around him after all this time, though? They both have different lives now. Wouldn't they be regular, mature adults about things now? I'm afraid to ask her, seeing how she reacted yesterday. I'll have to wait for the right time. Whenever that may be.

"Luce, it's for you!"

Mom's voice echoes from the front door. We haven't really talked this morning. She hasn't been ignoring me or anything, but she's been quieter than normal. At least she let me turn some music on to drown out the silence.

I turn my music off and go downstairs, aware of the paint smudges on my arms and possibly on my face.

Mira's standing in the entryway, chatting away with Mom. I glance around but don't see Jack. Part of me is a tiny bit disappointed. I liked walking home with him on Saturday. And I really wanted to talk to him yesterday.

If Mom wouldn't have freaked out.

"Thanks for taking Lucy around on Saturday. She needs a good friend. We left Wyoming pretty quick, and—"

"Mom . . ." I say, interrupting her. Partly because I want her to stop making friends with my friend and partly because I don't want her to mention anything about Dad. If she does, Mira will know I lied to her.

"What?" she asks. "It's lonely moving to a new place where you don't know anyone." She gives me a small smile to make me feel better, but I can see she's just as lonely as I am.

How did I not notice before? Of course she's lonely. She lost Dad to drugs and Gran died right after. She's probably hurting more than I am, and I've been so angry about everything and haven't made it easy for her.

Like she's told me so many times: there are worse things. I need to stop being so angry.

"You okay?" Mom asks, her expression filled with concern.

"Yeah." I frown at her. "Are you?"

"I'm fine."

She has speckles of blue paint in her hair. I probably do, too. "Okay." I turn toward Mira. "What's up?"

"I thought you'd like to come shopping with me. Jack never comes with me, and I don't have a sister, so it gets boring by myself."

"Sure. Let me change my clothes and grab my shoes." I glance at Mom. "Can I go?"

She hesitates a moment. I can see the way she's conflicted about me leaving again, but finally she nods. "Don't be gone long."

"Okay!" I run upstairs, change my clothes and slip on my shoes, then take a quick look in the mirror.

Ugh.

I wash a few dots of paint off my face and arms, comb through my ratted hair, and dab some concealer on my face to cover the small forest of zits that popped up on my chin overnight. I put a little mascara on, as well.

After pulling my hair into a ponytail, I hurry downstairs.

"Ready," I say, slinging my purse over my shoulder and sticking my phone inside.

"Great! See you, Mrs. N.!"

I laugh at that. "Bye, Mom!"

"Bye. Text me."

"Yeah, yeah," I mutter as I shut the door.

Once we're in Mira's car, I let out a breath. "Thanks for saving me from boredom today."

"No problem. I figured you didn't have anything to do. Besides work on your house, I guess."

"Nope. No plans at all. Ever, actually. I do need to help her out more, but she knows how to do everything and I don't. She's a pretty good handy-woman. I'm not."

"I wish I could just build things out of scratch. I tried to build a birdhouse once, but it looked more like a bro-ken-down cabin in the woods instead. The birds left it alone." She frowns. "The spiders didn't, though."

I make a face. Not a fan of spiders. "Did you burn it to the ground?"

"Of course."

"A girl after my own heart."

We both laugh.

Mira adjusts her rearview mirror a little, then focuses on the road again. I glance out the window, smiling at the cute houses and trees lining the roads. This really is a charming city.

"I saw you at church yesterday," Mira starts. "But everything was so crazy that I didn't get a chance to talk to you. Why didn't you come to class?"

"I don't know. My mom wanted to leave after sacrament meeting. She wasn't feeling very good for some reason."

"Next week then."

"Of course."

It feels good to have someone to talk to who isn't related to me. Not that I don't love talking to Mom, but sometimes you just need someone else who will listen. I know I could call Ashley, but it's different talking on a phone rather than in person.

"Glad I could help then. Just curious, what were you planning on doing all summer before you met me?"

I glance out the window. "Not sure."

Mira laughs. "You were just going to sit around?"

"My mom wants me to get a job, but we haven't gotten that far yet, so yeah. Sitting around sounds about right, until then." I think of my list and hesitate a moment, wondering if I should tell her about it. We're friends. I think. So, I go for it. "There is one thing I was going to do, I guess."

She smiles. "I like where this is going . . . Go on."

She stops at a stop light as I reach into my back pocket, then unfold my summer list. "Ooooh, what's that? I love lists. I'm definitely a list-maker. For pretty much everything. I don't usually use paper, though. Don't you put everything on your phone? Then it will all be in one place."

"My phone? No. Paper."

"Why? Technology trumps everything." The light turns green and we start moving again.

I smooth down the paper, noting the lack of sunshine in the car. The sky is overcast again and it's kind of weird not having the sun shine through the window, warming my arm like it normally did in Wyoming. Still. The scenery makes up for it. I focus on Mira again. "I disagree. What if your phone dies? You have to find a charger to turn your phone on again and what if you don't have one in an emergency?" I pat my list. "Paper never fails."

"Unless there's a fire," she says with a smirk. "I still choose my phone."

I smirk right back. "Tell me that again when all the power on Earth goes out and all we have left are pens and paper. Who will be laughing then? Oh, that's right. Me." I think of my favorite mug stuffed full of pens and the dozens of notebooks I keep stashed in my room. Maybe I've gotten just a *bit* carried away.

"You watch too many movies," she says, laughing.

"Maybe. But just you wait. It's gonna happen someday. Paper and pens forever."

"Right . . ." Another chuckle and I grin. "And when we lose power and can't use our electronics anymore, all we'll want to do is sit around writing in notebooks with pens."

I consider that a moment. "We'll forage for food a bit, too, I'm sure."

"Forage?" She laughs. "While we're fighting off zombies in the meantime."

"Just give me a weapon and I'll take care of them. But nothing stupid like a shovel or a hoe. A real weapon. Like a sword or something. Or a gun. But then I'd have to find bullets." I frown. "Scratch that idea."

"A sword? Since when do people use swords?"

"Trust me. They'll come back when the zombies come and we run out of bullets and our firearms are no good. I'll be ready with my swords."

She shakes her head. "That I would love to see. I bet you can't even carry one. I bet Jack couldn't even carry one. Do you know how heavy swords are?"

"I'm stronger than I look."

She laughs. "We'll stick together then, you and I. Fighting off zombies with swords and writing love notes to other survivors."

"Deal."

Her smile is huge as we pull into the store parking lot. "Seriously, you're officially my favorite."

"Salem Center?" I ask as I look up at the brown building in front of us.

"Yep. Lots of stores means lots of shopping."

"So it's a mall then."

"Yep."

"Cool."

We get out of the car and I follow her inside. As we walk through the doors, she glances at the list I'm still holding in my hand. "Now, about this list. On paper." She smirks again. "Tell me about it."

"Just a list of things to keep me busy this summer. Or, it's like a . . . I don't know what to call it. A try new things list? A summer bucket list I guess?"

"I love this! Details, details!"

"Oh. Okay. It's kind of dumb, but—"

"No, not dumb. Nothing is dumb, besides ex-boyfriends, but we're not gonna go there. Now spill. What's on your list?"

I stare at her. "How many ex-boyfriends do you have?"

She shrugs, then glances at me. "A few. Maybe."

I laugh. "Me too."

"Anyway, enough about my nonexistent love life. Spill!"

"Okay. So, these are just things I want to try. If I get enough courage to do it. Like, meet someone new was one of them, since I didn't have any friends here."

"Check," she says. "Cross that baby off. Next?" She turns into a store and starts searching through the sales racks for shirts. She holds a few up in front of the mirror on the wall, then puts them back and moves on. "So? List?"

"Oh. Um, let's see. Do something new with my hair, or style, go swimming in the ocean at night, find a great hike, do something crazy that I've never done before, go to an outdoor concert . . ." My face turns red. "See? They're stupid things. I didn't know what else to put. Especially being in a place that's so unfamiliar."

"They aren't stupid at all! We should do one today! Like the hair one. What do you want to do with it?"

"I'm not sure. It's been long for as long as I can remember, but I'm afraid to cut it."

"Then cut it!"

A few people look over at her since she pretty much yelled that through the store. I don't mind, though. I don't know them and they don't know me.

"That makes no sense! Why would I do something if it scares me?"

"Why wouldn't you? If people never did things that scared them, nothing would ever get done in the world."

I nod. She has a point. "So . . . you're saying I should cut my hair then?" I twist at my ponytail, wrapping it around my finger. What would I look like with shorter hair? Could

I really go through with it? What would Mom do? I don't know if the consequences are worth the action.

"No, I'm saying if you want to do something different, then don't be scared of it, just do it."

"You don't seem like you're scared of anything." She doesn't. She seems content and happy with life. Confident with who she is.

"Oh, I'm scared of things. Trust me. I'm just good at keeping my cool in front of people."

I stand there, contemplating what I should do. Hair can grow back. If I don't like my new style, I'll just wear a hat the rest of the summer while it grows back. Unless it doesn't grow as fast as I'd like.

Would I really hate a haircut that bad, though? I frown. If I hate my hair, I'll just avoid mirrors for a year. But if I like it . . . it could be the best thing that ever happened to me.

If hair can actually be a best thing that could ever happen to someone.

I clear my throat as I make a decision. "Know any good salons?"

Mira grins and grabs my arm, pulling me along with her. "I know just the place."

CHAPTER 11

"We must prove to the world that we are all nincompoops"
—Baroness Emmuska Orczy, *The Scarlet Pimpernel*

"My Mom's gonna kill me," I say as Mira and I walk up the porch steps to my house.

Mira runs her hand down the back of my head and flips my hair up. "Now why would she be mad? You look amazing!"

I touch the newly cut strands of my short hair near my shoulders. "It's so short."

"It's not that short. It still goes past your shoulders. Just not much."

"She cut eight inches off!" I twist a little strand around my finger, biting my lip at the thought of Mom's reaction. She's gonna freak out. "And the color . . . I should have left it at just the cut and not worried about the color. I've never colored my hair before. Never. And then I do it without even asking her?"

"It's only on the ends. She'll barely notice the purple since your hair is so dark. Oh, it's so gorgeous! I love it! What's a summer without a little color?"

"You're right. I do feel good. I feel . . . brave, actually. I've never done anything like this before. It's daring and new. Thanks for the motivation."

"You're welcome." She nudges me in the side. "You big rebel, you. And those boys at the hardware store were totally checking you out."

"Uh . . . pretty sure they were checking you out."

She waves my comment away. "Lies. You ready to go in? Oh, you need to cross your new hair off your list. That's two down, right?"

"Right." I smile, happy at how excited she is to help me with my list. I haven't exactly told her everything on the list, only a few things. Hopefully she can help me with more of them.

"Let's go in now. I can't wait to see the look on your mom's face!"

"I can," I say with a sigh. I open the door. "Mom?"

"Oh, you're home!" Her footsteps come from the kitchen. "Did you have—" Her voice cuts off as she stares at my hair with wide eyes. "Oh!"

"Mom . . ." I start. "It's not permanent. I mean, it's kind of. It stays in for at least a month. But . . . it will wash out later. I hope."

She's still staring, probably not listening to my rambling, then walks up to me and pulls on a strand. She studies the purple and, to my surprise, she smiles. "I like it."

"What?" Mira and I both say at the same time. Then Mira starts laughing hysterically. "I knew I liked you, Mrs. N.!"

Mom is still studying me. "It's a surprise, for sure, but I really like it. The pop of color is pretty."

I stare at her, then put my hand to her forehead. "Are you feeling okay? Do you need to see a doctor or something? Where's my mom?" I knock on her forehead. "Are you still in there?"

"What do you mean? Why are you looking at me like that?"

"Oh, I don't know. Maybe because you think it's totally fine that I colored my hair without talking to you first?"

She stares at me a moment. "Well, you're getting older. You're almost eighteen, so you can make *some* of your own decisions now." She frowns. "I'm not sure you can go to school like this, though. And if you ever got a tattoo or pierced something not meant to be pierced, there would be lots of words. And lots of grounding."

"Don't worry about those things. I'm too scared of needles. And it's June. I still have two months, Mom. The color won't last that long anyway."

"That's good." She hugs me. "I'm just happy you've found some friends. I've been worried about you. It's nice to see you happy and taking some chances. Even if you really should have asked me first."

"Mom," I say with a groan, since Mira is still standing there, giving me a sly grin.

Mom pulls away. "I need to get back to work. You can hang out upstairs or whatever. Your room needs one more coat of paint, so don't touch the walls."

"Thanks," I say. I gesture for Mira to follow me upstairs.

"But we'll still talk about this later," she says as she walks in the kitchen. "About a few more things we can and can't do without asking permission from parents."

"Great."

I knew it was too good to be true.

CHAPTER 12

"The dearest ones of time, the strongest friends of the
soul—BOOKS."
—Emily Dickinson

The first thing Mira does when we get up to my room is stare at the disaster. When she recovers, she gestures to the books stacked in various places. "Wow, you have a lot of books."

"Yeah. They're usually on the bookshelves, but since we're painting, I kind of had to move them. Sorry it's a mess in here."

She steps around piles of books and somehow makes it to my bed.

"No worries. You're obviously remodeling. You should see my room." She cringes. "Favorites?" she asks, running her fingers along the spines, stopping every now and then to pick a book out of a pile and look at the cover.

"Hmmm ... that's the hardest question. I have a deep love for the Harry Potter series."

"Who doesn't? What house?"

"I'm a Ravenclaw."

She jerks her thumb toward herself. "Hufflepuff. All about that puff pride."

"Oh, I'm seriously so happy right now that you know what your house is."

"Of course I do! Who doesn't?" She laughs. "Do you lend your books out?"

I hesitate. "I'm weird. I only lend them out to really good friends who will take care of my book babies."

"Noted. I have a love of books, too, just not so many in my actual house. I prefer e-books."

"Print is my jam."

"They take up so much space, though."

"They do, but remember when the apocalypse comes? Paper will trump technology. I don't have to plug my books in to make them work."

She laughs. "True, true. I still like reading them on an e-reader. You can have hundreds of them on it and e-readers aren't as heavy, so my hand doesn't cramp. When did you start buying all these?"

"I started collecting them a few years ago when I started really getting into reading. I have a lot of classics. I actually adore them. Well, most of them. And I do have an e-reader, but it usually just sits there and the battery runs out before I get to use it, so I always end up plugging it in and letting it run out again. I rarely remember to use it."

She chuckles and reads the spines of my Classics pile, since I kept them all together. "*Jane Eyre*, *Pride and Prejudice*, *Emma*, *Little Women*, *To Kill a Mockingbird*, *Black Beauty*, *Moby Dick*. You do have a lot!" She doesn't read the rest but continues to skim the titles. "Oooh, *Anne of Green Gables!*" She pulls it out of a pile on my bed and flips through it.

"Obviously you haven't liked this one." She rolls her eyes at the worn pages.

"I adore Anne. But that one's my mom's old copy."

"I'm more of a Gilbert fan myself," she says, a sly smile on her face. "Speaking of Gilberts and all ..." She pauses, shooting me a grin. "What do you think of Jack?"

My cheeks heat. "What?"

"Jack. You know. Cowboy hat, tall, my cousin?"

"He's nice."

"Nice? Well, yeah. But he's super cute. Even though he's my cousin, I can tell you a lot of girls like him."

"Why do you want to know what I think of him?"

She sighs. "Jack's had a rough year. He just needs a friend. And most of the girls his age don't deserve someone like him. He's a good guy, loyal to a fault and treats everyone better than they should be treated. I just want him to be happy."

"He seems like a good guy. From what I've seen." I missed hanging out with him today. Even though he's quiet, I like when he's there.

"He is. He's also a Gryffindor."

I laugh. "Is that a deal-breaker or something?"

"Maybe." She pulls her phone out and glances at the time. "I've got to go. Tuesdays are always crazy for me."

"What do you have going on?"

"Oh, nothing to worry about. I just have a meeting to get to. I'll call you when I get home, though, okay? We were thinking about going to the beach tomorrow. Would you want to come? It will be a bunch of our friends, so you'll get to meet new people, and I promise you can ride with me. I won't leave you to fend for yourself."

"Yeah, that sounds fun. I'd love to check out Oregon's beaches. I've heard they're beautiful. And I do need to go swimming in the ocean at night."

"We'll cross that baby off your list then!" she says, beaming. She heads toward the door. "I'll call you later then, okay?"

"Okay. I'll let you know what my mom says about that. She gets worried, so she may not let me go."

"She has nothing to worry about."

"I'll tell her that then." I smile.

I walk her to the door and tell her goodbye. She gets in her car and drives away.

I wonder what she had going on but know she has no obligation to tell me. We barely met two days ago.

Still, I do wonder.

I'm also curious about Jack. Why he's had a rough year. Does he have a girlfriend? It sounds like he doesn't, but I have no idea.

Right now, I have to convince Mom to let me go to the beach with my new friends. I'm pretty sure how that conversation's going to go.

Not well.

CHAPTER 13

"We sometimes encounter people, even perfect strangers, who begin to interest us at first sight, somehow suddenly, all at once, before a word has been spoken."
—Fyodor Dostoyevsky, *Crime and Punishment*

I make sure I'm awake early and ready before Mira picks me up the next morning. After a long discussion and more painting the night before, Mom finally gave in and let me go to the beach. I just have to text her every now and then so she knows I'm safe. Which, I will be. What does she think I'm going to be doing? She's so paranoid sometimes.

I'm just stuffing my towel in my beach bag when the doorbell rings. "I've got it," I yell as I hurry downstairs. I pull open the door and my breath catches.

It's not Mira. It's Jack.

"Hey," he says.

"Oh. Hey." I tuck my hair behind my ear, embarrassed at my crazy excited door opening.

"Um . . ." He shuffles his feet. "Mira asked me to pick you up. She's running a bit late, so we're meeting her at Ashton's house. There are a few other people coming with us. She probably already told you all this, huh?"

"Yeah." I smile. "It's okay, though."

"I thought so. You ready to go?" He glances at the bag in my hand.

"Yeah. Just a sec." I hurry to the kitchen where Mom sits at the counter, working on her laptop.

She looks up when I enter. She looks tired. Worried. But she smiles to make up for it. "Was that a boy I heard?"

"No. Definitely not a boy. Nope."

"It's that one boy. Jack, isn't it?" She gets up, a huge smile on her face.

"No. Mom," I hiss, panicked. I try to grab her arm to stop her, but she's already half way across the kitchen and into the entry way before I can stop her. And what's worse? She's in her pajamas.

At least she's in a good mood, I guess.

But still. She's in her pajamas.

"Hi, Jack. I'm Lucy's Mom. I didn't really introduce myself the last time you were over here, since Mira and I were talking." She shakes his hand. "I've heard a lot about you."

No. No, she did not just say that.

"It's nice to meet you, Mrs. Nelson."

"You're headed to the beach then?"

"Yes, ma'am."

"You two be careful, okay?"

"Mom, it's not a date. There's going to be a big group of us."

"Sure there is." She turns and winks at me. Winks!

I want to run back upstairs and hide under my bed.

She turns to Jack again and studies him. He swallows, looking a bit uncomfortable. "You look so much like ..." She trails off. "Never mind. It doesn't matter." She turns toward me and I'm sure my face is beet red. "Have fun, you two. Don't be late. And please text me when you get there, Luce. Don't forget."

"I won't, Mom," I say. I grab Jack's arm and pull him toward the door to get him away from Mom as fast as I'm able.

He's laughing as the door shuts behind us. I quickly let go of him and fold my arms, my bag hanging from my elbow. "Your mom's nice."

"Yeah, you'd think that," I grumble.

"You look like her."

I sigh. "I know."

"It's not a bad thing."

He clears his throat as I glance at him and he looks away, embarrassed. Me? I'm flattered. He may be shy, but he knows how to give a compliment. I know Mom's pretty. I've never thought of myself as that, but I get compared to her more than I realize.

He's quiet as we reach his old blue truck and opens the passenger door for me. "Thanks," I say, surprised at the gesture since we aren't on a date. We're not. Even though I wouldn't mind, actually.

"You're welcome," he says with a small smile.

I kind of like this shy, uncertain, boy. He's real. He doesn't do anything weird to try to impress me. He's a gentleman, a hard worker, and just his quiet self. And I really like that.

He looks different today. No cowboy hat. His dark hair is gelled and spiked. He's also wearing board shorts and a T-shirt, instead of his usual jeans, button-up shirt, and boots.

He looks ... uh ... hot, to put it bluntly. I've never really notice until now. Not that I'll tell him or anyone else that fact.

"I like your hair, by the way," he says as he gets in and starts the truck. "It looks good. I like the purple."

"Thanks." I pull my hair into a little ponytail, feeling self-conscious. "It's weird to have it so short. I mean, it's still long-ish, but it's just different. Different for me, I guess." I cringe. Why am I still talking?

"It's nice."

"And the color? That was Mira's fault." I pause. "She's very convincing."

"No surprise there."

"I mean, I really like it, it's just so not me. But I like it. It's new and interesting and fun. Maybe it'll grow on me." I glance over at him, embarrassed at talking so much again, but he doesn't seem annoyed at all.

I glance at my phone to distract myself, frowning at how low the battery is. Obviously, I forgot to charge it last night. Hopefully it will last the day.

There's a text from Ashley, asking what I'm doing today, and I quickly text her back and tell her about the beach, then put my phone away. I don't tell her about Jack. Or Mira. Or anything really. She hasn't really asked, and I haven't posted anything online but a picture of my book-shelves. I don't want to lose Ashley as a friend, but long distance is really hard and she keeps posting things about Dayson and her new "besties." It hurts more than I want to admit. Maybe I'll ask her to come out to Oregon for a week before school starts again. Who knows if she'll want to leave her new boyfriend, though.

The drive is quiet. I thought I'd be a little more nervous riding in his truck with just him, but it's not really awkward at all. It's normal. Like we've been friends for a long time. "So, how long does it take to get to the beach?"

"About an hour. Not too bad. We usually go about once a week in the summer. That or cliff jumping."

"Cliff jumping. So, you do this dangerous thing often then." I've never done that before. "It sounds like an adrenaline rush." Maybe I should do that. Take my mind off things and do something dangerous.

"It is, but it's actually really fun. I was a little nervous the first time I jumped off the cliffs we went to, but once you do it, it's no big deal." He smiles and glances at me. "You should try it. Mira told me about that list you're working on."

I don't know what to say, so I just sit there as my face turns red.

"Try something scary was on that list, right?"

"Yeah."

"Sorry. I didn't mean to make you uncomfortable."

"Oh, I'm not uncomfortable. I'm just embarrassed about my list."

He laughs. "What's there to be embarrassed about? I think it's great!"

"Thanks." I feel a little better. "But I'm still going to kill Mira for telling you anyway."

"She actually didn't mean to tell me. She was writing up a list of her own and told me she got the idea from you. Then I pressed her a little. She didn't tell me everything on it. Just the 'do something scary' thing because I like to cliff jump and she thought I could maybe take you. Nothing else. Promise."

"Good." If he knew about the summer romance thing? Yikes. That would be embarrassing. And it's not like I told her about that one, either. I'm just being paranoid.

"You inspired her, and me, if I'm being honest. I think it's great."

"Well, if that's the case then she's forgiven. I guess." We're quiet for a moment. "Speaking of lists, why don't you make one?"

He laughs, then glances at me with a grin. "Maybe I will."

"You'll have to add 'read a book' to it."

He looks thoughtful. "Can I pick said book?"

I shrug. "Sure! I don't care what you read. Just that you read something."

"I'll think about it."

I chuckle. "Deal. And I won't even be mad if you still don't like reading. Promise. We can watch a movie instead!"

"Perfect. And really. If you want to go cliff jumping, I can take you. There's a place about a half hour from here. It's fun. We really do go all the time."

"I may just take you up on that. That definitely fits the 'do something scary' bill."

"That sounds great. Besides, you'll be having fun with friends while you do it. I'll make sure you're safe. Our friends, they just like to have fun, hang out, and try new things." He shrugs. "We don't have all the time in the world, you know? After high school, we have to grow up."

"You can still have fun as adults," I say.

"Yeah, probably."

"You're a pretty deep thinker, aren't you?"

He chuckles. "Not really. Sometimes, I guess. My mom is really getting on me about picking a college to apply for once school starts. And of course I want to go to college. I just want to enjoy my last year of high school. You know?"

"I'd like to meet your mom. She sounds great."

"You'd like her. She'll probably map out your whole future too once you get to know her. She loves helping people. And she's good at getting people excited about things they never thought they wanted to do."

I've thought about my future but not to that extent. I'll worry about it when it gets here. Which is probably the wrong approach. Maybe if Dad would have planned, he wouldn't have gotten into trouble. But he didn't get into trouble until later, so maybe that wouldn't have mattered.

He was the provider when I was little, went to school and loved his job. Then he began his downward spiral after he had a steady, yet stressful job. Mom had to step up then. She worked hard and still works hard to give us what we need. "I'm planning on going to college. I want to be an English teacher." That much I know. Other than that, it's a big fat question mark.

"Because of the books?" He grins.

"Because of the books. And words. And the English language. It can be so beautiful and I want to teach my students that they can find beauty in words." I smile to myself. "Even the ones who don't like to read." I glance at him, and the corner of his mouth turns up.

"There's Mira," he says as he turns into a random driveway. She's standing next to her car, a group of her friends gathered around.

"You ready?" he asks as he puts the truck in park.

"I think so?"

He takes my hand, surprising me, and squeezes it. "You'll be fine. Just be yourself." He lets go, and I watch as he gets out of the truck, my hand still tingling.

Be myself. Everything will be fine. I've got this.

I hope.

"Lucy!" Mira yells as I step outside. "Get over here and meet our friends!"

I take a deep breath, grab my bag off of my seat, and shut the truck door.

This should be interesting.

Mira, Ashton, and four people I don't recognize watch me walk across the driveway. I don't love being the center of attention, so I'm relieved when Jack falls into step next to me.

"Guys, this is Lucy Nelson. She's new here." She turns toward the group. "This is Summer," she gestures to a girl with red hair and really light skin. She gives me a happy wave. "This is Brody," she continues, gesturing to a guy who looks like he stepped out of a K-Drama. He's gorgeous.

"Hey, Lucy," he says.

I give him a small wave.

"Kay's already sitting in Brody's car, it looks like."

We look over to see a dark-haired girl waving from the passenger seat of a silver Honda. The windows are down, so she can hear us. I didn't notice her until then, though.

Brody shrugs. "She wanted shotgun and was determined to get it, I guess."

"I always get what I want," she yells.

Mira shakes her head. "Whatever. And this is Tiffany and Alex."

I smile at the couple leaning against Mira's car. They both smile back, their hands entwined. "They've been dating forever."

They're super cute, I decide. Opposites in just about every way. She's short and petite and he's quite tall. Her blond hair is cropped short and she's wearing a bandana over it. He's super muscular with dark skin and curly hair.

"Dibs on Brody's car," Alex says. He gives Tiffany a squeeze, then goes over to the car Kay is already sitting in and puts two bags in the back seat.

Mira rolls her eyes. "Him and Brody are besties."

I nod and smile, though it's shaky. Everyone is still studying me and I feel a bit out of place. All these people know each other and I'm the odd man out. Or woman. For the first time, I feel like a charity case. Like they invited me just to be nice.

Mira puts her arm around me. I don't know if she senses my distress or what, but she gives my shoulder a squeeze. "You're riding with me." She glances at everyone else. "Brody's car has one more seat, and I have three more. Pick a car."

She steers me toward the passenger door while everyone starts talking and pretty much pushes me inside. "You're gonna have fun," she says, like I'm a little kid. "Everyone is super nice. You'll be fine."

"Okay?"

She frowns at me. "I can tell you're freaking out on the inside."

"I am not!"

I am.

"Sure," she says, the sarcasm thick. "You'll be fine. Promise. We don't bite. They don't either. Well, maybe Brody does, but that's besides the point."

I stare at her, my eyes wide.

She chuckles. "I'm joking. Calm down and breathe."

"I am calm!" I like to tell myself that.

I cringe as she gives me a look and shuts the door.

CHAPTER 14

"Now is no time to think of what you do not have. Think of what you can do with what there is."
—Ernest Hemingway, *The Old Man and the Sea*

Jack, Ashton, and Summer are crammed in the back of the car and chat away as Mira and I take turns picking radio stations.

Two things I've learned about Summer in the first ten minutes I've been with her: First, she's super nice and really positive, kind of like Mira, but not as sarcastic or funny. Second? She has a thing for Jack.

How do I know this? Her body language tells me everything I need to know. The way she leans more to his side of the car. The way she touches his shoulder when she's teasing him. And how she's been talking to just him and giggling the entire time we've been in the car.

It makes my eye want to twitch.

"What do you want to listen to?" Mira asks.

"Anything but country," I say.

She puts on some rap.

Not my first choice, but I deal.

"So, where are you from, Lucy?" Summer asks.

I glance back as Summer scoots closer to Jack, who's sitting right behind me.

"Idaho, originally. Then we lived in Wyoming for a few years before moving here."

"And you're a senior?"

"Yep."

"Oh, that's so awesome! And so hard. I can't imagine moving my senior year. You must be so lonely." She pauses. "Why'd you move here during one of the most important school years of your life?"

Her choice of words is interesting, but I ignore it. "My mom's from here. We're actually living in her childhood home. Her mom died and left it to her."

"Ooooh, that's so cool! I've only lived here for three years now, so I don't know a lot of the original residents." She giggles. "Well, besides the Kelly family. Everyone knows them." She bumps Jack's shoulder with her own and I turn back to face the front of the car. A wave of jealousy crashes into me, and I stare out the window trying to shake it off.

Summer doesn't stop talking.

"So, it's just you and your mom then?"

I glance back at her, curious how she knows that.

She shrugs. "Mira told me she saw you and a woman she thought was your mom the day you moved in."

"Oh. Yes. Just me and my mom."

"Where's your dad then?"

I suck in a breath. The silence is deafening. I don't want to say anything about him. I don't want to lie again. I don't know what to say.

So, I sit there, the silence dragging on, until I feel a gentle tap on my shoulder.

"Lucy? Could you change the station? This song sucks." Jack says, breaking the silence.

Grateful for the interruption, I start flipping radio stations.

Summer doesn't repeat the question and starts singing to the song I stop on instead.

"Oh, this song is the best!"

She has a nice voice. Which makes my eye want to twitch again.

"I hope y'all like turkey sandwiches," Mira says. "That's what I brought for lunch."

I turn toward her. "You didn't have to bring lunch for me."

Mira waves me away. "We always trade off. And I wasn't gonna let you starve. What kind of friend would I be?"

"I'll pay you back," I insist.

"Nope."

"Seriously, Mira. I will."

"Lucy. It's a sandwich and a bag of chips. It's no big deal. Promise." She smiles. "But if you feel like I need a shake or smoothie or something, I won't protest. Today or any other day."

I chuckle. "Deal."

"How long have you two been hanging out?" Summer asks.

"A few days," I say.

"Forever," Mira says at the same time.

We both laugh, and I hear Jack's low chuckle behind me.

121

Summer doesn't say anything else.

"Is there a reason Ashton hasn't said anything?" Mira asks. "He asleep?"

I look back at him, his head slumped against the window and eyes closed. "He's asleep," I confirm.

She rolls her eyes. "Not surprised. That kid isn't a morning person. And he can fall asleep anywhere. And I mean anywhere. Sitting up, standing up, riding a horse. I think he needs to go see a sleep specialist. That's one reason I wouldn't let him drive."

"My mom can sleep anywhere, too. Just not while driving, thankfully," I say.

"Lucky," she says. "I have a hard time sleeping."

"It takes me at least an hour to fall asleep every night."

"Me too!"

"You two have a lot in common," Summer says, not mean, but there's a tiny edge to her voice. "Should I wake up Ashton then?"

"No. Let him sleep. He'll be more fun when we get there," Mira says. "Trust me."

I wonder if Mira really does have a thing for Ashton, but I decide to ask her later. When Summer isn't in the car.

We reach the beach about an hour later.

As soon as I step out of the car, the cool, salty air hits me in the face. I walk over to the edge of the road and stare down the hill at the blue water. There are rocks jutting out of the ocean, some covered in green, others just rocks. The whole scene is beautiful, and I pull out my phone to take a picture.

"Beautiful, isn't it?" Jack says, startling me.

"It really is."

"You've never seen the ocean?"

"I've seen California's beaches, but this is different," I breathe, watching the foamy waves come in and taking in the pretty cliffs surrounding our little cove. A lighthouse sits on one of the cliffs, a calming light on a dark night, I imagine.

The world is a beautiful place even when it's filled with so much darkness.

A shout makes us turn. The other car pulls up next to ours, and Mira and Jack's other friends jump out.

Mira takes charge. "Everyone, this is Lucy's first time at the beach. Well, our beach, I guess. Don't ruin it for her, m-kay?"

"Mira . . ." I start. "I'm fine!"

"Sure," she says. I laugh at the look she gives me. "Lunch is in the cooler. We'll eat in a bit."

Ashton, who finally woke up, grabs her attention then.

"Well, what are we waiting for?" Summer says. "Let's go!"

Some of the boys let out a whoop and start down the hill toward the water. I follow them, my bag in hand, down a winding dirt trail until we reach the sandy beach. It's cooler than I expected. I brought a hoodie and debate on putting it on, but notice no one else cares, and most of them are already running toward the water in their swimming suits.

The breeze tousles my hair and I take in a lungful of clean, fresh air. Even though I've seen the ocean in person before, the rolling waves are mesmerizing to watch. I wonder what makes them come in and out and in and out like that. Why the ocean doesn't stand still like ponds and lakes, especially since it's so huge. I wonder at the life under the water, so many different fish and sharks, dolphins and whales. The ocean is a vast place, full of life.

It's fascinating, the ocean. So many stories, so many books. It's also terrifying.

I think of *The Old Man and the Sea*, how Santiago fights to get his great fish and how it gets taken from him by sharks after all of his hard work. You never realize all the dangers lurking in the water.

Oakley's fiancé pops into my head. He lost a leg to a shark. I shiver. How would it be, I wonder, to be fine one moment and the next . . . your entire life has changed? You could be bitter and resent your life, or you could move on.

I sigh. I need to move on.

I think of *Moby Dick*. How Ahab hunts the great white whale and how his obsession ultimately leads to his downfall. His death. All because he was fixated on getting revenge for his lost leg.

Obsession.

Addiction.

They are kind of the same thing. I've seen it. I've lived it through watching Dad, always moving, always muttering to himself when he was in a bad way. He stopped caring, stopping loving, and focused everything he had on getting his next fix. He used to be so kind and caring; I have so many good memories of him. I need to write them down.

Draw some pictures of some of our better times. When I can pick up a pencil again.

I let out the breath I'm holding and kick at the sand a little.

Obsession. Addiction. One in the same. I know it's like a disease. Addiction takes away your agency and messes with your head so you're not thinking straight. You're not yourself. But still. The pain of watching him. Wondering where he was when he didn't come home or when he didn't show up to pick me up from school when he was supposed to.

Not understanding why he didn't care.

I close my eyes, surprised at the burn of tears threatening to fall. I snap out of my thoughts. I'm here to have fun. This is not a place to think of past hurts. It's a place to enjoy the beauty of life. Of my dreams. Of a new start.

I set my bag down and look around. Everyone's already in the water or playing in the tiny waves covering their feet. Summer is hanging onto Jack's arm, pulling him toward the water. Mira is on Ashton's shoulders, screaming as he flings them both backward into the waves. I don't know what the others are doing. I don't really care. I take this moment for myself.

The water is only a few yards away and I smile as it edges forward and hits my toes, covers my feet. It's a lovely, strange, cold feeling with the sand beneath my feet. I sink a little into the mud as the water pulls away, leaving my toes surrounded by wet foam. The water really is colder than I expected, and with the cool breeze blowing, my body shivers. I don't care, though. I take a few more steps into the ocean, closing my eyes and breathing in deep.

The salty air is so calming. I needed to come here today. I need to start healing.

"Hey," a voice says.

I turn and see Jack coming toward me, Summer nowhere in sight. Thankfully.

Not that I don't like her. I have no reason not to like her. She's nice, but . . . there's that jealousy again. I push it away. Or try to. I have no claim on Jack. I just barely moved here and she's known him for a long time. I don't even know him that well and don't even know if I like him or not.

"You okay? You're just by yourself over here so I thought I'd come see how you're doing."

I give him a small smile. "You love to sneak up on people, don't you?"

"Not really. Just you. You have fun reactions."

"Very funny." I sigh.

"So, are you okay?"

"Yeah, I'm fine. Just thinking and enjoying the water on my feet."

He stands beside me, the tiny waves rushing back into the ocean. "Thinking? Nice thoughts?"

"Ha!" I don't mean to laugh, but it just comes out. Humorless. "Sure."

"You sound convincing," he says, dryly. "Do you want to talk about it?"

I shake my head. "I'm alright." I give him a smile since the concern in his voice is real. "Thanks."

"Is it your family? Your dad?"

My stomach drops. "I don't know." And I don't. I don't know what I want to say to him. I do, but I don't. I want to tell him the truth about Dad. I want to talk to someone about it. About what's really going on. But I'm too scared of what he'll think of me. I'm scared he'll hate me for lying to him. Why didn't I just tell the truth when he asked?

"Maybe I can help?" The waves lap against our feet and I shiver and wrap my arms around myself. "I haven't lost a parent, like you, but I did lose my best friend last year."

I look over at him. He stares at the water, looking solemn. I try to forget the fact that he thinks I'm grieving over a death and instead focus on his friend. "How?"

"Ben suffered from depression. Bipolar disorder. You name it. He had a hard life. Parents divorced, physical abuse. He seemed like the most positive and happy kid at school, though. People had no idea about his home life. I did, since we were close, but no one else did. One day, it got to be too much for him to handle. I should have known what was going on. I should have been able to help him." He kicks softly at the wet sand as the water is sucked away from our feet again. "But it was too late. He was gone."

Suicide.

I've never had to deal with something like that before. I don't know what I would do if I knew someone who took their own life. It would be devastating, to say the least. And by the look on his face, it was.

He's lost someone. *Actually* lost someone. I've never lost someone like that. Yes, Dad is gone, but not in that way. How have I been so selfish? Thinking my life is ruined because of Dad? I'm still alive. I'm healthy. Mom's still here. We have a nice home to live in. I've made new friends. Yeah, it sucks knowing I won't see Dad again for a while and he'll probably never really be in my life again, but all I've been focused on this whole time is how this has all affected *me*. What about the couple Dad accidentally killed? How does their family feel? How does *Dad* feel?

I know what I feel right now. Ridiculous.

"I'm so sorry," I whisper.

"Not your fault. I wish I could have done more. There are so many things I could have done. That everyone could have done. It really messed up our town for a while. He was only sixteen." He sniffs. He's not crying, but I can see the moisture in his eyes. "No one talks about it anymore. It kind of got swept under the rug because no one wants to mention it. We always do that around here, when someone dies young. It isn't forgotten, but people don't like to talk about it. But the stuff Ben went through needs to be talked about more. There are resources and things that can help someone struggling like that. No one should ever feel so lonely or hopeless that it makes them want to end their own life. It's not okay and shouldn't have ever happened."

I nod. I don't know what else to do. What to say. I'm surprised he's telling me this. He doesn't know me well. But he seems to trust me.

Trust.

I take a deep breath and stare at the foam surrounding my toes. After a moment, I glance up at him. "I'm sorry, Jack. That's so hard."

He smiles. "I know he's okay now, but it still hurts. I kind of backed away from my old friends and started hanging out with Mira and her friends. Even though they are all a year younger than me. They just . . . they each have things they're dealing with, too, so they sort of get me. My other friends wanted to pretend nothing ever happened. But how can you forget a person? Or pretend they didn't exist or have problems? Everyone has problems. People just need to talk about them more so we understand each other. You know?"

"Yeah." He's right. And at that moment, I want to tell him everything. I trust him, too.

I'm so afraid of how I'll feel once the truth is out, though. How I'll feel once everyone knows my big secret. Will they treat me differently, like some of my old friends did? Will their parents tell them not to hang out with me anymore? Because that also happened with some of my other friends.

Am I really so afraid of what people will think that I need to keep the lie going? Mom has told me countless times she doesn't care what people think and neither should I.

I open my mouth to let it all fall out, but I stand there, mouth open.

"I," I start, but then I shake my head. It won't come. My stomach is in knots and I take a few slow breaths to calm my racing heart.

Jack doesn't seem to notice, since he's still lost in thought. "Anyway. Sorry. I just wanted you to know that you're not alone. We all have something we're dealing with. And I'm sorry about your dad."

My chin quivers and I blink back the tears that threaten to fall. How can he care about me so quickly? And not romantically or anything, but as a friend? We barely know each other and he opened up about his problems to make me feel like I'm not alone? He's a better person than I am. Much better. I'm just a selfish girl. Why haven't I seen that until now?

"Thank you," I manage. It comes out almost as a whisper and sort of shaky, but I get it out. The guilt of not telling him the truth eating me alive.

"You're welcome. If you ever need someone to talk to, I'm here. Talking helps."

It does. And I'm a coward for not talking. It would be so easy. *Just open your mouth, Lucy,* I tell myself.

But I say something else instead. "I know. And thank you. For telling me your story. I'm sure it was hard."

He shrugs. "You're pretty easy to talk to. Which is weird." His eyes widen. "Not that you're weird, I just . . ." He hesitates. "I like talking to you." He looks away.

I smile at his embarrassment. He's cute when he gets like that. It makes me like him even more.

Even more? Do I *like him* like him?

"I like talking to you, too," I say before I can stop myself.

He glances at me and his cheeks turn pink.

A bigger wave crashes into my legs, not enough to knock me over, since they're still pretty small, but enough to make me lose my balance for a second. That's when I realize, since I haven't moved for a while, that my feet have sunk a little deeper in the mud. As the tide rolls out, leaving us standing in the mud again, I attempt to move. Instead of gently pulling them out, I lift one foot quickly, realize I'm off balance, and before I know it, my feet fly out from under me. A second later, I end up face down in the mud. The water comes back, and little ocean waves hit me in the face, drenching my hair and forcing a high-pitched squeal out of me.

Nice.

I glance up and notice Jack staring at me in shock. "Are you okay?"

After *my* shock wears off, I'm laughing as I shake sand out of my hair and wipe the freezing water off my face. "Uh . . . I have no idea what just happened."

He's laughing now as he helps me up. I'm so embarrassed from falling over nothing that I don't really speak for a moment. Instead, I shake my hair out of its ponytail and run my fingers through the bits of sand stuck in it. After a second, I put it back in the elastic and wipe some of the water from my cheeks.

"Really, Lucy. Are you okay?"

I let out a snort, which only makes things worse, and sends him into another fit of laughter. Finally, I nod. "Yes, I'm fine. I did not mean to do that. Any of that."

He sets a hand on my back, making heat flood through me. "Well, it was pretty entertaining anyway."

"Thanks," I say, wiping sand from my arms, legs, everywhere. Why? Ugh. "I really hope no one else saw that."

"I'm pretty sure I'm the only lucky one."

"Great," I mutter.

Someone screams and we hear a huge splash and lots of laughter. He nods his head. "Why don't we go join in whatever they're doing?"

I hesitate, so he reaches for my hand, pulling me along with him, then when we're side by side, he lets me go.

"You're already a little wet. Might as well get in."

"I'm okay. I'll just put my feet in."

"Don't let them sink!"

"Ha. Ha." I roll my eyes at him and fold my arms as we splash through the shallow water. "I could live here."

He laughs. "You do live here."

"No, I mean by the beach. I could buy a beach house and live here. It's beautiful."

"It is."

"Heads up, Kelly!" someone yells.

Jack looks up just as a huge ball of mud splats across his chest. I can't help it—I burst out laughing as Jack's wide eyes look around to find the culprit.

Brody.

Then he's running, splashing into the water and tackling Brody under the waves while the rest of us die laughing on the beach.

CHAPTER 15

"I know not all that may be coming, but be it what it will,
I'll go to it laughing."
—Herman Melville, *Moby-Dick or, The Whale*

We stay until it gets dark. My phone has long since died, and I hope Mom's not freaking out. Mira is insistent that I swim in the ocean at night to cross it off my list, so we wait a little while longer. And talk. And wait some more. We sit on the beach as the tide rolls out. It's colder now. I tug a hoodie over my swimsuit and pull my knees under it before wrapping my arms around them.

Summer has been by Jack's side since our little talk on the beach, so I watch them chat across from me as we all sit in a circle in the sand.

Mira sits next to me and Ashton is on her other side, their hands really close to each other in the sand, but not quite touching. I'm not sure where Tiffany and Alex are, possibly making out somewhere, and Kay and Brody are on my other side. They're both flirty, I've noticed. Not only with each other, but with everyone. Especially Brody. He still has his shirt off, even with the cool breeze, and I have to keep telling myself to look away or else I'll stare at him all night.

I don't want to be the creepy girl.

As I sit there, I wonder if Mom ever came to this beach. If she ever came with her friends at night or took pictures of the ocean. Maybe Susan was with her. I wonder about Susan again. Do they have a cemetery somewhere? Maybe I'll look for her grave if there aren't a million headstones to search through. Or maybe I could do an internet search for newspapers from Salem?

I glance at my dead phone, wishing it were charged so I could look right now.

A hand lands on mine and I jump as it jars me out of my thoughts.

"Why didn't you just tell me you wanted to hold my hand?" Brody says, linking our fingers together.

I let out a sort of hysterical laugh and try to pull away. He pulls me closer and lets go of my hand but puts his arm around me and pulls me against his chest. "We can cuddle if you'd like." He grins.

Mira laughs. "Leave her alone, Brody." She reaches across the circle and pushes him over, making him let go of me. "He's harmless," she says, rolling her eyes. "Promise. He just likes to show off."

He puts a hand to his chest. "Me? Harmless? And a showoff? I thought we were friends, Mira?"

She chuckles and rolls her eyes again before going back to her conversation with Ashton.

I catch a glimpse of Jack as I scoot away from Brody. He's watching me, paying no attention to Summer talking his ear off next to him.

"Well," Mira says, checking her phone. "It's time. Let's take a quick swim in the dark and get out of here. Parents will start to worry."

When she says it, several of them laugh. "Right," Brody says. "I could come back next week and my parents wouldn't even notice."

Kay shakes her head, as well. "Same. My mom works late every night. She'll be home after I'm asleep. Usually at two in the morning." She glances at me. "She's a nurse, so she works weird hours and I know she won't check on me when she gets home. She always goes straight to bed."

"Are you home alone then?"

"Most of the time. My older brothers are all married, so it's just me left." She shrugs. "It's no big deal."

But it is a big deal. Under the grin, I can see it in her eyes. She's lonely. Like me. Like Jack. Even Mira seems to carry something. All of these people have something to bear. Of course, I don't know what all of it is, but it's *something*.

It brings me a small amount of comfort to know I'm not alone.

Mira helps me to my feet. "Let's do this."

"You're really going in there?" Summer asks. "It's freezing!"

"Yep." Jack stands, surprising both of us. "Well?" he says as we stare at him. "Let's go!"

Summer jumps to her feet. "Okay, let's go!"

"I'm gonna go find Tiff and Alex," Brody says. "Not that I'm looking forward to finding them, but I can't leave them, so ..."

Ashton sighs. "I'll go with you." They start walking toward the cars, muttering something about the couple always running off together.

Kay picks up her towel and a few bags. "I'll be in the car. Have fun freezing your butts off."

I take off my hoodie, throw it on the ground next to my bag, and follow Mira out to the water, which is further out now. Jack and Summer are behind us. Our footsteps make prints in the sand, which for some reason, I adore, and I finally stop when my feet touch the water.

Kay's right. It's freezing. My toes feel like icicles as the water runs over them.

"Okay, looks like I can cross one more thing off," I say with a smile.

Mira shakes her head. "You specifically said *swim* on your list. Not put your feet in."

I shake my head and rub my hands up and down my arms, missing my hoodie. I would have worn it down here, but I didn't want to chance getting it even a little wet. "No way. It's too cold out here now."

"You should have been more specific then," she says with a sly smile. "*Put feet in ocean at night.* But you said *swim.*" She pumps her fist in the air, yelling, "Swim, swim, swim," over and over.

"Maybe we can do a rain check? When it's warmer?"

"Oregon will never be warmer. It's summer already!" She glances at something behind me and her eyes grow wide before she grins.

Almost at once, I'm scooped off my feet as Jack carries me toward the ocean, his arms beneath my shoulders and knees.

"Don't you dare!" I yell. "It's too cold!"

He laughs as I struggle to get out of his grasp, but man, his grip is tight. There's nothing I can do but wrap my arms around his neck as he heads deeper in the water.

"You are in so much trouble!" I scream as the cold water hits my legs. "It's too cold! You are so going down!"

He doesn't say anything, but he does cringe, which is satisfying. I can tell it's too cold for him, too. "You ready?"

"What? For what? Don't you—"

He falls backward, taking me with him, and cold water rushes around me, making my whole body tense. I pop back up, gasping as my face hits the surface, and then stand. The water is about waist-high on him and it's up to my chest.

"What did I ever do to you?" I push him in the chest, but of course he doesn't move. "Why would you turn on me like that?"

He laughs at that. "You said you wanted to swim, so I thought I'd help you along!" He grins, then floats on his back for a moment before standing back up, waiting for me to join him.

I sigh. "Fine. I'm wet anyway." I take a breath and brace myself for the cold again as I dive under the water next to him. We're not far out, so I don't dive deep, just enough to submerge my whole body. I do a few strokes when I hit the surface and run right into him. He's laughing as he grabs my wrists to pull me up and, after I get my balance, I realize he's still holding onto me.

"Just so you know, this means war," I say.

"Oh, I'm ready." He lets go of one of my wrists and a wave hits me, sending me forward. I set my hand on his chest to steady myself and look up, his eyes on mine.

"We ready to go yet?"

Jack clears his throat and drops my hand. "Yep."

Freezing and a little annoyed at Summer's interruption, I make my eyes leave Jack's chest and I scramble back to the beach, trying to run through the waves. My progress is slow and I hear Jack laughing behind me.

"Stop making fun of me!" I yell back at him. "Just because you have long legs and can run through the water faster doesn't give you the right to laugh at me!"

"Yes, it does!"

"Seriously, he is so going down."

Mira hands me a towel when I reach her, a knowing look on her face. She grins, then looks back at Jack, then at me again.

"What?" I ask, wringing out my hair.

"Oh, nothing. Nothing at all." She starts back up the beach, and I struggle to keep up with her as I wrap my towel around myself.

"You're in big trouble, you know that?" I tell her.

"You should be thanking me right now."

"Why?"

She shrugs but shoots me a wicked smile.

"I didn't realize you were really going swimming," Summer says to Jack as she reaches him.

He breathes in the salty sea air and glances at me. "Nothing like a late-night swim on a night like this, huh, Lucy?"

"I'm starting to regret that decision." It's cold. And I'm wet. Not a good combo.

Summer doesn't say anything, just follows us to the cars where everyone else is waiting.

A breeze hits me, and I shiver as I grab my hoodie and bag off the beach. I run to catch up with Mira. I need heat, stat.

"Shotgun!" Ashton yells when we reach the top of the hill.

No one protests. Everyone is either too exhausted or freezing to death. I am the latter.

As we approach the car, Summer climbs in the left side. I know she wants to sit by Jack, so I wait for him to get in first.

He appears next to me. "I can't do the middle. I have to be able to look out the window or I'll get carsick."

Before Summer can object or scoot over, he nudges me into the middle seat. I can feel her eyes on me as I buckle my seatbelt, but I don't look at her. I glance at Jack, who looks content, and he smiles down at me before he climbs in.

He's so close to me. But of course he is. We're crammed in the back of a little car. But I can feel the heat from his body next to mine. Goosebumps cover my arms and legs. I rub at my arms, trying to warm them up. Jack's leg touches mine, and I can't really scoot anywhere, but he doesn't seem to mind. His long legs barely have anywhere to go. He should really be the one sitting in the front.

I don't mind, though. Not at all.

"Ready?" Mira asks.

"Let's go," Jack says. He leans toward me. "You're cold."

"I'm fine." I shiver. "Okay, maybe a little."

He nods and rolls his window up. Then he hands me his towel and slips a shirt over his head. "Wrap that around you."

"I can just put my hoodie on."

"You're wet. You'll just get your hoodie wet. And that seems like a priceless hoodie."

I roll my eyes but laugh anyway. Summer shifts next to me.

I look up and meet Mira's eyes in the rearview. She smiles knowingly. I give her a *look* before she rolls her window down and yells at the car next to us. "We'll follow you this time!"

Brody lets out a whoop from the other car and takes off. Mira follows him.

"So, how long are you planning on living here?" Summer asks. "Are you just here to finish high school? Then you'll go off to college somewhere?"

Her question is innocent enough. "I'm planning on college, yes. Probably somewhere close, since my mom will still be living here and I don't want her to be by herself all the time."

"Cool." She nods then stares out the window.

She doesn't sound like she thinks it's cool at all.

The drive home is quiet. Mira and Ashton talk up front as Summer stares out one window, and Jack the other.

I feel like I've unintentionally ruined something between them.

Even though I don't want to, I do feel bad about it. From the way Summer has acted all day, I know she likes Jack. I don't know about him liking her, but still. I feel like I need to trade one of them seats.

"You warmer now?" Jack asks quietly.

I shift, moving my legs a little to keep them from aching or falling asleep. "Yes. Thanks for letting me use your towel."

"You're welcome. Anytime."

I lean my head against the seat and close my eyes. Exhausted. Driving at night always makes me tired. Being at the beach all day has doubled my tiredness.

Jack bumps my shoulder softly and I look at him. "You can lean on me. I mean, if you're tired." He swallows. "If you want."

If it's possible, we've already navigated closer to one another. "You're so nice."

"I try." He laughs, deep but quiet. "Honestly, I get that a lot. Always the nice guy."

"Which is not a bad thing." At all.

He runs a hand through his hair and sinks a little lower in his seat. He's still leaning toward me, and I can't help but be drawn to him. I don't know what it is, but he's like a magnet. I lean away just a little. Summer is sitting right next to me, and I'm sure listening to our entire conversation.

"Girls always go after the bad boys," he says, his lips in a half smile.

"Bad boys are overrated. *And* a bad example. They're not my type. Anymore, I guess."

He smiles at that, looking a little more confident. "What is your type?"

I shrug. "The nice type. Caring, good listeners, not in it for just one thing." My cheeks heat and I sink lower in my seat, too. What the heck am I saying?

Shut it, Lucy.

He nods, still smiling, but looks straight ahead. I glance at his profile. He has small, complementary features. Small ears, nose, thin lips. His eyelashes are longer than mine, I realize, which makes me jealous. I can barely see mine, even with mascara on, I swear.

"How far away are we from home?" Summer asks, still staring out the window.

"About thirty minutes," Mira answers.

Ashton says something I can't hear to her and she swats at him. They both laugh.

"They do like each other," I whisper to Jack.

"Yeah. They're stupid, though, and won't do anything about it."

"We'll have to help them along then."

He chuckles. "I've tried."

"You didn't have me as a partner in crime before now."

"True."

Summer sighs next to me, and I lean away from Jack and close my eyes again, resting my head on the headrest.

The car grows quiet and my exhaustion creeps in again.

The next thing I know, a light is shining in my face. I'm disoriented and blink a few times as my eyes adjust. I look up and see Jack grinning at me. "Wake up, sleepyhead," he says.

The car has stopped and one of the doors are open. Everyone's still inside, though.

I realize my head is on his shoulder and sit up so fast, my head spins. "I'm . . . oh, I'm so sorry! I didn't mean to fall asleep on you."

Then I feel moisture on my cheek.

"Oh my gosh, I drooled on you!" I wipe off my cheek, see the little wet spot on his shoulder, and bury my face in my hands.

Jack's laughing so hard he can barely breathe, as are Mira and Ashton.

I'm mortified.

"I promise, it's fine," Jack says. He puts an arm around me, giving me an awkward hug, since I'm bent over on the seat.

"No," I say, shaking my head. "Nope. Girls don't drool." I let out a small cry. "Girls don't drool!" I shake my head, crack a tiny smile since Jack is still laughing, then sigh. "I'm disgusting."

"You're not. I drool all the time."

Mira pipes in then. "One time, I was supposed to be taking a test in chemistry, and I fell asleep on my paper. When I woke up, there was a huge drool puddle on my test. I rushed and finished it, then walked up to the teacher's desk and quickly put it in the middle of the test pile so no one would see it."

Jack laughs. "See? Girls drool, too."

"Yeah, it's cool!" Mira says, laughing.

"Really. A little drool never hurt anyone," he says, nudging my shoulder with his.

I groan again. "This is just the worst."

"Come on, let's get your stuff," Jack says, still laughing.

I hear Summer let out a frustrated breath and get out of the car.

"Great," I whisper. I've already blown it with one potential friend. Because of a boy.

"What's wrong?" Jack asks, opening his door.

I don't want to talk about Summer with him, so I shake my head. "Nothing." I grab my bag and climb out after him.

"I can take you home," Jack says, gesturing toward his truck.

Summer stands next to the other car, not looking at either one of us. "Why don't you take Summer home? I'll catch a ride with Mira. I need to talk to her anyway."

Summer turns around and looks at me then, her expression curious.

"Nonsense," Mira says, coming up behind me. "I need to take Ashton home, and Summer is right on the way. Jack can take you so you don't have to wait any longer."

I hesitate but finally give in. "Okay."

Everyone gets into their own cars, and Ashton and Summer get back into Mira's, and they all shout goodbyes as they drive away.

"Ready?" Jack asks.

I nod and follow him to his truck.

It's not that I don't want to go with him. I actually think I might like him. Not think. I do like him. But I don't want to cause problems.

And I just drooled on his freaking shirt. How romantic.

Why do I have to be so . . . me?

Jack opens the door for me, of course. I climb in and set my bag on my lap. I look at my phone. Still dead. Hopefully Mom will be cool about it, since it's later than I thought.

"Thanks for taking me today. I mean, letting me come with you," I say as he starts down the road. "It's nice to have some friends."

"They're fun. And they seemed to get along with you just fine."

"I hope so."

He pulls into my driveway and I stare out into the darkness of the trees. We reach the house, and he puts the truck in park.

"Thanks for bringing me home."

"It was my pleasure."

The air is thick with some kind of tension and my heart has picked up speed. I have to remind myself this wasn't a date. He's not like other guys. He's not going to try anything. And he doesn't. He waits patiently, a small smile on his face, while I grab my stuff and open the door.

I jump out and am about to shut the door, when he says, "Wait."

I look up at him and he's just about to say something when Mom opens the front door.

145

"Lucy!" she yells. She is not happy. "Inside. Now."

I glance at Jack, embarrassed at Mom's tone. I'm obviously in trouble. And Jack heard it.

"I'll see you later," I say as he gives me a sympathetic smile.

He backs out of the driveway and I meet Mom at the door.

She folds her arms. "Where have you been?"

"The beach? You already knew that."

"It's eleven-thirty. I thought you'd be home hours ago."

"I'm sorry. My phone died and I couldn't text you."

"You could have used someone else's phone to let me know what was going on! You're smarter than that!"

"Sorry . . . I didn't think of it. We weren't planning on being gone all day."

"Why are you so late then? Were you on the beach at night? Was it dark?"

I stare at her, confused at why she would care. "Well, yeah, but—"

"Do you have any idea how dangerous the water is at night? And how come you were only with that boy? You said you were with friends."

"Mom! Why would I lie to you? We were with a whole group. He just brought me home. We rode there with Mira and a bunch of her friends."

She rubs at her temples. "Just . . . go to bed. I've been worried sick about you. I was waiting for a call from the police that you . . . just . . ." Her eyes are watering and instead of talking back to her, I wrap her in a hug, remembering how many times Dad would leave and wouldn't

146

call. How many sleepless nights we had, especially Mom, wondering if he was okay.

She hugs me back.

"I'm sorry, Mom. I didn't mean to scare you. We were fine. Safe. I promise."

She strokes my hair. "I just worry about you. I've already lost ..." she trails off. "I can't lose you. Please let me know if you're going to be late next time? And promise me, never go swimming in the ocean that late again. Promise me. There are no lifeguards or anything. What if you got sucked underwater?"

I sigh. "I'm fine, Mom. But I promise."

She pulls me into a fierce hug. Like she won't ever let me go. I don't know what's gotten into her. She's never been like this. I mean, she worries, but not like this. The pain on her face and haunted look in her eyes.

I realize right then how stupid I've been. I won't ever make her worry like this again. Not after what Dad did to us. I know she's remembering things and being extra overprotective of me because of him. And why wouldn't she be? I'm all she has left. Just me and her. If something happened to me, I don't know what she would do. She'd never get over it, just like I'd never get over losing her. I feel awful making her worry so much.

I give her one last squeeze before letting her go. "I'm going to go to bed. Sorry again."

"It's okay. Get some sleep." She kisses the top of my head, her hand lingering on my cheek, before her arm falls to her side. "Goodnight."

"Goodnight, Mom." I walk upstairs, our exchange running through my head.

Once I get to my room, I plop down on my bed and plug in my phone.

After a few minutes, it restarts and I see a bunch of missed texts from Mom and Ashley and a few from Oakley, as well. It's too late to answer them now, so I put my phone down and pull out my summer list. I cross off *swimming in the ocean at night* and look at the rest of the items.

My eyes stop at number ten.

10. Find out who Susan is and visit her grave.

Susan. Could this all have to do with Susan too? Mom's paranoia, her freak-out tonight, how she's been so protective of me. I know it's partly Dad's fault, but I wonder if Susan is involved somehow.

They were obviously best friends and something happened between them.

How did Susan die?

I pick up my phone again and search *Susan*, obviously, but since I don't know her name, I search *Salem, Oregon, death.*

Salem comes up. A lot of articles about deaths in Salem, Oregon, obituaries, accidents, but they're all recent. No old records. I search for about fifteen minutes, clicking on a bunch of links, but come up with nothing.

How could there be nothing?

Maybe the library would have old newspapers or something. Or I could still check the cemetery.

But I still don't have Susan's last name, and I know Mom won't give it to me. I'm going to have to do a lot of old-school digging to figure this one out on my own.

CHAPTER 16

"If you look for perfection, you'll never be content."
—Leo Tolstoy, *Anna Karenina*

There are two things I truly hate.

Grapefruit and flip-flops.

Why flip-flops, you ask? I can't stand that little plastic piece that goes between my toes. It's so uncomfortable. And my feet get all dirty when I wear them. Also, they make me trip. A lot.

And grapefruit, for obvious taste bud reasons. Too tart. And weird. Why the heck did they name it grapefruit when it tastes nothing like grapes? I don't get it. They should just name it *gross* instead.

As I head downstairs the next morning for breakfast, what do I find in the living room? Mom eating a grapefruit, dressed in sweats, her hair on top of her head in a messy ponytail, and yes, you guessed it, flip-flops on her feet.

Bright orange flip-flops.

"Please tell me you haven't left the house this morning," I say, taking in her appearance.

151

She nods toward the kitchen where several grocery bags sit, waiting to be put away.

I groan. "Mom. What if someone saw you?"

"Lot's of people saw me. A few people I knew when I lived here before, and lots I didn't." She smiles, lifting the spoon to her mouth and eating a piece of grapefruit. "I was at the store, Lucy, so of course there were people there. I'm not the only one who goes to the store in the morning."

"And you didn't care that they saw you like that?"

She shakes her head. "Why would I care about what people think of me? It's not their place to judge."

"They still do judge, though," I mutter under my breath. At least she's in a good mood this morning compared to last night.

"I don't care if they do," she says.

"I know you don't." Then my eyes fall on her shirt.

Or, more importantly, *my* shirt.

"Mom?" I stare at her. She stares back, an innocent look in her eyes. "Why are you wearing my shirt?" The question comes out whiney, but I can't help it. It's my favorite book-ish shirt!

"It's fantastic." She looks down, admiring my *Talk Darcy To Me* shirt.

"For me. It's fantastic for *me*!"

"Hey, I'm allowed to like *Pride and Prejudice*, too. I read it and loved it before you did."

"But you're old . . ." I trail off at the look she gives me. "-ish," I finish. "You can't wear stuff like that! You're a mom!"

She grins. "A *single* mom."

"Oh my gosh. You're killing me, Mom."

She stands and bows. "My work here is done." She starts toward the kitchen. "Oh, and I *totally* rock the old-ish look."

I stare at her as she struts into the kitchen then let out a sigh and follow her.

She puts her plate in the sink and I sit at the counter, watching her. "Grapefruit?" she asks, knowing very well that I hate them.

"No."

"Your loss," she says.

I stare at her twisting a strand of hair around her finger as she looks at her phone. I don't know how she doesn't care about what she looks like right now. Or the fact that she actually went out in public like that. "How are you so confident with yourself?"

She puts her phone in her pocket and is quiet for a minute. She grabs a rag and wipes off the counter, her brows pinched in thought. "You know, I haven't always been confident. When I was your age, I didn't care what people thought and was confident with myself and with pretty much everything, honestly. Through the early parts of my marriage, I was that person, too. But when Dad started having problems, it changed me. It got to the point where I worried about everything. What other people thought of me, how they saw me. What they were saying about Dad behind my back. Our marriage. You. When we have certain trials, everyone seems to have a lot of opinions

153

and don't always keep them to themselves like they should. People are nosy. And some like to tell you how to live your life. Which, in turn, made things worse for me and my self-esteem."

"Really?" She sounds like I feel too often. I worry. All the time. "How did you get over it?"

She shrugs as she sets the rag on the table. "I woke up one day and finally realized this was *my* life. I had a beautiful daughter to take care of and I wanted her to see the confident me again. Not the person I was becoming. With everything I've been through, concerning your father especially, I realized the happy person I used to be was missing. I knew I couldn't find myself again alone, though, so I started to open up to people. I told my story. I went to counseling. My support group back home, remember? Talking with those people who had different, but similar experiences as I did made me realize everyone is dealing with something. Experiences change you. But you can still be who you want to be if you work for it. So I worked for it. And realized people matter. Even if they suffer from an addiction or were married to an addict, or whatever. Every person matters. Everyone is struggling with something we usually can't see. But if there's a way to help others, with things I've gone through, I'll help them. And to do that, I can't worry about what other people think of me. I can love myself, no matter what has happened in the past and I can be who I want to be. My choices are and were my choices and I'll own them. They've helped me grow. The good and the bad. They've made me and us," she gestures to me, "stronger."

I think about my lie. About Dad. I'm not as strong as she is. I especially worry how people will see me once the truth about Dad comes out. I don't know why. It's not like he's here or is a threat to anyone. And I'm not a threat either, but still. The truth sucks sometimes. "Why is it so hard, though? I don't want people to know things about my life. Especially the past."

"You don't have to tell anyone anything if you're not ready. But someday, you'll be ready, and you can provide comfort to those who are going through the same thing. And you'll be okay to talk about it. You won't care what people think. It might take a while to get to that place, but you'll get there. Promise."

"Going to the store in your pajamas is very different than telling people my dad's in prison."

She laughs and puts the rag in the sink before washing her hands. "It is, but they are kind of the same. I don't care what people think when I go to the store like this. It's comfortable and it's me. But it makes others uncomfortable because they think I should dress another way or they think I don't care about my appearance. Which I do, but why should I get all dressed up to go shopping for groceries? Shouldn't I want to be comfortable?"

I chuckle. "Yeah, you have a point."

"And with your father. He has struggled with addictions for years. He's where he is because of his own choices, not mine. I tried everything I could to help him. I tried so many times to get him the help he needed, but when it comes down to it, I can't change him. I couldn't make him go to rehab if he didn't want to. He's an adult. He's the only one who can change himself. And I couldn't wait around for something he may never do."

Tears fill my eyes and I look away from her, blinking them back. She's right.

She comes around the table and wraps her arms around me. "I'm sorry I freaked out last night. I know you're having a hard time. I've just spent so many nights worrying about your father, among other things, and I don't know what I'd do if anything ever happened to you. You're all I care about. You're my whole world. I just worry. That's all. I'm sorry."

"I know you do," I whisper.

"Things will get better. I promise."

"Thanks, Mom."

She pulls away and tucks my hair behind my ear. "You know, maybe I'll go chop my hair and dye it purple. Not just a little purple, though. The whole thing. Then we'd be twinsies."

I roll my eyes. "Mom, please don't say *twinsies*."

"But it's so fun!"

"And no purple hair."

She laughs. "I'm teasing. I love you, Luce."

"Love you, too."

My phone beeps and I pull it out of my pocket.

It's a message from Mira.

Mira: The girls are getting together to
ride horses today. Wanna join?

Me: I have no idea how to ride a horse. So,
probably not. Thank you though.

Mira: Will teach U.

Mira: Come on.

Mira: It'll be fun.

Mira: Promise.

Mira: Hello?

Mira: I know you're reading these. I can
see that they've been read.

Mira: Luuuuucccccyyyyyy

Me: Okay! I'll come.

Mira: I knew you'd see things my way.
Meeting at noon at the stables. K?

Me: K

Mira: Wear pants.

I laugh at that.

Me: How did you know I was going to
come pantless?

Mira: I had my suspicions.

I laugh out loud again and set the phone down. "Mira wants me to come over. Is that okay?"

Mom, like always, hesitates before smiling. "I guess. Just be home before dinner, okay? We need to take the wallpaper down in the living room."

I let out a happy sigh. "Finally. Finally, we can repaint that hideous yellow room."

"It'll be a good time. Also, girls' night tonight. We're watching a chick flick and eating all the snacks you want."

"Sounds great, Mom."

CHAPTER 17

"Oh! if people knew what a comfort to a horse a light hand is . . ."
—Anna Sewell, *Black Beauty*

Mira waits for me near the stable doors, a huge grin on her face. "Riding horses is the perfect thing to do to cross something new off your list. Wasn't it *learn a new skill? Do something scary?*"

"This could work for either since I wasn't really expecting to work with an actual animal when I wrote them. I'll probably cross off *learn a new skill*. Even though I'll probably make a fool of myself trying to ride a horse."

"Still. It's gonna be great. We're just going to ride around for a while. Nothing hard. Yet."

"Yeah . . . easy for you to say. I've never ridden a horse."

I follow Mira into the stable where the girls from the beach are waiting. Tiffany, Kay, and Summer. Of course. They all smile as I enter, saying quick hellos.

"Am I the only one who's never done this?" I ask.

Everyone nods, looking apologetic.

"I only learned about a year ago," Tiffany says. "It's not too bad. Alex hates it. He never comes riding with me." She leans toward me. "He's kind of a wimp."

I laugh at that.

"How long have you been together?"

"Three years."

"You're super cute together."

She blushes. "Thanks."

"You ride?" I ask Kay.

"I've done jumping for years," Kay says. "I used to compete, but I don't love it, so I stopped. I just ride for fun now. My older brother competes nationally, though. He still likes the thrill. I couldn't handle the pressure. For me and my horse."

"She's excellent," Summer says. "I've grown up with horses, but I've never competed in anything. Several of our horses board here. The Kelly family takes such good care of their boarders. They love them like their own." Summer walks over to a stall and pets a chestnut horse. "A lot of people don't appreciate horses for what they are. They're so intelligent and loving. They just need someone to respect them and care for them like they deserve."

"They are beautiful," I say.

She smiles. "They are. We've rescued a few. I wish I could rescue them all. Seeing a mistreated horse makes me sick. I want to open a horse refuge when I'm older. I'm going to school to be an equine veterinarian."

She notices the look on my face.

"A horse doctor," she says with a wink.

"Sorry. I don't speak horse lingo."

"I totally get it." She smiles and it's genuine.

I think of Black Beauty. He had a hard life but ended up with humans who finally cared about him like they did when he was a colt. This place holds happy horses that are well cared for and loved. I can tell by the way Mira and Jack treat their animals and how clean everything is. Kelly Stables is truly a wonderful place.

"I'll be honest. Horses scare me a little bit."

She smiles, nodding. "They can be intimidating if you haven't been around them a lot. But most around here are very tame and love human affection. Give them a good grooming or a treat and they'll be your best friend."

"I'll try to remember that."

I'm impressed with Summer's kindness and ambition to go to school to care for horses. Even if she has feelings for Jack and maybe thinks of me as a threat, since I sort of have feelings for him too, she's still been nice to me. I vow to be nice back and to be her friend. I need friends. I don't need to make enemies over a boy. No matter how cute he may be.

I turn toward Mira, who's talking to Tiffany near the door. "So, how am I going to learn how to ride if everyone knows how to do it already? I don't want to be a burden and slow you down."

Mira rolls her eyes. "You're not a burden at all. I invited you today so you could start some lessons. Not actual lessons with a class, but learning enough that you know how to control your horse when we take them to do fun things."

"Like?"

"Let's get going." She ignores my question and walks over to me. "We have a good teacher for you and everything."

"Who?"

"Jack, of course! He's our resident horse trainer, instructor for kids and teens, rodeo rider, the works. Along with Ashton, but he had football something or other today. Uncle Mike taught Jack all he knows, so he'll take good care of you."

I glance around. Jack's not in the stable.

"He's outside." She grins. "Come on!" She grabs my arm and pulls me along with her.

Great. The last time I saw him I drooled on his shoulder. I'm so embarrassing.

There are five horses tied to the fence outside, all saddled and bridled. At least, I think that's what it's called. Jack's standing by a dark brown horse, holding its reins. It's really shiny, has white hair only by its feet, and has a braid in its tail with flowers in it.

"You like her tail?" Mira asks. "Did it myself."

"She's beautiful."

"You'll learn to ride on her. She's the nicest horse we have. And the most obedient."

"Mira!" Tiffany calls, and she leaves me with Jack and hurries over to see what she wants.

"Hey," Jack says as I walk up. "Ready for a new adventure?"

"Not really." I fold my arms across my chest, trying to calm my nerves. "I'm still not over drooling on you."

"I promise I won't hold it against you."

"I'm such a train wreck."

He laughs as he strokes the horse next to him and it moves its head, nudging him sweetly. "This is Bronte. She's very calm, easy to learn on. I picked her out just for you."

He's wearing a cowboy hat today, with a white collared shirt, a few buttons undone and jeans. He wears brown cowboy boots to complete the ensemble.

Standing there in my tennis shoes makes me feel unprepared. I should probably get some boots. But for now, I pretend like I know what I'm doing and don't care what I'm dressed like. "Bronte? As in, the Bronte sisters?"

He shrugs. "My uncle has a thing for books, I guess. Like you. That's why I think it's so funny that you love reading. Our horses are named after literary characters."

My mouth drops open. "No. Way."

"Yep. We have Bronte here, Sherlock, Atticus, that's Mira's horse, Bellatrix, Elinor, Tybalt," he says with a pause. "Oh, and Eyre, Severus, Matilda, Gandalf, and Darcy."

"Oh my gosh, I'm in love with this place. Bookish names for horses? This is the best ever." I glance around. "Also, you have one named Darcy? Which one is he?"

He chuckles at my excitement over my favorite book boyfriend's name.

"I'll show you when we're done. He's a little full of himself sometimes."

"Fitting. And I approve of all of those other names, too. Your uncle is very well read. And awesome."

"He's a good man and loves his horses. And, like you, loves his books. I still don't understand it, though."

"I'll change that."

"I'd like to see you try."

I fold my arms and meet his dark eyes. "Challenge accepted."

He chuckles. "You ready? Bronte's itching to get going."

I watch Jack with Bronte. He's so gentle with her. He strokes her nose, rubs his hand down her cheek, then pulls the reins over her head and lets go so they're resting in front of the saddle.

For me to hold.

Panic starts to sink in now, and I think I'm going to throw up.

"You ready?" he asks.

I glance around and notice all the girls are already on their horses, walking them around the pen.

"You coming riding with us, Jack?" Summer asks.

He shrugs. "I'll see how Lucy does first."

She nods, gives me a small smile, and leads her horse away from us.

"Meet you guys in a few minutes," Mira says as they unlatch a gate across the pen. "Good luck!" She winks at me and gets back on her horse. They all walk their horses through the gate and head out into the pasture, leaving us alone.

I'm suddenly feeling very nervous. And not just about the horse. There's tension between Jack and me, and I don't know how to handle it. Or react to it. I wonder if he feels it too because it's pretty much crushing me.

Especially since last night.

Then I think of Summer. I don't want her to hate me, so I fight the tension and the confused feelings I'm having. I look at Jack and realize he's staring at me, an amused expression on his face. If he only knew what I'm thinking about, he'd probably run far away.

"Okay. First thing you need to do is actually get on the horse."

I frown as he steps to the side, gesturing for me to stand by Bronte. "Yeah, I was hoping there was a way around that part."

He laughs. "We're here to ride the horses not look at them."

"You are . . ."

He puts a hand on my shoulder. "You'll be fine. I promise I won't let anything happen to you. Okay? Just trust me. Bronte is really our most passive horse. She does what she's supposed to and hasn't let us down once."

That makes me feel a little better. And I do trust him. "Okay." I step around the horse and stand by her side. "Now what?"

"Put your left foot in the stirrup, then swing your right leg over her back."

"You want me to, what now?"

"Left foot in stirrup. Grab the saddle horn, and when you're ready, swing your leg over her back and pull yourself up." My shortness does not come in handy at this moment. I can barely get my foot in the stirrup to start. Maybe because I'm wearing skinny jeans. Bad move on my part. Mira just said "pants."

I'm sure I look ridiculous as I struggle. "Uh . . . a little help?"

He laughs again. "Okay. I'm going to kind of push you on." He holds up his hands in defense as my eyes widen. "I teach kids how to ride horses all the time, so I'm used to helping shorties up. Or if you're uncomfortable with me helping you, I'll get you a step stool." He chuckles nervously.

It's so cute when he gets embarrassed.

"I don't need a step-stool, just help me up, Mr. Professional."

He chuckles again as he stands beside me. "Grab the saddle horn," he says, showing me what exactly the saddle horn is—a knobby part of the saddle in the front that I can wrap my hand around. "Right there with your left hand." I reach up and grab it. "Hold it tight since you have to pull yourself up. I'll help where I can."

I sigh, still standing awkwardly with my foot in the stirrup. It's almost like I'm trying to do the splits. "I think there's a problem if I can't even get on the horse in the first place."

"You'll get on. You've just never done it before, so it's a bit awkward. And horses are pretty tall in their own right." He pauses. "Shorty."

"Very funny." The leather of the saddle horn is cool on my hand. "Okay, ready."

"Now pull yourself up as you swing your right leg around her back. One, two, three!"

I pull and swing, just as he says. I feel his hand push lightly on the small of my back, and before I know it, my leg clears the saddle and I'm sitting on a horse.

A real horse.

I fight the urge to freak out and wrap my arms around her neck to hang on for dear life.

She hasn't even moved yet.

I take a deep breath. I'm fine. Totally fine.

Not many people would think this is weird or crazy or even awesome. But I do. Bronte decides at that moment to move forward maybe an inch. I wrap both hands around the saddle horn, my eyes wide, my fight-or-flight instinct kicking in. I need to get off this thing. Bronte is all muscle, so powerful, and could seriously buck me off in two seconds and crush me. I try to slow my breathing and pretend like I'm cool and calm. Collected.

What a joke.

Jack must see the terror on my face, since he reaches up, patting my hand. "You're fine, I promise." He grabs the reins. "I'm going to lead her around for a few minutes and then I'll hand the reins over to you and you can try."

"What? You want me to actually lead this thing?"

The corner of his mouth twitches, and I can he's trying really hard not to smile or laugh at me. "She's gentle. Pull the reins this way, she'll go right. This way, she'll go left. Hold them straight, she'll go straight. If you want her to turn, pull hard to the right or left. She'll do whatever you make her do. And she won't run unless you make her."

"Oh, I'm not planning on making her do anything but stand here. Trust me."

He moves the reins back over her head. "Hang on. I'm going to walk her around for a little bit."

"Okay." I hang on to the saddle horn as Bronte starts a slow walk, following Jack and totally ignoring the weird girl silently freaking out on her back. Once we get going, though, it's not too bad. The slow gait is kind of nice. The cool, horse-stink breeze in my face makes me feel like I know what I'm doing. Sort of.

I could be a cowgirl. For sure.

I chuckle to myself. Right.

Jack stops after we've gone around the little pasture twice. "Okay. Your turn." He hands the reins back to me. "Give her a little tiny kick and she'll start walking."

"You want me to kick her?" I ask, horrified at the thought.

"Not a hard kick. Just a little click of your heels."

I stare at him for a second. "Aren't you coming?"

"You don't want to try it yourself?"

"You really trust me to steer this thing? I have no idea what I'm doing. What if she bolts and I fly off the back?"

"She's not going to bolt. And I'll ride with you, but on my own horse. Bronte will follow Sherlock anywhere. Stay here."

He makes sure I'm settled and disappears into the stable.

Bronte moves a little. "No. Don't do that," I say. "Keep your hooves on the ground." She shakes her head, her brown hair cascading down her neck. "You're a good girl, right?" I stroke the side of her neck. She steps forward again. "Bronte," I warn, as if I'm a mom scolding her child. Like she knows what I'm saying. I'm like a fly to her. She can flick me away if I get too annoying.

Relief shoots through my body as Jack appears on Sherlock. He rides him up beside us. "Okay. Hold the reins now." I hesitate, then grab them. "Pull back on them if you want her to stop, but don't pull too hard or she'll rear up."

"Well *that* makes me want to pull them. And I thought Sherlock didn't like people."

"Most people." He smiles. "He's mine."

"Oh, I don't feel special anymore then." I try to keep my smile off my face.

He shoots me a look. "Come on. Let's go join the others." He leads Sherlock in front of us, and even though I don't do anything, Bronte follows him. I hang on to the reins, but not tight, since I do want her to follow him.

He goes slow, which I'm thankful for. "You okay?" he asks, looking back at me.

"Surprisingly, yes!"

"Good!" He steers Sherlock toward the girls who are riding over near my house. You can see it through the trees.

"You're riding!" Mira shouts as we approach.

Jack stops Sherlock and I pull on the reins, lightly, and Bronte does the same.

"How's riding for your first time?" Mira asks.

"It's actually not bad."

I glance at Jack, who grins and then looks away.

"We'll just ride around for a little bit, and next time we can hit the trails."

"Trails?"

"There are a few horse trails around here that go up in the mountains. So pretty."

"You take them in the mountains?" I stare at her. I could just imagine falling off a horse and rolling down a mountain into a river or something.

I think I read too many books.

"Of course we take them in the mountains. Horses aren't just for rodeos."

"That sounds . . . fun."

She doesn't look convinced. "It will be. Promise." She glances at her watch. "I've gotta get out of here soon."

"Oh? Do you have plans?"

"Just somewhere I need to be at two. It won't take long. Maybe an hour."

"Oh." I want to ask her where, but she would have told me if she wanted me to know.

"Keep riding for a while and get used to Bronte. I'll be back later and we can hang out."

"Okay."

She says goodbye to the other girls and kicks her horse into a run to make it back to the stables.

"Where is she off to?" I ask Jack.

He watches her go, a sympathetic smile on his face. "That's her story to tell. Not mine."

I nod and wonder what Mira is hiding.

As I watch her go, I wonder why Salem seems to be hiding so many secrets. Past and present. No matter how many more I find, I'm determined to figure them all out.

CHAPTER 18

"It's such a happiness when good people get together."
—Jane Austen, *Emma*

My legs hurt. We've been riding for at least a couple hours. I haven't tried trotting or galloping. I know I'd fly off the horse if I tried any of that nonsense, so I just follow Jack around—or I guess Bronte follows Sherlock around—until we're ready to go back to the stables.

The girls kind of keep to themselves, since they already know how to ride horses and they still don't know me very well. They check up on us once, but then race off to another area of the pasture.

I don't mind. I actually enjoy spending time with Jack. He pulls Sherlock back so our horses are walking side by side. "So?"

"So what?" I ask.

"You getting the hang of it?"

"I think so. She's pretty easy to control," I say, turning her to the right to start back down the edge of the pasture again.

"She's a good horse."

"Sherlock seems like he's good, too."

He shrugs. "Depends on the day. He's good for me because I know how to control him and keep him calm, but with other people, he can be pretty impulsive."

"Sounds difficult."

"Sometimes."

"So, do you do rodeos and stuff?"

"Sometimes."

I raise an eyebrow. "Like bucking horses? Or bulls?"

"No. I do team roping. Ashton and I are teammates. We rope steers, if you've ever been to a rodeo. I rope the legs, he ropes the head. So, he's the header, I'm the heeler."

"I've been to a few rodeos. I did live in Wyoming, after all." I think of the roping events and remember how hard it looked. "I don't know how you get both feet roped. Isn't it hard?"

"Really hard. But it's fun. Ashton and I are pretty good. We've been roping for a long time."

"I'd like to see that someday."

"Sure."

A raindrop falls on my nose and I look up. I didn't notice the few wispy clouds from earlier had turned into darker ones.

"You about ready?" he asks as another drop falls on my forehead. "Looks like it's going to rain."

"Yeah. We should probably get back."

I follow Jack back to the stables and he stops and slides off his horse, just as the heavens open up.

I swear, it's just my luck.

He hurries over to me. "Okay, to get off, just do the same thing you did to get on."

I nod as rain pelts me in the face. Bronte doesn't seem to mind; she just stands there. I set down the reins I'm holding and grab onto the saddle horn again. I swing my right leg off, sort of, then get my left foot tangled in the stirrup. Before I know what's happening, I slip off the wet horse and fall right into Jack's arms. He steps back to steady himself, loses his balance, and we both fall in the dirt, which is now turning into mud. I'm mortified.

Again.

"Jack!" I yell, wiping rain out of my face. "Oh, no. I can't believe ..." I trail off, wanting to crawl in a hole somewhere, but he's laughing harder than I've ever heard him laugh before. He hasn't let go of me and I'm lying on top of him as the raindrops start to soak us. His hat has flown off and his dark hair is wet and has dirt sprinkled in it, which is also quickly turning into mud.

"That was graceful," he says, through another round of laughter.

"I'm so sorry! I don't really know what happened!"

And I didn't. One minute I was on the horse, the next I was tackling my horse-riding teacher to the ground. It looks like we've been mud wresting or something with the water and mud pooling around us.

His arms finally unwrap from around me and I stand, slowly, attempting to wipe the mud from my pants and arms. He stands then, even muddier than me. The back of his white shirt is covered in mud. I can't even help him get it off and I feel bad I stained his shirt.

I turn around and see Bronte just standing where I left her, possibly sleeping as the rain soaks her. She doesn't care what's going on around her at all. Sherlock stands near her, pawing the ground with his hoof.

I face Jack again, wiping wet hair from my face. "Seriously, Jack. I'm so sorry. Are you hurt?"

He wipes off the back of his pants with his hands, but it doesn't do much. "I'm fine. Don't worry about me. I'm just glad I was right there or you would have landed face down in the mud."

"It would have been better than smashing you in it!"

He shakes his head. "Nah, I'm fine. Promise." I bend over and pick up his hat. I hand it to him, mud and all. "Thanks," he says, shooting me a grin.

"You're welcome."

He's still smiling, holding his hat and searching my face. I gulp.

"You two okay?" Summer asks, coming up behind us, still on her horse. The rain has slicked her red hair to the sides of her face. "We should probably get the horses back in the stable."

I look away from Jack's piercing eyes and clear my throat. "Yeah. I'm fine."

"Yep," Jack says. "We're good. And we'll be there in a sec."

"Okay." She glances between the two of us, then clicks her horse to keep moving and disappears into the stables.

I don't know what to do now, so I just stand there, meeting Jack's eyes again.

"Let's get the horses inside. Take Bronte's reins and follow me."

I don't ask questions, just do as he says, and the rain keeps coming down.

We're soaked when we make it to the stable. The girls are already there, taking off saddles, brushing down their horses, and wrapping blankets around themselves.

"You're a mess," Tiffany says to Jack.

"I know." He doesn't tell her why, just starts laughing again. "Lead Bronte into that stall and shut the door. I'll take care of her in a minute."

I do as he says.

"You're pretty messy yourself," Tiffany says to me. She hands me a little compact mirror and I gasp at how hideous I look. Sprinkles of mud have splattered all over my forehead and left side of my face and my hair is partly out of its ponytail, strands of brown and purple are stuck to my skin. I try to wipe the mud off, but it just smears everywhere instead. I don't do anything to my hair. There's no point.

"Oh, I look wonderful," I say, giving up and handing the compact back to her.

She laughs. "You two make quite the pair."

I glance over at Jack, who runs a towel over his face and then through his hair. He grins.

"I'm heading out," Tiffany says. "I've gotta be home in five minutes. My horse is fine, so don't worry about her. I came in before it started raining."

"Okay. Later, Tiff," Jack says. After she walks away, he turns to the rest of us. "Let's get these horses cleaned up," he says.

I know he's not talking to me, but I still feel the need to help. I don't know what to do, though, so I just stand there as Summer and Kay help instead. I feel useless as I watch them towel-dry the horses and brush them out.

"Can I do anything?" I ask Jack as he checks on Bronte.

He hands me a towel. "Just dry off her back while I do the rest. Make sure her hair is standing up and not slicked down so she can dry faster. It's not cold outside, but we do need to get most of the moisture off of her so she'll be comfortable."

I start drying her like he says. I move up her back, into her mane, and rub at her neck. She turns her head to look at me and I pet her cheek. She's so sweet.

After we get her as dry as we can, Jack opens the stall door and lets us both out.

"Thanks," he says.

"Sorry, I don't really know what I'm doing."

"Hey, you offered to help, so that's good enough for me. I'll teach you how to care for horses if you're interested sometime."

"I'd like that."

He's still covered in mud and I know I am too.

"I should probably get home and take a shower to get all this mud off of me."

He shoves his hands in his pockets and walks me to the parking lot. "I'm not letting you walk home in this weather." He opens his truck door. "Get in."

"No way. I don't want to ruin your truck."

"You're not that muddy."

"I'm wet, though."

"So am I." The rain is still coming down, though not as hard as before. Still, it's soaking me more as we argue. If you can call it arguing.

"Fine. Just a second." He shakes his head and walks back in the stable. He comes back a few seconds later with some towels and sets them on my seat and his. "There. Now you don't have to worry."

I climb in his truck, raindrops sliding down my face. I wipe them away as I close the door and Jack climbs in the driver's seat.

He starts the truck and pulls out of the parking lot. I don't see any of the girls. They're probably still working on the horses.

It's quiet while we drive, the rain pitter-pattering on the windshield. I wipe away more raindrops that slide down my cheeks and know I probably look like a drowned rat. For some reason, I'm not really embarrassed about it. Probably because he looks just as bad as I do.

Actually, that's a lie. He looks muddy and wet, but he wears it really well. Which is ridiculous to think about. But it's true.

He speaks then, pulling me out of my thoughts. "Thanks for letting me teach you today. It was pretty hilarious actually."

I punch him softly in the arm. "Was not."

"The rain made things interesting. But if I'm being honest, that dismount you pulled off should go down in the record books. It was the funniest thing I've ever seen."

My face turns red and I can't help but laugh, even if I'm totally embarrassed. Again. "Not *ever*," I say.

"Pretty close!"

"Well, you were a good teacher."

His eyes widen. "I did not teach you to get off a horse like that."

"I improvised."

"Obviously."

"Yeah, yeah. I don't know why I always embarrass myself around you. I'm really good at doing that."

"I'm just lucky."

We both laugh, then the truck grows quiet again, the silence ringing in my ears.

"Well, thank you anyway, for teaching me how to ride a horse. Even if I was scared out of my mind. And sort of bad at it."

"You're welcome. And you weren't that bad. Promise. I've seen worse."

I stare at him, not convinced.

"Okay, maybe you're in the top three, but still. You'll get better."

"Thought so."

He laughs. "You can come riding anytime. I teach kids some mornings, and work on roping when I can, but if you ever want to come over ... I mean, come see the horses, that's fine." He pauses. "Do you have my number?"

"I don't."

He pulls into my driveway and parks the truck before we exchange cell numbers. I don't know if I'll be brave enough to text him.

"Great," he says.

I smile. "I think you need to go get cleaned up. You're a walking mud ball."

He glances down at his clothes, stained with mud. "And whose fault is that?"

I sigh. "Mine. I'm sorry about that. Again. I owe you ... something, I guess. For ruining your clothes. And your pride."

He laughs. "My pride?"

"Okay. *My* pride."

"I'll think hard about what that something you owe me should be."

I open the door. "Don't make it too crazy."

"No promises."

I roll my eyes and he laughs. "Thanks again," I say. "And tell Mira to call me if you see her."

"I'll tell her." He watches as I jump down. "Maybe I'll see you later?"

"Yeah." I smile. "Maybe."

CHAPTER 19

"Every man has his secret sorrows which the world knows not;
and often times we call a man cold when he is only sad."
—Henry Wadsworth Longfellow

After explaining my muddy appearance to Mom, I head to my room to grab some clean clothes. I need a shower, stat.

As I grab a few things from my dresser, I spy something white on my desk.

It's another letter.

"No," I say. "Not now." I pick it up, turn it around in my hands for a moment, run my fingers over my name in his handwriting, then let out a deep breath and shove it in the drawer on top of the other one.

I put my face in my hands, suddenly tired and lonely and upset.

I'm not writing him back. I don't want anything to do with him.

But I know deep down that's not true.

I miss him.

I miss Dad.

The stories he'd tell me as a child to help me go to sleep at night. The tickle fights, the nights we'd stay up singing songs as he strummed on his old guitar. The memories flood back.

There were good times. Lots of them.

I miss so many things about Dad before the drugs. The late-night ice cream runs, making up songs while he played his guitar. He'd listen to me talk about my problems or my successes while he painted something beautiful like a mountain scene or a beach. I'd watch, fascinated as he dipped the paintbrush in one color, mixing it with another, before he slid the brush against the canvas, nodding at my words and letting me talk. He was always listening, even if I thought he was more concentrated on his work.

In sixth grade, he came to my art show and bought my drawing of flowers in a vase that I'd done with pencil and some oil pastels. It hung in our living room for a few years, but one night he threw a beer bottle in its direction and the glass in the picture frame shattered and everything fell to the floor.

We haven't bought a new frame yet, but I do keep the picture rolled up under my bed, waiting for the right time to hang it again.

At first, we just thought he was busier than usual at work since he wouldn't come home until the early hours of the morning. He'd finally come in ragged and tired, but then he wouldn't sleep. He'd stay up all night, watching movies, attempting to paint or write songs for his guitar.

Maybe Mom knew something was wrong. But I was so naïve.

At first.

Then he started disappearing for days at a time. He'd come home and he would be so angry. Mom and Dad would yell and scream. He never hit her. That I know of. But still. The yelling.

When he'd sit down to paint, I'd notice his once steady hand would slip and shake. He mixed the wrong colors, stared at the canvas for far too long, the paintbrush held tight in his shaky hand. Instead of smooth lines, the paintings would turn out choppy and uneven, so different from the beautiful and flawless outdoor scenes I was used to seeing. I thought maybe he was tired or something, but the shaking got worse as time went on. He was twitchy. Nervous. Looking over his shoulder or jumping every time there was a noise. It didn't matter what we were doing, or how much Mom tried to help him, the paranoia only grew.

After a few months, we noticed things in the house were disappearing. Game systems, a television, tools, money. He lost his job and decided to take care of himself again, try rehab. Got a new job but lost that one, too. We had a glimmer of hope again with the next job, but he soon lost that one, as well. He'd turned back to the drugs.

I researched symptoms. Paranoia, depression, angry outbursts, and so, so twitchy.

They all pointed to one thing. Something I never thought anyone in my life would actually seek out.

Meth.

How could my dad be on something like that? I didn't believe it at first. Or at least, told myself I didn't. But I knew it was true. What else could it be? So, months went by.

Things got worse. Mom filed for divorce and Dad begged him to take her back but would disappear again and he'd get caught in the same cycle.

An endless cycle.

When he came around, he still managed to find time to tell me he loved me and to sit and listen to me talk. His face was all wrong, though. Tired, dark circles under his eyes, the skin not as tight as before and the bones in his cheeks poked out more than I remembered.

This person was not my dad anymore; it was only a shadow of him. But I held onto that shadow, determined not to let him slip through my fingers and fade away.

Then, one day, he was gone.

The phone call was the worst. I didn't hear the voice on the other end, but I did hear my mother. Her sobs, her anger and sorrow as she curled into a ball on the floor and didn't move until morning. I didn't bother her. I just stayed in my room, wondering what was wrong but too afraid to ask.

I didn't want to know.

She told me the next day after all her tears had gone.

Even though the accident happened after she had filed for divorce, she still loved him. She still does.

His arrest was all over our state's news. The newlywed couple he hit while under the influence died. A second-degree felony. Up to fifteen years in prison.

It's only been six months.

I don't know when I'll see him again. If I'll see him again. If I want to see him again. Mom made it very clear that we were starting over somewhere new after I finished my junior year of high school. And now here we are. Starting over. Far away from him and our old house and town and all the memories they held.

If he hadn't made those stupid choices, that couple would still be alive. They'd be living their new life together, making a family, having adventures.

He'd still be here with us, too.

I stare out the window, thinking of the letter from their family. Wondering what it says. Thinking about Dad's letters, knowing he's waiting for me to respond.

What is it about a letter?

I know I can't write him back yet.

I can't open that family's letter either.

I do want to know what both of them say but ... not yet.

I'm not ready.

CHAPTER 20

"Live! Live the wonderful life that is in you! Let nothing be lost upon you. Be always searching for new sensations. Be afraid of nothing."
—Oscar Wilde, *The Picture of Dorian Gray*

Jack calls me a few days later.

He doesn't text. He calls.

No one calls anymore.

I adore it.

"Hey," I answer, plopping down on my bed.

"Hey. What are you up to today?"

"Nothing. Already helped my mom take that hideous yellow wallpaper down. We're painting tomorrow, since she has a lot of work to catch up on."

"Cool." He pauses. "Hey, I was wondering if you want to go swimming and maybe cliff jumping today. There's a place close to here with some natural pools, waterfalls, and great places to jump."

"Really?" My stomach sinks.

"Yeah. It's kind of a . . . we're doing a group date sort of thing and I'd like you to come with me. If you're up for it?"

"A group date, huh?" I smile.

He chuckles. "Yeah."

"Sure. I'd love to!" Cliff jumping?

"Great! Sorry it's late notice, but my Uncle Mike didn't need my help today. I wasn't even planning on going, but then Mira told me to take you out, so I told her I would." I can hear the smile in his voice. "Because I want to take you. Not because she told me to. Just so we're clear."

"I wasn't doubting," I say. His nervousness is so cute.

"Good. Let's say noon? I'll pick you up. Ashton already picked up Mira. We'll meet them there."

"She went with Ashton?"

"Yep."

"Awesome. Okay, I'll go get ready. See you then."

"See you."

I smile as I hang up.

This day is starting out pretty perfect.

Then I realize we're going cliff jumping.

How did he manage to talk me into doing that?

I'm such a sucker.

And I'm probably going to make a fool of myself.

Again.

The upside? I can cross *Do something scary* off my list.

I hurry and change, then go downstairs and talk to Mom.

"Where do you think you're going?" she asks, looking up from her laptop in the kitchen.

"Jack asked me to go on a date."

She raises an eyebrow. "A date."

"A *group* date," I clarify. "Not just the two of us."

"Where are you going?"

I hesitate. Mom would never let me go cliff jumping. She's so overprotective already. "Just swimming. They're going to some natural pools or something. There are waterfalls there, too." Which is true, so technically I didn't lie. I just didn't mention the cliff jumping part.

She studies me. "Do you know how long you'll be gone? We really need to go pick up some job applications around town."

"I'm not sure. Most of the day, probably."

Her eyes fall on her computer again, though she doesn't type or anything. She's quiet so long I'm afraid of what her answer is going to be. Finally, she looks up again. "If you text me when you get there and when you're leaving to come home, you can go."

"Really? Thanks, Mom!"

She points a finger at me. "And if you're really going with a group."

I let out an annoyed breath. "Mom, I'm really going with a group. I promise. You can even ask Jack when he gets here."

She nods. "Okay. If you forget to text, you're grounded."

"Deal." I race back upstairs to get ready.

The drive to wherever he's taking me is comfortable. It's been about fifteen minutes and we have about fifteen minutes to go. Which is good. I like spending time with Jack.

A lull in the conversation prompts me to ask a question I've been meaning to ask him for a while. "Will you tell me about your friend Ben?" I look at him, hoping I don't put him in a bad mood because of it. I just really want to know about his best friend. It would be hard to lose a best friend. Or a dad for that matter. "I mean, if it's not too hard to talk about."

He smiles. "You would have liked him. He was . . ." He shakes his head. "Crazy. Kind of like Mira, actually. Just without the sass."

"Sounds dreamy," I say.

He shoots me a look and I laugh.

"I'm joking. He sounds like a fun guy."

"He was." He's quiet for a moment. "I wish I could have helped him more. I didn't know he was so bad until . . ." He shakes his head. "I still remember every single tiny detail of that day. I was in first period when my mom came to get me. It was like a bad dream. Like everything was moving in fast motion and I was stuck in this slow reality, trying to process things. It was really coming out of that fog."

"I know the feeling." He reaches over and squeezes my hand then lets go quickly. Too quick. My skin tingles and I want to reach for hand and hold it again.

"I know there's nothing I could have done, but I still feel guilty. He was my best friend and I didn't know how bad he was. I should have known. I should have gotten him some help."

"You never know what's going on in someone's head, no matter how well you think you know them."

He nods.

"It wasn't your fault though," I say.

"I know." He smiles. "It's nice to have someone to talk to who wasn't close to the situation. No one else really understands. It helps to talk about it sometimes."

"You're welcome."

"You can always talk to me, too."

"I know. I have a bad habit of holding things in. But I'm trying."

"You miss your dad?"

He has no idea. "Yes." I really do. But he thinks he's dead. Not sitting in prison in a different state. My stomach twists at the lie that I've woven. The lie I still haven't owned up to. I miss my dad and I could still see him if I wanted. Yet, I don't. I'm pretending he's gone, just like Jack's friend, Ben. How can I do something so selfish and pretend he's not there? How can I lie to my new friends? To myself?

It's quiet and I look out the window, wishing my hand were still in his. Wanting to tell him the truth. My heart beats fast in my chest. I take a deep breath. What will he say once I tell him the truth? Will he think less of me? Will he think I'm going to turn out to be a horrible person because of Dad's choices and actions? I open my mouth to say it, but a new song comes on the radio just then and he reaches over to turn it up.

"Great song," he says. "Do you like Blue Fire?"

I smile. "I do."

And just like that, the lie stays hidden.

I lean back against the headrest and close my eyes, defeated.

Jack doesn't know the comfort he's given me. Even though the lie hovers in the back of my mind, the truth is, I know I can talk to him when I'm ready. I just need to find the courage to do so. I need to stop being afraid of the truth coming out and how it will affect my family. Especially me. Because last time, with Dad being all over the news? It wasn't pretty.

And Jack trusting me enough to tell me about Ben?

He trusts me.

I feel sick all over again and stare out the window, wishing my guilt would go away and knowing I'm the only one who can make it so.

CHAPTER 21

"Our doubts are traitors and make us lose the good we oft might win by fearing to attempt."
—William Shakespeare, *Measure for Measure*

We arrive a few minutes later. Jack grabs my bag with my beach towel and carries it for me as we head toward the water.

It's beautiful here. Trees everywhere. A few areas I'd call pools are filled with blue green water, with a few cliffs surrounding each area, some higher than others. Some people are jumping off a waterfall, as well, though it's not really high. The cliffs make me nervous, though.

Mira is in the water with a group of people and shrieks in delight when she sees us. She scrambles out of the pond and runs over to us, throwing her arms around me and soaking my shirt.

It's a good thing I already have my swimsuit on underneath.

"Oh! Sorry," she says, attempting to wipe the water off my shirt, but it's already soaked in.

"It's fine. I'm getting wet in a minute anyway."

"True. I'm so happy you came! Everyone's already swimming if you want to join us." She gestures to the pools and a few of them wave. Summer's here with Brody, but Ashton is dunking him under water while she stares at Jack as he takes off his shirt and sets it on a rock with his towel. He puts my bag next to it.

"Well?" he asks. "Let's go."

I smile, suddenly embarrassed. I know I'm in my swimsuit, but I have to strip down to it.

I pull my shirt off, since that's the easiest, but taking shorts off in front of a really cute guy is kind of—no, not kind of, *really*—uncomfortable. "Turn around," I say to Jack.

"Okay?" He laughs but does as I say.

Mira laughs as well.

I slip my shorts off and stuff them in my bag. "Okay. Ready."

We follow Mira over to the closest pool. The water is so green now. It looked blue from further away.

Jack looks at the water a moment before diving right in.

There are a few people I haven't met before talking to Summer and Mira, and Mira quickly introduces me to them, but I forget their names the second after she says them. Ten more people are ten too many to remember names for.

Jack grabs my hand under the water after I get in and tugs me toward the waterfall. "Come on. Let's go jump."

"Is it safe?" I ask.

"Very. Promise. The waterfall isn't high."

I swim after him until we reach some rocks and then follow him out of the water and up a tiny trail. He takes my hand as he crosses a few slippery rocks until we're staring down at the pool.

He's right. It's not high.

"Ready?" he asks, still holding my hand.

"Uh . . ."

He jumps, pulling me with him.

We hit the water together, and as my head pops up at the surface, he's already there, laughing.

"That wasn't so bad," I say after I choke up some water. Really. It wasn't. It was like jumping off a diving board. "Next time warn me, okay? My mouth was wide open!"

"Sorry." He smiles then points at one of the cliffs. "That was your trial run. Now we'll tackle the cliffs."

"I don't know about that."

"It's really not bad," Mira says. "I've done it. And if I can do it, since I'm a huge wimp, you'll be able to do it."

"She really is a huge wimp," Ashton says, coming up behind her.

She splashes him in the face. "Am not."

Jack whispers in my ear. "She really, really is."

I look up at one of the cliffs for a moment and then at the smooth water below. My eyes float back up to the cliff's edge. There's a girl, probably my age, standing at the top. After a moment's hesitation, she jumps. Her body is straight, her arms to her sides, and she hits the water with barely a splash. When she comes to the surface, she laughs and calls up to the next person, her boyfriend it looks like, and once she's out of the way, he jumps.

"You want me to jump off of that?" I ask, swallowing the sudden lump in my throat.

Jack laughs. "Yep."

I glance toward the water again. "No rocks at the bottom?"

"Nope." He smiles and puts his arm around me. He's getting more comfortable, which is nice.

"I've heard of people dying from cliff jumping."

"Only if they're stupid. So, not often." He frowns then but shakes his head, ridding himself of whatever he was thinking, and smiles again.

"Come on," he says, grabbing my hand and pulling me out of the water, up a trail, and toward the cliff.

Before I know it, Summer's behind us with Brody right behind her.

"Wait up," she yells.

"Race you to the top," Brody tells her, and he takes off running up the trail. Summer sneaks a glance behind her at Jack but then hurries after Brody.

"Is he always like that?" I ask.

"Yep."

We're on the cliff now, just a few more feet to climb. I step on rocks jutting out of the cliff and pull myself up. "I don't know about this," I say once we reach the top. Summer and Brody are nowhere to be seen. I look down and see them swimming in the water.

Wow. They weren't scared to jump at all.

"I'm not sure if I can do it."

"You don't have to if you don't want to."

"I want to." I sigh. Do I? Do I really? "What do I do?"

Jack nudges me toward the edge. "Okay. A few things to remember as you jump. Point your feet. Keep your arms tight to your sides. If your arms are flapping around, they'll be really sore tomorrow. And if you don't point your toes, the bottoms of your feet will slap the water. That hurts. Trust me."

"So, I can't plug my nose?"

He shrugs. "You can if you need to, I guess. Just keep your arm close to your body if you do. It's better if you don't, though. Just breathe out through your nose when you hit the water and you won't get water up your nose."

"Right."

We step onto the ledge after another jumper hits the water. I peek over the side and my heart starts racing. What am I doing? How did I let him talk me into this? The water is so far below. Is this even legal?

Jack seems to sense my hesitation. I feel his hand on my back. "Do you want me to go first?"

"No. I can do it." My voice is tiny and shaky and I swallow. My chest tightens and I take a shaky breath. I push back the panic that I can feel welling up.

I can do this. I'll be fine. I'm not going to die. This cliff is not that high. I'm brave. This is fine. Scary, but fine. It's fine.

Stop saying fine.

"Lucy." His voice is so soft. So kind. So . . . worried.

He takes my hand. "You look terrified. You don't have to do this, okay? I can walk you back down right now and we can just swim around instead. I'm sorry I talked you into this."

I take a breath as he squeezes my hand.

He leans closer. "You don't have to jump, okay?"

"I know."

He gives my hand a tug to pull me away from the cliff's edge, but I stand my ground. He lets go, still looking worried.

I look at the water again then glance back at him. "I can do this."

"Lucy," he says.

I shake my head. "I can."

I am brave.

I can do hard and scary things.

I jump.

CHAPTER 22

"When I discover who I am, I'll be free."
—Ralph Ellison, *Invisible Man*

Freefalling is amazing, but then I hit the water faster than expected. It doesn't hurt, since I do what Jack tells me and keep my arms to my sides. I also keep my eyes closed and swim up as soon as I splash down. My ears fill with pressure and hurt a bit until I kick my legs and finally get myself to the surface. I take a deep breath of air, spot Mira and her friends watching and clapping for me, and then I do something unexpected.

I laugh.

The adrenaline from doing something so daring, so *extreme* for me, is ... thrilling. I swim out of the way so I can stand and watch Jack jump. He hits the water with barely a splash then joins me seconds later.

"You did amazing," he says, standing up and pulling me into a hug. "Did you hurt yourself? Are you alright?"

"I'm fine. It was actually really fun. Can we go again?"

"Of course!"

"Nice job," Summer says, wringing her long hair out.

"Thanks." I give her a smile. She smiles back. I call that a win.

Brody is watching Summer, his mouth half open. She really is a cute girl and Brody obviously notices. He watches her a moment longer before he reaches out and pushes her back into the water, soaking her hair once more. He glances at me, I'm guessing wanting to do the same thing, but I see a slight shake of Jack's head out of the corner of my eye and Brody backs off. Instead, he makes Mira his next target.

"Seriously? I didn't want to get my hair wet!" she yells, jumping on his back and trying to dunk him. "Ashton, help me!"

Ashton obliges and it turns into an all-out war until they finally dunk him, but only with Summer and another kid's help.

I watch them, feeling good about things. I'm sort of part of a group of friends again. My old group was fun, yes, but I always felt like I wasn't myself. Here, I feel more like myself since I'm not relying on someone like Ashley to make the first move and talk to someone new. She was always the adventurous one and I went along for the ride. Mira sort of reminds me of her, but she's different, too. She includes me but doesn't force me to pick a guy or do something I'm not comfortable doing. She's helped me grow more confident.

I wonder how Ashley's doing. I haven't talked to her for a while. She's probably making the most of her summer.

Just like I'm trying to.

I'm here with a bunch of people who seem kind and easygoing. I'm excited to learn everyone's names. Because right now, I sort of feel like I belong.

It's a really good feeling.

Maybe I can get away with my lie. Dad will never be here. No one will ever know. If I can keep my secret, things could stay like this forever. No one will judge me for having a felon for a father. No one will pity me or walk away and not look back because their parents say I'm a bad example. If my dad had issues, I probably did, too, is how people think.

If the truth never comes out, no one will think something's wrong with my family. With me.

My stomach clenches.

The guilt is trying to claw its way out. I should have told Jack when I had the chance.

"Jack, let's show these girls what we can really do," Brody says, shaking out his wet hair out sending water droplets everywhere.

Jack looks at me. "You okay if I go real quick?"

"I'm fine."

He takes off after Brody as they climb up to the top of the cliff again.

"So," Summer says, gliding through the water toward me. "You and Jack, huh?"

My cheeks heat. "I don't know . . ."

She smiles. "It's okay, Lucy. I'm not mad."

"Really? I can tell you like him. I'm sorry, I—"

She holds up a hand, stopping me. "It's not a big deal. Yes, I do like him, but I've liked him forever and he hasn't noticed me at all. When you came along . . ." She sighs. "He only has eyes for you. And it's okay. I'll get over it."

"I'm sorry." I feel lame.

"Boys aren't worth fighting over. If two people have a connection, they should try it out. See where it goes. I won't get in the way of that. And Jack's had his chances to like me back. He just doesn't." She shrugs and smiles as she looks up at the cliff. The boys are standing on top. "Are we good then?" she asks.

"Yeah. We are."

How can someone be so kind? So happy for someone else, even if it makes them unhappy? I need to be more like her.

She gives me a small hug, which is awkward, but nice.

And the guilt I felt about stealing Jack from her, if you could call it stealing, fades away.

We watch the boys as they look down and wave, then Brody jumps, doing some weird pose in midair, then going back to arms and legs straight as he hits the water.

I laugh as he comes up, spitting water everywhere. Then look back up at Jack. He meets my eyes, then lets out a whoop and jumps. He does a flip then hits the water the way he's supposed to.

"What the heck was that?" I cry as he swims over to me.

"I should be in the Olympics," he says.

"That was pretty great, but just one flip? Lame," I tease. "I've seen better."

He grins and bumps my shoulder with his own, his eyes lingering on mine. "Ready to head back up?"

I glance at the cliff and smile. "Yes." I climb out of the water, tripping on a rock as I do so, but manage to keep my balance. For once. "I'll race ya!"

The drive back from cliff jumping is uneventful, other than I'm exhausted and wet. My towel is draped over the back of Jack's seat and tucked under my butt so I don't ruin his truck.

There's an easy, calm feeling between us. But there's that tension, as well. I like him. I admit it. He hasn't said anything about how he feels, but others have implied he may feel the same, but I won't push it. I'm not one to rush things.

"Thanks for taking me today," I say as he pulls in my driveway.

"Thanks for coming. I had so much fun. And you were amazing at cliff jumping."

"After I figured out I wouldn't hurt myself, I was fine."

"You did great."

He stops the truck. "I'll let you out. Stay put. This is a group-ish date, after all."

I chuckle and he gets out and walks around the truck, opening my door. He reaches out a hand and helps me down. He lets go too soon once again.

He walks me to the porch and we stop at the bottom of the stairs.

"Thanks again, Jack. I had so much fun."

"You're welcome."

He's nervous.

So am I.

I'm surprised at the emotions bubbling inside me. I really, really want him to kiss me. Which is ridiculous. I barely know the guy. But I guess I do know him better than I did a week or so ago. Each moment we spend together, I get to know more about him.

"Can I . . . hug you?"

I'm so shocked at the question, I burst out laughing. "Of course."

He leans forward, a little embarrassed as he chuckles quietly, and wraps me in a tight hug, but then lets go before *I'm* ready to let go. I'm still in his arms, and I notice his eyes flick from my own, to my lips, then back.

He wants to kiss me, too.

But then he lets go and my dreams are dashed.

Not really.

But I *am* disappointed.

At least he didn't give me a high five or something. That would have been awkward.

"Talk to you tomorrow?" he asks, shoving his hands in his pockets.

"Definitely."

He nods then gets in his truck and drives away.

I open the door and go inside, my heart thumping a million miles an hour. Still.

He wanted to kiss me. I know he did.

"Lucy?"

I move into the living room where Mom sits, reading a book. She has her glasses on, her hair looks messier than normal, and she's munching on potato chips.

"Hey, Mom."

"Did you have fun on your date?"

"It wasn't a real date. Just friends."

"But couples . . . you said it was a group date."

I shrug. "It was. Sort of." A few couples but a few singles, too.

She nods. "Thanks for being home at a decent hour. I don't like you at the beach this late."

"Oh. I didn't go to the beach."

"What? I thought you said you were going swimming?"

"We did. We went to this place with these gorgeous pools. I told you that, didn't I? There were a lot of people and Jack even talked me into going cliff jumping." The minute I say it, I wish I could take it back.

Mom's expression changes in an instant. Her eyes widen and her book falls from her hands. She jumps to her feet, startling me, and then she has me by my shoulders. "You did what? Tell me you didn't. Tell me you didn't go cliff jumping."

"Mom?" Her fingers dig into my skin. "Ouch. You're hurting me."

Her fingers relax at once, but she still has a hold of me. "Lucy, this is very important. Tell me you didn't go cliff jumping."

"I did? Sorry, I didn't know you were against it. Why are you freaking out so bad?"

She lets go of me, her face pale. She paces around the room, running her fingers through her messy hair. "I can't believe you didn't tell me. I can't believe you went and . . . why? Why didn't you tell me?"

"I didn't think it was a big deal?"

"A big deal?" she shouts. "It's a huge deal!" She paces the room again. I've never seen her like this. I don't know what I've done or why she's acting this way. "We're going job hunting tomorrow. I told you when we moved here we'd find you a job. That will keep you busy and you can meet friends that way."

"I'm fine with getting a job, but I already have friends, Mom!"

"No! Those friends could have gotten you killed!"

"Seriously? Why are you always so paranoid about everything? I'm almost eighteen! I'm allowed to have some fun! It wasn't a big deal!"

"I'm still your mother and I still make the rules in this house."

"But your rules are so controlling!" I stand there, breathing hard, my brain working overtime trying to figure out what's going on and why she's acting so crazy. "You don't let me do anything! You barely even let me leave the house unless you know exactly what I'm doing. And even then you freak out!"

"I've let you do a lot of things this summer, Lucy."

"Yeah, after making me go through a checklist of rules every time I leave the house! You don't have to be so protective, Mom. I'm not five years old!"

"You're still a child! You could still get hurt!"

"So could you!" Her reasoning doesn't make sense. I stare at her.

Then I remember my list.

Susan.

Does this have something to do with her? Is that why she's so paranoid? Was she with her when she died?

"Mom?" This is probably the worst time to bring her up, but I know deep down, her reactions to dark water or cliff jumping or whatever has to do with Susan. Is that how she died? "Can you please tell me about Susan? This has to do with her, doesn't it? How did Susan die?"

Her face goes even paler. "Don't bring her name up again," she whispers. "Please, Lucy. Don't talk about her. And I forbid you to ever go cliff jumping again. Do you understand me?"

I back away from her. She looks like she's gone crazy. "Mom, we were careful! There were tons of people there!"

"It doesn't matter! It's dangerous! You could have . . ." She trails off, closing her eyes a moment. She takes a deep breath then points a finger at me. "Promise me. Promise me you'll never do that again. I don't want you anywhere near that place. Do you understand?"

I stare at her, her glasses perched almost on the edge of her nose, her hair in disarray. "Why?"

"It doesn't matter why. I'm your mother and you obey my rules."

"Your rules make no sense!"

"They do to me!"

"I'm not promising anything."

"Lucy."

"Tell me why? Why are you so insistent about this? Why won't you ever talk about anything that's happened in this town? Your childhood? I know something happened. I know there was a reason you never wanted to visit Grandma here, why you didn't want to move back here. And I know it has to do with Susan."

Her eyes grow wide and she opens her mouth to speak again, but I beat her to it. "You can't expect me to just sit here and pretend everything is okay, when clearly, it's not! You're going crazy, Mom! I've never seen you like this, not even when we were dealing with Dad. Something happened and I want to know what!"

She stares at me. Her eyes glaze over and it's almost as if she's staring through me now. She shakes her head. "Go to your room."

"Mom—"

"Go!"

We stare at each other for a few more seconds before I turn and run upstairs, slamming my door behind me. I throw my bag of wet clothes in the corner and get ready for bed, determined to help Mom overcome whatever is eating at her.

If she'll let me.

For her sake and mine.

CHAPTER 23

"I am longing to be with you, and by the sea, where we can talk together freely and build our castles in the air."
—Bram Stoker, *Dracula*

The next few days pass by and Mom is still not herself. She took me to town and we picked up a bunch of job applications, but that's about it.

I've filled out a few. I know I should get a job to help Mom with bills, but I don't want to get one just to "keep me busy," as she put it. I want to work where *I* want to work—not where she wants me to work and for all the wrong reasons.

So, the days go by. Me, looking for more jobs online. Searching some social sites, checking up on Ashley, who is quite obsessed with her new boyfriend and apparently doesn't have time to talk to me at all.

I should probably text her, but I don't. She's drifting away, and I'm sure she doesn't really have time to think of me right now.

Mira and Jack have work to do, so I read a lot, help Mom with some projects even though she doesn't talk to me unless she has to, and also cross a few things off my list.

Lucy's Summer Bucket List

1. Read twenty-five books.
2. ~~Go swimming at the beach. At night.~~
3. ~~Learn a new skill.~~ (Horseback riding.)
4. ~~Meet someone new.~~
5. ~~Do something crazy. Something I'd never normally do.~~ (Cliff jumping)
6. Find an awesome and challenging hike. (Research)
7. ~~Try a new look. Dye my hair? Cut it? Something daring.~~
8. Outdoor Concert. (Need to research.)
9. Summer Romance. (There must be kissing for it to count.) *Jack?
10. Find out who Susan is and visit her grave. (Mom knows. Keep asking.)
11. Forgive Dad.

Things are getting done, and what's left are the hardest items. I guess some of them aren't *that* hard—I just have to do some research—but the Dad one and the Susan one are driving me crazy.

Another letter came. Along with Oakley's wedding announcement. She looks gorgeous in it, standing on the beach wrapped in Carson's arms.

I can't wait to see her in August.

I put my summer list away, bored. I woke early this morning for no reason. I'm not sleeping well lately. Too much going on in my head, I guess.

Mom's not up yet and I don't want to bug her, especially with how she reacted after news of my cliff jumping and how she's been acting ever since. I write her a note and leave it on the counter, telling her I'm going out. Hopefully she'll feel better when I come back.

Maybe.

I walk down the driveway, not really knowing where I'm going, and finally stop at the fence lining Kelly Stables. I lean against it, watching a few horses graze. I don't see Sherlock anywhere, which makes me sad. He's my favorite.

I see people across the field, Ashton I think, giving riding lessons to some kids. I think I spot Jack on a horse, but I'm not sure. There's no cowboy hat in sight and that's what he's usually wearing when he's working or riding.

A few minutes later, someone rides across the field toward me and I smile.

"Hey," Jack says, sitting on a huge black horse. He stops just shy of the fence.

"Holy . . ." I trail off, staring at the horse. It's enormous.

Jack laughs at my reaction. "This is Darcy. I figured you'd want to meet him, seeing how much you love *Pride and Prejudice*."

Darcy sniffs my hand when I reach out to stroke his velvet nose. "He's beautiful. And huge."

"Yeah, he's pretty awesome. A little spirited, but he's a good horse."

I keep stroking Darcy's nose and he doesn't seem to mind at all. I glance up at Jack. "Aren't you working?"

"Not right now."

"What are you doing later?"

Jack cocks his head to the side. "Why later?"

"I assume you're working later, which means sooner. Than later."

"Huh?"

"I have no idea."

He chuckles and glances behind him. "You know what? Come with me."

"What? Now?"

"Yes." He sets the reins to the side and drops to the ground. Darcy shakes his head in annoyance but stays where he's at. "Come with me." He holds out a hand.

I take it.

He smiles, his white teeth gleaming, and pulls me over to the horse. "Now, Darcy's a little taller than Bronte, so I'll give you a boost."

"No way."

"Oh, come on."

I sigh. "Fine."

I barely get my foot in the stirrup, when Jack asks, "Ready?"

"Uh . . . No?"

He doesn't say anything else, just lifts me up, pushing me onto the horse. I barely even have to do anything.

My cheeks flame as his hands leave my thigh. "Thanks."

He climbs up behind me.

"I thought horses couldn't hold two people?"

He situates himself in the saddle behind me. "Not for long, no. But we're not going far."

His breath tickles my ear and his arms wrap around me, taking hold of the reins. "Ready?"

"For?" I'm nervous. This horse could seriously take me out with one little gallop.

Jack chuckles and kicks the horse to move. Darcy takes off, bouncing me all over the place. I can't help it—I let out a high-pitched scream.

Jack laughs behind me and wraps one arm around my waist, pulling me closer to him.

I realize we're not running that fast, but still, it's jarring. After a moment of being jostled, I find a rhythm and relax.

"This isn't so bad," I shout.

He laughs in response and steers us toward the stables. He pulls on the reins, bringing Darcy to a stop.

Jack gets off first, then helps me down. I don't flatten him to the ground this time, but I still end up in his arms as my feet hit the ground.

I look up at him, smiling. "Much more graceful this time."

He grins. "Sort of. I guess."

I smack him softly and he laughs.

"So, I have an idea. You mentioned one of your items on your list was to find a good hike, right?"

"Yes," I say slower than I mean to. "Why?"

"Let's just say, I know the perfect place. You don't have anything to do today, do you?"

"Nothing. I have to drop off a few job applications, but I'll probably do it tomorrow."

"Great. A hike it is then. Let me go change and I'll take you home to change. Then we'll go."

After he gives Darcy to one of the stable workers, I follow him to his truck and feel excitement bubbling as he drives us to his house. I haven't been to his house yet, and I'm not sure if I should stay in the truck when he stops.

"You coming?" he asks, a smile on his face.

"Yeah." I unbuckle and jump out of the truck to hurry after him.

His house is beautiful. Old, like mine, but everything has such a classic farmhouse feel. The floor is hardwood, the walls are a soft white with pictures of chickens, baskets full of eggs, and paintings of flowers hanging on each one.

A lovely woman about Mom's age comes down the stairs, a basket of laundry in her arms.

"Hey, Mom," Jack says. "This is Lucy."

"Oh!" She nearly drops the basket before Jack grabs it out of her hands and sets it on the floor. She tucks a strand of blond hair behind her ear then holds out a hand. "Hi, Lucy. Jack's told me so much about you."

I glance at him and he rolls his eyes, but I can see the tips of his ears turning red.

"I'm taking Lucy to Silver Falls today," Jack says. "She's never been before, and I thought she might like the waterfalls."

"Oh, you'll love Silver Falls. It's so beautiful. One of the crown jewels of Oregon, in my opinion." She turns to Jack. "Be safe, son, okay?"

"Mom," he says, as she kisses his cheek. "We'll be fine."

She smiles then turns to me. "I have to worry. He's my baby."

"Mom," he says again, this time with a groan.

She and I both laugh.

"Don't worry. Jack's seen my mom in her pajamas, so . . . yeah."

"I met your mom at the store the other day. She's a lovely woman. My husband actually knows her. I'd introduce you two, but he's at work right now."

I raise an eyebrow at Jack.

"He helps out at the stables, but he works at a law firm for his full-time job."

"Oh."

"Let me go get changed. I'll be right back." He bounds up the stairs.

"You can have a seat, honey," Jack's mom says.

She gestures toward a little bench in the entryway. It's covered in padding, with black and white spots on the material, like a cow.

I sit.

"It was so nice to meet you. You're welcome to come over anytime. We'd love to have you for dinner. Maybe next week?"

"Oh, thank you. That would be nice."

She nods, gives me a smile, and heads down the hall.

I glance at a clock on the wall with apples on its face. It's only 7:30. I'm actually surprised I'm up this early.

Jack doesn't take long. Before I know it, he's hurrying down the stairs, dressed in a white T-shirt and shorts. "Do you like turkey sandwiches?"

"Why?"

"We're gonna be hiking a for a while, so we'll want some lunch."

"Okay, yes, turkey is fine."

I follow him into the kitchen, which is cute with lots of windows and a little nook where the light spills in. The nook would be perfect for reading.

"Can I help with anything?" I ask as Jack hurries around the kitchen, puling things from the fridge and cupboard.

"Nope. I'm good."

Ten minutes later, he has a backpack full of food and water. "Ready?"

"Are you sure you don't want me to carry anything?"

He shakes his head. "I invited you. I carry the food."

"Fine," I say, defeated, but smile just the same.

"Bye, Mom," he yells as we head toward the front door.

"Love you!" is the reply.

"Your mom is so nice," I say. I love how she adores him. And he obviously loves her, too.

"She's pretty great at embarrassing me." He laughs and opens the truck door for me.

"I know the feeling."

When we get to my house, I just run inside and he stays in the truck. The house is quiet, yet the car's outside so I know Mom's home. I don't know if she's still sleeping or what, but I don't dare wake her and face her wrath if she's still in a mood. I change into a tank and some shorts, write another note and tell her where I'm going, making sure I have my cell with me before I leave.

When I get in the truck, rock-and-roll blasts from the radio. I look at Jack in surprise. "You like rock music?"

He smiles, a little sheepish. "Mira has tried to get me to like country, since she calls me a country boy, but I just can't get into it."

"Want to listen to Blue Fire?"

"Of course! It's too bad they broke up. I like Jaxton Scott's new stuff, though."

"Me too."

He plugs in his phone, turns the volume up, and peels out of the driveway.

CHAPTER 24

*"'My idea of good company . . . is the company of clever,
well-informed people, who have a great deal of conversation;
that is what I call good company.'
'You are mistaken,' said he gently, 'that is not good company,
that is the best.'"*
—Jane Austen, *Persuasion*

The first thing I notice about Silver Falls State Park is that it's green. So green that I pull my phone out and take pictures before we even leave the truck.

"You know, they'll probably be clearer if you get out," Jack says.

"Yeah, you're probably right. It's just so beautiful!" I get out, marveling at all the trees, snapping a few more photos on my phone. "Where are we hiking?"

"We're going to hike the Trail of Ten Falls. It starts right there. It's pretty long, probably about three to four hours. Is that okay?"

I nod. "I like a good challenge. My dad used to take me on hikes in Wyoming. We did some pretty impressive ones."

"So you're up for it then. Excellent. This one is worth it. The ten waterfalls are awesome." He hitches the backpack on his shoulders and pulls out his phone to check the time. "Ready to go? Do you need to do anything before we start?"

"Nope. I'm ready."

He starts walking and I hurry until we're walking side by side. He surprises me and grabs my hand as we start up the trail together. He doesn't let go.

I don't mind. Not one bit.

The trail is pretty much dirt and rocks, but the trees and the foliage? Breathtaking. Moss and vines snake up the trunks of the trees, covering them like a warm sweater. The ground is blanketed in green as well, and the air smells so good. A little like rain from all the mist. "I've never seen anywhere like this place before."

"I love it here. I like coming early because the crowds get worse the later it gets. This way we'll get some good pictures and we won't have to wait for people to get out of the way."

"It's pretty busy then?"

"All the time. All year round."

"Really?"

"Yep."

The first waterfall we reach is the South Falls waterfall. It's so beautiful I can't even speak. It's huge. There's even a trail to walk behind the falls. Jack guides me around, careful as we step on wet ground. I take in the power of the water, crashing onto the rocks as we walk. So crazy. Before I know it, we're behind the waterfall. I reach my hand out, letting flecks of water dot my skin, breathing in the cool, misty air.

"This is fantastic," I say.

Jack laughs. "It's pretty awesome. And this is just the beginning of the hike." He grins. "Think you can keep up?"

"The question is, do *you* think you can keep up?"

He laughs and squeezes my hand. When we make it to the other side, I pull out my phone and snap a few more pictures, then Jack pulls his out and takes one of the both of us. I'm sure I'm smiling weird. I'm super great at ruining selfies.

I'm surprised how easy the hike is. It's not difficult, like some, with rocks and things to climb over. It's pretty smooth, just inclines in some places, and sometimes the trail is damp from the spray of the waterfalls.

The North Falls we hit next. I can't get over how green everything is. The trees, the bushes, the moss, everything. It's like I've stepped into a fairytale or something. I keep waiting for fairies to flit back and forth from the trees or for a unicorn to step through the bushes.

It would not surprise me one bit. That's how beautiful it is.

"It's magical here," I say, earning a laugh from Jack.

The only time he's let go of my hand is to take a picture or adjust his bag, otherwise he's picked it right back up. I like the feel of my hand in his. It's perfect. Again, like a fairytale.

He's quiet a lot, taking in the scenery, watching the water spill into the ponds. I wonder what's going on in his head. He's very observant, and from what I've noticed, a really deep thinker.

I appreciate that.

Most of the time, if silence passes between me and someone else, I get all awkward and have to fill it.

It's different with him. The silence is comfortable. He's easy to be with. He doesn't try to show off or get my attention in obnoxious ways. He's quiet, thoughtful, gentle.

I wish more guys were like him.

And I'm not gonna lie: I'm a little nervous about today. It's our first real date-like outing, and I'm still not sure if he really likes me like that.

But I definitely like him.

He wouldn't be holding my hand right now if he didn't like me, right?

I can never tell what a guy is thinking. And the same is true with him.

We reach Double Falls. The ground is really wet around here, but I stop and take a picture anyway. The water spills over a high cliff and moss covers the rocks at the bottom where the water hits. How does moss grow in such random places? You'd think there would be nothing but slick rock, but no, green pops out everywhere.

We walk a bit further and reach a little area with rocks to sit on. A good place to take a break.

Jack stops and takes off his backpack, handing me a water bottle from inside.

"Thanks," I say, taking a drink. I screw the cap back on and hand it back to him.

"Ready? Do you need a snack or anything?"

"I'm good."

"Great. Let's keep moving then." He smiles, takes my hand, and we keep walking.

We pass a few more waterfalls, each one of them breathtaking in their own right. This is the perfect place. The perfect hike. And I wouldn't want to share it with anyone other than Jack.

The Middle North Falls has another trail that goes behind the waterfall. I've decided seeing the other side of the waterfalls are my favorite part. The water splashing my face, the mist rolling off the water as it rains down from the cliff. I love it all.

Jack stops and we watch the water pouring down for a moment. He squeezes my hand.

"This is seriously perfect. Thank you for bringing me here."

"You're welcome."

I scoot closer to him. "Do you bring girls here often?" I ask, teasing.

He shakes his head. "Never. I don't . . . I don't date much."

"Why not?" Actually, I'm not surprised. Mira said as much.

"No time, I guess. The girls at my school aren't right for me, either."

I glance up at him and he smiles. He hesitates at first, but lifts his other hand, pushing a loose strand of dark hair behind my ear. I'm sure I have lots of hair falling from my ponytail. Now that it's shorter, it's harder to keep it contained. He turns to face me, still holding my other hand.

"I don't know if I'm good at . . . all this," he says, gesturing to our clasped hands. "If you couldn't tell. Like I said, I don't date much. Or at all."

"It's okay. I can help things along," I say, laughing. I squeeze his hand then let him do the rest.

He chuckles as his hand slides slowly down my cheek, his eyes on mine.

He's going to kiss me. I know it. My whole body feels like it's on pins and needles as I wait.

I don't even know how to explain what's happening. I never imagined being kissed behind a waterfall. The soft spray of mist in the air, the sound of water splashing on the rocks. No one's around. We're very much alone. It's a perfect moment. Perfect and sweet and my body trembles in anticipation.

Much better than being kissed under the bleachers at the high school.

Lame.

He leans forward and I close my eyes just as his lips touch mine. It's a feather of a kiss, but a kiss just the same. He wraps his arms around my waist as his lips linger on mine for just a moment. My hands move around his neck, like we're dancing. It's maybe ten, fifteen seconds before he pulls away.

And it's glorious.

He doesn't say anything, just searches my face, and then I smile, my lips tingling. I want him to kiss me again, but I don't think he will. Not yet at least. He lets out a breath of what sounds like relief and squeezes my hand again before we continue on the trail.

CHAPTER 25

"You don't need scores of suitors. You need only one . . . if he's the right one."
—Louisa May Alcott, *Little Women*

We finish the hike in about four hours. I'm sure it took so long because of me, since I had to stop and take a picture of every waterfall.

Jack doesn't seem to mind. In fact, he's been more talkative and playful since the kiss behind the waterfall.

I can't stop thinking about it.

You know those kisses in the movies when the couples pretty much eat each other's faces off? It wasn't like that at all. No sloppy messes.

Just a sweet, chaste kiss that made my body tingle from my head to the tips of my toes. It was perfect. I want to kiss him again.

Like now.

Preferably not right after eating, though, since we're sitting in a little green alcove off the trail with our lunch.

"You make a mean turkey sandwich," I say before I take another bite.

"What can I say? I'm a master chef."

I laugh. "You know, you have to actually cook something to be a master chef."

"I actually do like cooking. I make dinner all the time."

"Oh yeah?"

"Yeah. I don't tend to shout it out to the world, but I do like cooking. Not really baking much, besides cookies, but cooking actual meals."

"Interesting." I will definitely be asking for a gourmet meal from him sometime soon. "So, what do you want to go to school for?"

"I haven't decided yet. I thought about being a vet, but after Ben died, I think I want to be a counselor. Like at a school or something."

"You'd be great at that."

"You think so?"

"You're a really good listener."

He laughs. "I get that a lot." He takes a bite of his sandwich, chews, looking thoughtful, then clears his throat. "I know I'm quiet. Especially compared to the people I hang out with these days. But I like observing. Watching people. When I don't have something to say, I don't feel the need to add nonsense to a conversation, you know?"

"I've never thought about that."

"I like being around people. Especially good friends. They give me a lot to think about. And when I want to say something, I'll say it, but it's not necessary when it doesn't need to be said."

"Makes sense."

He chuckles. "I've always been the quiet kid. The nice kid. Most people would hate that. I don't mind."

"You are seriously one of the nicest people I've ever met."

"I learned a lot from my parents. They're very giving, kind people. My mom especially. If anyone at church gets sick, she's taking them meals the next day. She's very thoughtful."

"She seems wonderful."

"Was it hard for you and your mom when your dad died?"

I'm so caught off guard by the question, I drop my water bottle in my lap. It spills everywhere, soaking my pants. I grab it and put the lid back on and stand, trying to wipe some of the water off.

"Seriously? Now it looks like I peed my pants."

He smiles.

"Don't you dare laugh."

The corner of his mouth twitches.

"Does it look bad?" I turn in a full circle, and when I meet his eyes again, he chuckles.

"Yeah, it pretty much looks like you peed. Sorry."

I groan. "Why do dumb things always happen to me in front of you?"

He laughs and hands me a few napkins.

"Thanks."

I pray he doesn't ask the question again. I've already lied to him enough. I don't want to make up more lies about feeling grief and acceptance for someone who has passed when they are very much alive. I have grieved for the loss of my previous life, for the loss of my father as he was, but . . . it's not the same.

I mean, in some ways, it's kind of like he really has died. But still.

He's out there. Waiting for me to write back.

"Lucy?"

Jack's voice pulls me out of me thoughts.

"Yeah?"

"You okay?"

I nod. "Yeah. Just mad at myself for spilling my water."

He reaches for my napkins and empty sandwich bag and stuffs them into his backpack. "You ready to get out of here?"

My lips quiver. I want to tell him about Dad so badly. "Jack, there's something I need to talk to you about."

He leans back a little. "Okay?"

I look at him. Really look. His expression is curious, yet full of worry. Worry about what? That I'll tell him I don't like him or something? Maybe he thinks I'll confess to having a boyfriend after all. But no, it's worse than that.

"I . . ." I can't. "Can we just stay here forever?"

He lets out a breath and laughs. "We don't need to leave yet."

I nod as I take in a deep breath of fresh, misty air and calm down. Why can't I get the right words out? Why is this so hard?

I glance around, trying to take my mind off things, make it less awkward and quiet. "You know? I could possibly live here."

"Like, right here?"

"Yes. Like, live in this park. But then I'd become someone like the guy in *Jumanji* who wears leaves for clothes and stuff."

"That would be interesting." He laughs and takes my hand again.

"It would. . . . I'm ready to go now. Promise to bring me back here, though?"

"Promise."

CHAPTER 26

"Love, she thought, must come suddenly, with great outbursts and lightnings—a hurricane of the skies, which falls upon life, revolutionises it, roots up the will like a leaf, and sweeps the whole heart into the abyss."
—Gustave Flaubert, *Madame Bovary*

We don't go straight home.

Jack drives me around Salem, pointing out all the places I should visit, even though I live here now.

Gran used to take me around town when we'd come visit in the summers, but I was younger and didn't really pay attention too much. Still, I loved riding in her old beat up car with her as she prattled on about how I reminded her of Mom when she was younger or how she wanted to teach me how to crochet. She was an amazing seamstress, but I was never interested in sewing or crocheting. I was more interested in art. I do wish I would have taken her up on her offer to teach me, though, since I could have had that small part of her with me. Maybe I'll teach myself someday in her memory.

Jack shows me the library, which makes my reader heart giddy. It's a circular building, with the words SALEM PUBLIC

LIBRARY on the front. As I watch it pass by, a thought pops into my head. I need to see if they have any information on Susan.

"Hey, could we stop by the library for a bit? I need to check something out."

He shrugs. "Sure."

"And I can get myself a library card."

"I have one if you need to use it."

I glance at him, skeptical.

"What? I do go to school, you know." He chuckles. "My mom actually made me get one."

"Thought so."

He turns the car around and, before I know it, we're pulling into the parking lot. Once the car's parked, I follow him inside.

"Do you always carry a book with you?" he asks as he holds the door open for me.

I smile. "Not always. I didn't today."

"I noticed one in your bag when we went to the beach and when we went cliff jumping. Two different books, actually."

"Yeah, I like to have one available if I get bored."

"You thought you were going to be bored cliff jumping?"

I laugh at the horrified look on his face. "No! Of course not. There's always a lull in conversation, though, and what else could fix the awkwardness of not knowing what to say than picking up a good book?"

"I can argue with that, but I think I'd lose."

"Yeah, you would."

He laughs, hard, and shakes his head. "You're a force to be reckoned with when it comes to literature."

"Yes I am. And I'm proud of it." I glance around the huge library then. The walls are a happy robin's egg blue and there are shelves and shelves of books everywhere.

"Uh ..." Jack starts. "Do you want to stand here all day or were you looking for something specific?"

I snap myself out of it and laugh. "Oh, right." I walk up to the front desk and smile at the older librarian sitting there. She has grayish hair, a cute pair of pink-rimmed glasses, and long pink fingernails.

"Hi there," she says. "What can I do for you?"

"Hi, yes, I'm new in town and I was wondering if you had a Salem newspaper collection. From like twenty-five or thirty years ago?"

"We definitely have newer issues online, but the older ones we have on microfilm. Do you know how to use a microfilm reader?"

"Actually, I do." I flush at her surprised expression. "I used to work at a library."

"Oh? That's wonderful. We're actually taking applications for a part-time position if you're interested."

"Really?" My heart flutters at the possibility of working at a library again.

"Yes, you can check it out online or read this and bring your résumé by." She hands me a piece of paper with the job description on it.

"I'll take a look at it. Thank you so much." I try to keep my cool, though I can't seem to wipe the smile off my face.

She nods and gestures for us to follow her. "Now, let's find you a computer."

She stands and leads us to a small area with a few computers that read microfilm. She hands me a stack of boxes with several dates on them, tells me to be careful with the microfilm as she watches me take a roll out of one box, and after watching me hook it up, gives me a satisfied smile and leaves us alone.

Jack settles in the seat next to me. "So, what are you looking for?"

"Just something I'm trying to figure out." I look through a few slides. I'm really not sure what date I should be looking for. I just know Mom was a teenager when whatever happened to Susan happened.

"You're pretty fascinating, you know that?" Jack says.

I blush. "Not really, but thanks." I glance at a few mores slides before taking this roll off and getting a new one. "This may take a while."

"I have nothing to do today. Take all the time you need."

I shoot him a grateful smile and get back to the task at hand.

Jack sits by me for a while, then gets bored and wanders through the library as I work, checking up on me periodically. He finally settles down to read a stack of comic books in a comfy-looking chair behind me, and I'm *not* about to interrupt. He's reading. Which makes my bookish heart happy.

About two hours later, my eyes hurt and my back is sore.

"How's it going?" Jack asks, coming up behind me and pulling me out of my groove.

"This is the last one," I say as I flip to the first slide. After a few slides later, I freeze and stare at the headline.

Tragedy at Misty Falls

Susan Kelly dead at 17 after drowning accident.

"This is it," I whisper. I lean forward, my eyes wide, and read the account.

Police recovered Susan Kelly's (17) body on Friday after an accident at Misty Falls. Several witnesses saw Susan jump off one of the smaller cliffs around 5 p.m. She went under the water and never resurfaced. Her body was found a few hours later by search and rescue teams. Susan had graduated high school in June and was planning to start working toward her teaching degree this fall. Salem School District and Salem Police Department express their condolences to Susan's family during this difficult time. Salem Police Department voices concern for cliff jumping and urge people to be cautious since lifeguards do not patrol at Misty Falls at this time.

"So, she died while cliff jumping." I say, more to myself, than to Jack.

No wonder Mom went crazy when she found out I went cliff diving. I had my suspicions, but it feels more real to have it confirmed. Poor Mom. I had no idea.

Jack leans forward to look at the screen. "Oh, that's my Aunt Susan. That's funny that you just stopped on her newspaper article."

I whirl around to stare at him. "What?"

"Yeah, she's my aunt. She died before I was born. My dad still talks about her a lot."

"You knew who Susan was this whole time?"

He shrugs. "Well, yeah, I didn't know you were looking for a Susan, though."

Susan Kelly. Of course. I'm such an idiot. "So I could have just asked you who Susan was instead of sitting here for two hours," I laugh. "Wow. I'm such a nerd. I didn't even think about asking you. But your family has lived here forever, so of course they would know about this. Ugh. I'd make a pretty lousy detective."

He laughs. "Was this something on your list?"

"Yeah, well, it was on my mom's old summer list when she was a teenager. 'Visit Susan's grave,' she wrote. I'm pretty sure they were best friends before she died, but my mom won't talk about it." I look up at him. "Do you know where she's buried?"

"Of course."

"I may have you take me there one of these days." I turn back to the computer, take out the microfilm, and go scan a copy of the article. Once I print it off, I pay the librarian ten cents and we're on our way out the door.

"That was kind of a waste of time because I could have asked you who Susan was ages ago, but I'm glad I found this article. Now I can hopefully talk to my mom about it. One of these days."

He nods and opens the truck door for me. Once he's inside, he starts the truck and pulls out of the parking lot. "So, I've been working on a few things, you know, guy list things, and I wondered, what's your favorite book?"

I smile at him. "*Guy* list things? So you *did* make a list?"

"Maybe."

"I'm actually very impressed right now."

"Good. I thought you might be. Now, answer the question."

"But that's an impossible question to answer."

"Is it?"

"Yes."

"Pick one."

I groan. "Seriously. That is the most unfair question, ever. How can I pick only one?"

"There has to be one you value above the rest."

I wrack my brain. *Pride and Prejudice? Jane Eyre?* Although, I don't love Mr. Rochester like everyone else seems to. I do approve of their marriage in the end, though. They were meant for each other. Besides the whole age difference thing.

I shudder.

"Hmm . . ." Harry Potter? I adore Harry Potter. The twists, the character development. Snape.

"You okay there?"

I look at him. "Uh . . . yeah?"

"You just look like you're getting a headache or something."

"I am! And it's your fault."

He laughs again and reaches for my hand, entwining our fingers together.

All of a sudden, my brain doesn't hurt anymore.

"Seriously, I don't know what to choose. I do have a fondness for *Little Women* and *Anne of Green Gables*, I guess."

"A fondness?"

"Don't make fun of me."

"I'm not. I was just surprised at your word usage. That's all."

"Yeah, I don't know why I chose that particular word." I frown. "I'll probably have to say *Anne of Green Gables*. One reason is because I'm named after the author, another reason, my mom loves it just as much as I do, and the third reason, it was the book that got me hooked on reading."

"Fair enough."

"So, what's on this list of yours?"

"A question for another time, my friend."

"No fair."

He grins. "One step at a time."

After spending the day with Jack, he finally drops me off at home. He walks me to the porch, and instead of asking me for a hug, he just pulls me into his arms without a word.

The world feels safe when I'm with him. Like he can take all my worries away with his quiet countenance.

There are so many worries, though. So many. Too many for him to hold.

He looks down at me, a soft smile on his face. He runs his knuckles along my cheek, my jaw. I've been waiting for him to kiss me again all day.

"You know, I always told myself I wouldn't have a girlfriend until I graduated high school."

"Why?"

"Because I'm just spending money on another guy's wife."

I'm so shocked that I burst out laughing. "Oh my gosh, that's so funny. And kind of ridiculous. What fun would it be to never date anyone?"

He shrugs. "You're right. It wouldn't be very fun."

"And is that what I am? Your girlfriend?"

He shrugs again. "If you want to be?" He shakes his head, chuckling. "I'm seriously so awkward. Sorry."

"You're fine. That's why I like you."

"Because I'm awkward?"

"Because you're real. And I'm the one who's drooled on you and knocked you into the mud and fallen on my face in front of you, among other things, so I'm pretty sure I win the awkward award."

He laughs, louder than usual.

I take his hand. "And I'd be okay with the whole girl-friend thing."

"Really?"

"Yeah. I do worry what people will think, though. Specifically Summer."

He raises an eyebrow. "Summer? Why?"

Is he so clueless about girls?

"She totally likes you."

He stares at me in disbelief. "No, she doesn't."

"She does. She told me. When we went cliff jumping, actually."

"Well, it doesn't matter. I don't think that would work."

"She's super nice, though. Like, way nice. She was totally fine with me . . . uh . . . liking you. Which is weird. She's too nice, I think."

"You want me to date her instead? Because it sounds like you're trying to talk me into it."

My eyes widen. "Oh! No, I only meant—"

He silences me with a kiss. Longer this time, turning my insides into jelly and nearly making me melt to the floor. I slide my arms around his neck, pulling me a bit closer. When he moves away a few seconds later, he grins. "Believe me. I know what's right for me."

"Okay," I say, eyes wide and feeling a bit breathless. "That's fine with me. Whatever you want."

He chuckles and hugs me once more before stepping away. "I've gotta get going."

I'm still trying to find my words, but my brain's not working.

What are words anyway?

"Thanks for coming with me today," he says.

I snap out of it. "Thanks for bringing me. Having me. Or . . . taking me." I roll my eyes, frustrated with my inability to use the English language correctly. "Just . . . thanks." My face heats and he laughs.

"I'll see you tomorrow?"

"Definitely."

I watch him go before I walk inside.

I still don't see Mom anywhere. I do hear her in the kitchen, though.

"I'm home," I yell.

She doesn't answer. She's probably furious that I left the house today without her knowing. I don't feel too bad, since I left her a note. And I texted her, too. She probably needs space from me anyway. It's not like she's ready to talk to me. She's proved she doesn't trust me and doesn't want me to know anything about her life.

I'm not ready to talk to her either, to be honest.

I go upstairs, wrap myself in a blanket, pick up my next book to read, and block out the world for the rest of the night.

CHAPTER 27

"There is nothing in the world so irresistibly contagious as laughter and good humor."
—Charles Dickens, *A Christmas Carol*

I see Jack and Mira at church. Even though I sit by Mom during our first meeting, she doesn't say a word to me.

Talk about awkward.

I don't know what to say to her. I already apologized for going cliff jumping without her knowing. And I haven't asked her about Susan again. What else can I do?

She looks ragged lately. I notice dark circles are under her eyes today, and it looks like she didn't even try to get ready. Her hair's in a messy bun, but not a cute messy. Just messy.

Mom leaves right after the prayer, and even though she asks me to come home with her, I decide to stay with my friends.

Jack doesn't hold my hand or anything today. I do catch him staring at me several times during the next hour before I go with Mira to our young women's class.

"So? How was your date yesterday?" she asks as our teacher reads over some announcements.

"It was . . . nice."

"Just nice?"

I wonder if Jack told about . . . things. "Yeah, I had fun."

"No details?"

"What details do you want?"

She shrugs. "I don't know. I just know you two are cute together and want to live my love life vicariously through you."

"Ew, that's your cousin."

"It's not like I'm attracted to him. That's gross."

"My grandparents were cousins."

Her mouth drops open. "Are you serious?"

I laugh. "No, I'm just joking."

She puts a hand to her chest. "That seriously could have been the best and weirdest story ever."

"Sorry to disappoint you."

"Don't worry. I'll dig up something else on you."

I laugh, but it's more nervous than anything. I really hope she doesn't look anything up about me. Not that she'd find anything about *me*, but she could definitely find out something about my dad if she looked hard enough. My name wasn't in the papers with his because I was—and still am—a minor.

Once church is over, Jack gives me a ride home. No kissing, since Mom's probably staring out the window waiting for me, but he does hold my hand and tells me he'll call me later.

Sundays are his family's time to be together.

We used to spend Sundays together, too.

When I walk inside, Mom's not in the living room. I wander to the kitchen. She sits there with a cup of hot chocolate of all things, the whipped cream piled high.

"Hi," I say, testing the waters.

She turns. "Made it home?"

"Yeah."

"Okay."

I slowly walk toward her, bracing myself for another confrontation, but nothing comes. "Mom, are you okay?" I sit down next to her.

"Fine."

I stare at my hands. "I'm sorry about the other night."

She closes her eyes. "It was my fault."

"I'm the one who made you mad." I think of the things I said. The reason she was so angry. The article I found. Susan went cliff jumping and drowned. Of course she was upset and concerned.

She doesn't answer, just takes a sip of her drink, whipped cream getting on her face more than in her mouth. "I'm gonna take a nap. Why don't you go read or something?"

"Okay," I say slowly.

Usually we play games or do something together on Sundays.

She takes her drink with her and goes to her room, leaving me alone.

I want to talk to her about Jack. About Mira. About a lot of things. Even maybe bring up Susan again. Talk about Dad.

But she doesn't seem to want anything to do with me.

I don't know what more I've done, but it's obviously bad. I never told her to stay out of my life or anything. I was mad, yes, but now I understand her a bit better. Not that she knows I know, but still.

Instead of sulking, I go upstairs and scroll through my phone. No messages from Ashley. I stare at my phone as I scroll through her social media accounts. She's definitely not too busy to post on those.

I sigh.

I see a picture of an ocean sunset on Oakely's account. Posted yesterday. Before I can stop myself, I call her. I haven't really talked with her for ages.

She answers on the second ring.

"Lucy," she says, her voice excited. "It's been forever!"

"I know. How are you?"

"I'm good. Just walking on the beach right now, taking some time for myself. Mom's freaking out about the wedding, so I had to get out of the house for a bit. You know how moms can be."

Oh, boy. Do I ever. "Sounds exciting?"

She laughs. "It is. Everything okay? Are you adjusting well?"

"I'm doing well enough. Things are . . . interesting without my dad here. And my mom's in a weird place."

"I'm sorry. I do know how that is, though. Why is she being weird?"

"She's just so protective. And when I do something out of her control, she gets all quiet and won't talk to me. I don't really know what to do about it. I don't know how to talk to her. I really want to tell her I'm almost eighteen and I'm not going to die every time I leave the house."

She laughs. "I'm sorry. You haven't tried talking to her about it then?"

I sigh. "No, not really."

"Maybe you should."

"Maybe."

"Made any friends?"

"Yeah, I have. They're great."

"Good. . . . Boys?"

"One."

"Will I like?"

"Of course."

"Can't wait to meet him."

It's quiet for a moment. "I wish you lived closer. I miss seeing you."

"I miss seeing you, too. You'd better be coming to the wedding still."

"I am. Of course."

"Good."

"I'll let you go. I just wanted to chat for a minute. See how you're doing."

"Thanks for calling, Luce. I promise things will get better with your mom. I've been there. It's not fun. But talking through things might help. At least, it helps me. Most of the time anyway. You just have to wait for the right mood to hit her and then attack her with your niceness."

I laugh. "Okay. I'll talk to you soon."

"Soon," she says. "Bye, Luce."

"Bye."

I sigh and glance over at my desk. After a moment, I walk over and pick up my sketch book and a pencil. I open the book, put the pencil against the paper to draw something. Anything.

Nothing.

I can't do it.

I set them both on my bed and stare out the window instead.

CHAPTER 28

"What loneliness is more lonely than distrust?"
—George Eliot, *Middlemarch*

Mira comes over the next day to get the details on my date with Jack. If that's what it actually was. He never said it was a date. There was just some . . . kissing. That's all.

My eyes widen as I remember my list. I'll have to cross off *summer romance*. Even though I'd rather have it be more than just a summer romance.

And I'm not going to tell Mira about it being on the list.

I hope he doesn't get sick of me before school starts or realize he's in love with some other girl he hasn't seen all summer, leaving me devastated with no one to love.

I'm not in love with him. Yet.

And obviously, once again, I read too many books.

Speaking of books, Mira's looking through my bookshelves again as I change out of my pajamas behind her.

"So, since you wouldn't tell me yesterday about your date with Jack, you can start today by telling me how it went."

"It wasn't a date."

She makes a raspberry sound. "Right. I'll pretend you didn't say that."

She is not going to make my denial easy.

"We had a good time. On our outing between two *friends*," I say.

"Nice try."

"Mira."

"Did you have fun or not?"

I stare at her, her mouth curved into a twisted smile. "Fine. It was . . . nice."

"Nice?"

"Yes."

She sighs, and I hope she's done asking questions. She doesn't seem satisfied with my answer though. "We need to go cliff jumping again."

"Yeah we do. That was so much fun. I was so scared."

"You did great! We go a few times each summer, so pick a day."

"We both know I'm free any time until I get a job." I don't tell her about Mom's freak-out about cliff jumping. Or the fact that she won't ever let me go again. I'll find a way around it. I have to. I understand she's scared that what happened to Susan could happen to me, but that's not the way we should be living our lives.

"So . . . did anything happen on your hike that I should know about?"

I don't answer, just focus on putting on my socks. I knew she wasn't done.

"You like him," she says, as a matter of fact.

I still don't say anything. Especially about the kiss. Or kisses. She turns then, grinning as she sees my flaming face. "Really. Do you like him?"

"Mira . . ." I don't want to discuss my love life with Jack's *cousin*. She tells him everything!

"Your silence speaks volumes," she says.

I sigh. "Fine. Yes, I like him."

A squeal erupts from her lips and before I know it, she's tackled me to the floor.

"Stop," I say with a groan.

She laughs. "I can't! I'm just so happy! You two are so cute together and I totally knew you liked him forever ago."

"I haven't even known him that long."

"I know, but the chemistry is totally there. It's been there since you first met. I was there, remember?"

I roll my eyes. "What do you know about chemistry?"

She places a hand to her heart. "I know more about romance than you think." She sighs. "I've never seen him so lovestruck before."

"Lovestruck?" I laugh. "He's not in love with me. We're just getting to know each other. We just like each other right now."

"You're in-like."

I shrug. "Sure."

"Girlfriend and boyfriend?"

"Maybe." I slap my hand across my mouth. I didn't mean to say it.

"Ha! I knew it!"

I close my eyes and let out an annoyed groan.

"Did you know he's never had a girlfriend before?"

I open my eyes. I knew he didn't date much, but he's never had a girlfriend? "Really?"

"Really. Never kissed anyone either. I take it you know how, so you'll have to teach him." She wiggles her eyebrows.

"Why would you say that?"

"You've said you've dated guys before."

I let out a defeated breath. "Yeah. Losers."

"Same."

"Why don't we have a conversation about you and Ashton now? Get the focus off of me and your cousin. Because that's weird."

She stands, helping me up, then steps away and folds her arms. "Nope. That subject is off limits."

I laugh. "Come on, Mira. Everyone knows. You're always together. You always hang out, and the way you look at each other . . ."

"He's my friend," she says, insistent. "That's it. There's nothing going on between us and there never will be anything."

I sit down on my bed as she wanders around my room, distracted.

"Why are you so against the idea?" I ask. "You two are perfect for each other."

If chemistry between two potential love interests is a real thing, they have it in spades.

"It's not that I'm against the idea, I just . . ." She trails off, staring out the window.

"Have you two dated before?" I ask, curious about their history.

"No." She sighs. "I don't want to ruin things with him."

"Why are you so afraid?"

She hesitates. "I'm just scared I'll do something wrong. Or I'll make him mad. You know those stupid love story misunderstandings in books and movies?"

Oh, boy. Yes.

"I'm the queen of those." She sits down on my bed and wraps her arms around her knees. "I'm just scared if we break up or something, we won't be friends anymore. And he's one of my best friends. I'd have a hard time with that." She laughs, but it's not with humor.

"I get it. I do. I think you two would make a great couple, though."

"You sure know how to make a girl feel good about herself."

I shrug. "If you like each other and you've been friends for a while, you already have that foundation to build on. Things can only get better. In my opinion. You just have to take a chance sometimes."

She raises an eyebrow. "You sound like a therapist or something."

"I've seen one before. After . . ." I swallow. "My dad. You know?"

"Yeah." She takes a breath. "I know." She looks like she wants to say something else but then changes her mind.

"Anyway. Back to Ashton."

She shakes her head. "Not gonna happen."

"Oh, come on! What did we just talk about?"

She stands and wanders around the room again. "It's just, the timing's off. It's not the right . . ." she trails off, staring at something on my desk. Probably Oakley's engagement picture on her invitation.

"That's my cousin, Oakley. She's getting married next month."

She shakes her head and picks up a white envelope sitting next to the wedding announcement.

My whole body grows cold as she reads Dad's neat handwriting on the front.

"What's this?" she asks, holding it out to me.

I stare at my name and address, then just like the other letters, the word *Dad* in the left-hand corner with his prison return address underneath.

"It's nothing." I stand and reach for it, but she pulls it away from me.

"Dad?" she asks, her voice sharper than I expected.

I don't say anything, just try to get the letter again, but she's too quick. She moves around my bed and close to the door. "This is dated this week."

"I can explain, just give it—"

"Lucy," she says, quiet. "Is this from your dad? Did you lie to me?"

I stare at her as her eyes shine with tears, yet she doesn't blink, doesn't let any of them fall. "Mira . . ." I start, but she shakes her head.

"All this time you've been telling us how much you miss your dad. How we are so much alike because we've both lost parents. And he's really alive?"

I let out the breath I'm holding and sit down on the edge of my bed.

"Well?" she snaps.

Her anger makes me angry. My hands clench into fists as I stare her down. "Yes, okay?" I say, my voice raising. "Yes, my dad's alive and sitting in a prison cell in Wyoming. Are you happy now?"

She frowns. "No. I'm not, actually. You lied to me. And not just a little lie. Lucy, this is *huge*. This is a huge part of your life that you totally made up! I thought we trusted each other. I thought we could talk and help each other through things. I thought we were friends!"

"I do trust you, Mira! And you are my friend. It's just . . . you don't know what it's like . . ."

Her frown deepens and she folds her arms. "Don't I?"

"You couldn't possibly—"

"My brother's been in and out of jail for drug charges, theft, and DUIs, among other things. *My* mother *died* because she overdosed on prescription drugs that helped her with her depression and pain from her medical issues."

I stare at her. I had no idea.

"And you think I wouldn't understand? You think lying about a parent being dead to someone who has actually lost a parent is funny? Were you trying to get sympathy because you thought your problems were worse than mine?"

"No!" I stand and take a step toward her. "Mira, I'm sorry. I didn't want you to think less of me. I didn't know how to tell you."

"Think less of you? Is that what this is about?"

"No! I don't know. I honestly don't really know. I wanted to tell you. I tried to tell Jack, I just . . . couldn't. I don't want to feel like I did when my dad went to prison. Everyone was so weird around me. I just want people to be my friend because they want to. To like me for me."

"Then why did you lie? I don't understand! Pretending your dad was dead to fit in? What a horrible thing to do to someone. Make someone feel sympathy toward you because you pretended to share the same loss."

"Mira, please."

"Where do you think I go every Tuesday, Lucy?"

The question stops me. "I—"

"I go to a group therapy meeting for teens. Because I can't deal with my life. Everyone has hard things they're dealing with—not just you. And I trust those people because I *know* they have my back and don't judge me for what I'm going through. They trust me too! And they *don't* lie!" She stares at me, breathing hard, tears filling her eyes. "I don't know what else to say to you right now. I need to get out of here."

"Mira, wait!"

She storms out of my room and hurries down the stairs. I trail behind her.

"Mira!"

She throws open the front door and I grab it and shut it behind me, still following her. She walks toward her car, and that's when I see him.

Jack.

He glances between us, then heads for Mira, who wipes tears from her eyes.

"What's wrong? What happened?" He looks to me for answers, but I have no idea what to say. What do I say?

Tears trail down her cheeks as she turns toward me. "She lied to us, Jack. To all of us."

"What? What are you talking about?"

"Her dad's not dead. He's in prison! She made it all up."

Jack stares at her a moment, then looks at me in confusion before wrapping an arm around his cousin. "Lucy?"

"I . . ."

"Your dad's alive?"

I take a shaky breath. I can't lie to him anymore. To them. "Yes," I say, defeated. "Yes, he's alive. He's in a prison in Wyoming."

He's quiet for a moment. I can see the struggle he's facing as he looks at me and then to Mira. "Why would you lie about something like that?"

I stare at him, not knowing what to say. "I don't know."

Mira looks so angry she's shaking. "Let's get out of here. I can't . . . I can't do this."

"Wait," I say, as Jack starts to follow, but then he gives me a look and it feels like my whole world shatters.

Disappointment.

Regret.

"Jack," I say, taking a step toward him, but he keeps walking.

He doesn't look at me again, just takes Mira's keys, puts her in the passenger side of her car, and climbs in the driver's seat.

The car starts.

They drive away without looking back.

I stare at the empty driveway for a long time before walking back inside.

I ruined everything.

Mom meets me in the entryway, concern etched on her face. "What was that all about?"

We haven't spoken, so it surprises me when she does.

"Nothing," I say, numb.

Cold.

On the verge of a breakdown.

"Lucy," she says, warmer this time. She reaches for my hand and I pull away.

"I said nothing." I walk upstairs and slam the door to my room.

We both know it's far from nothing.

CHAPTER 29

"Solitude, isolation, are painful things, and beyond human endurance."
—Jules Verne, *The Mysterious Island*

I text Mira.

Nothing.

I call her.

Nothing.

I do the same to Jack.

He doesn't answer.

Jack.

My heart hurts.

The way he looked at me? I'll never forget that face. How I lost his trust in just one small moment. And what's worse is that I had the chance to make this right. I had a lot of chances and I blew it. Those moments of weakness, when I didn't want to tell him the truth because I was too afraid of what he would think of me . . .

And now he probably thinks I'm the worst person in the world.

I put my face in my hands. They're probably talking about me now. How I'm a liar and manipulator or whatever horrible things they can think of.

I shouldn't have lied.

I write out a long apology text to send them both, but I can't bring myself to send it. Apologizing over text isn't right. They deserve better than that.

Mom knows something's wrong. She asks, I don't answer.

It hasn't been the same since I brought up Susan during our cliff jumping argument and I don't know why.

I need to fix things with her.

I don't know how.

I don't know how to do anything.

I pick up Oakley's wedding announcement. If only she were here. She'd know what to do. How to fix things. She's always had a way with words, even when there's nothing to say.

Should I call her again?

I don't want to bother her with all of this. Not now. Not while she's planning her wedding.

Days pass.

I see Jack and Mira at church on Sunday, but neither one talks to me. They don't even look at me. They pretend I don't exist. Jack catches my eye once, but his expression is sad. He looks away.

I go home early. I can't handle being invisible.

No word from anyone. Mom's not even really talking to me, even though that's all my fault now. I turned her away this time.

How do I fix this?

I see Mira and Jack riding horses, since their field is so close, but other than that, it feels like they've just disappeared and forgotten me.

I'm sure Summer is happy I'm not in the picture anymore. She can have Jack now.

My heart aches.

I shouldn't have lied.

Everyone always disappoints.

But in this case, I'm the disappointment.

I thought this summer would be amazing. Crossing things off my list, hanging out with new friends, feeling like I actually have something to get up for every day. And it's been amazing.

Until now.

Why did I have to screw things up?

I really felt like I belonged for a little while. I had friends. My mom and I had a good relationship. Our house was finally coming together, feeling like a real home.

Instead, this has turned out to be a summer of lost things.

A lost dad.

A lost mom.

Lost friends.

I've even lost myself.

CHAPTER 30

"Angry people are not always wise."
—Jane Austen, *Pride and Prejudice*

The doorbell rings a few days later. I hurry down the stairs, hoping, but not quite believing, it will be Jack. It's too soon. I doubt he'll be the one to come talk to me when I'm the one who lied and I'm the one who needs to seek him out to apologize. Still, that little bit of hope lingers as I open the door. My mouth drops open at the sight of the girl standing on the other side.

My cousin.

Oakley.

She looks beautiful. Her hair is longer, a bit lighter from being in the California sun, and her tanned skin is flawless. She looks the same, yet so, so different. She looks happy, which is the most important thing of all.

"Lucy," she says, wrapping me in a hug. "It's so good to see you."

"And you," I say. "What are you doing here?" I try to fight the tears that burn my eyes as she hugs me tighter.

"Just passing through," she says as she pulls away, wiping at her own tears.

The last time we saw each other was at Lucas's funeral. Two years ago. She'd been distant then. Pale, quiet, and oh so very angry.

"Just passing through? I doubt that," I say, chuckling.

"I just had a feeling you needed me."

I sniffled. "I do."

She smiles and gestures to someone behind her. "There's someone I'd like you to meet."

A guy with light brown hair and brown eyes steps up the porch stairs. He's in shorts and a button up shirt, with the few top buttons left undone. The metal or plastic of his prosthetic leg is black and he's wearing tennis shoes on both feet. It's amazing how far medical technology has come; he walks as though he was born with this leg.

"You must be Carson," I say, holding out a hand.

He nods and takes it, giving it a good shake. "I've heard a lot about you, Lucy. Oakley's been dying for me to meet you."

"I've heard a lot about you, too," I say, a blush creeping to my cheeks. Oakley wasn't exaggerating when she said Carson was charming and handsome. His pictures don't do him justice.

I stop my staring and clear my throat. "Come in. Mom will be excited to see you."

I motion them inside and lead them toward the kitchen. The smell of fresh baked cookies permeates the house and my stomach growls.

Mom is taking a pan out of the oven as we walk in, and when she sees Oakley, she just about drops it.

Instead of freaking out about seeing her, though, she doesn't look all that surprised. I look at Oakley as she gives Mom a conspicuous smile. I look back and forth between them. "You knew she was coming."

Mom shrugs and comes around the counter to give Oakley a hug.

"It's nice to meet you, Carson," she says, shaking his hand.

"You too, Ms. Nelson."

I stare at them. "How? Why? What?" I stammer.

Everyone laughs at my confusion.

"Why didn't you tell me they were coming, Mom?"

She just smiles. A real, genuine smile that I haven't seen for a while, and Oakley answers instead. "We know how much you love surprises."

"Um . . . no." I chuckle. "But I'm so glad you're here."

After consuming a few plates of cookies, Carson stays in the kitchen to help Mom clean up, and I motion to Oakley to come outside with me.

"Just a sec," she says. "I need to grab something from my suitcase." She runs up the stairs and I head out to the porch swing.

A few minutes later, Oakley sits down next to me. She hands me a dark blue hoodie that says Huntington Beach on the front. "Thought you might like this," she says. "It's really soft. I have like five of them in different colors."

"Thank you! I love it." I lay it across my lap, rubbing the soft material.

Oakley hands me a sand dollar next. It's beautiful, even with a few chips here and there. "I love these and thought you would, too."

"Thanks, Oakley."

I study the sand dollar. I don't know what tiny creature lives in them, but they're so beautiful and delicate. I'm afraid if I touch it too hard it will crumble to dust.

Oakley produces something else and I stiffen. It's a stack of letters. Addressed to me and unopened. Of course.

"I found these in your room when I was putting my stuff up there earlier. They were just sitting on your desk, so I looked. I'm sorry." She's silent for a moment as I stare at them in her hands. She flips through them, then sets them on her lap. "Want to talk about it?"

"No," I say, folding my arms and turning away to stare into the trees. "Where's Carson?"

"Still helping your Mom. He likes to help. And meet new people."

"He's perfect for you, Oakley."

She sighs. "We're not talking about me right now."

"Oakley . . ."

"What's going on, Lucy? When I talked to your mom, she said you weren't doing great."

I let out the breath I'm holding, still not looking at her, and laugh, though it's not funny at all. "Well, first of all, my dad's in prison. That's what's going on. Or haven't you heard yet? The whole family knows. Everyone knows."

My fingers trace the letters on my hoodie. I want to get up and go inside. I hate talking about this. Hate thinking about it. But it's Oakley. She's been through hard things, too. So I sit. And fidget. And trace. And try not to cry or run away.

"Lucy, of course I've heard. But that's not what's really bothering you." She pauses and I hear her move the letters around again. "What are all these? I don't mean to snoop, but why are they all unopened? Is there a reason?"

"They're nothing." I don't even look at them.

"Believe me. They're not nothing."

"You wouldn't understand."

She stiffened. "Try me."

"I can't read them, okay?"

I don't mean to snap at her, it just happens.

"Why not?"

"I just can't, okay? It's too soon. I'm not ready to read what he has to say to me." I put my face in my hands. "I'll never be ready."

She's silent for a moment, though I can hear her flipping through the letters. "Can I tell you something?"

"As long as it doesn't involve my dad, then sure."

She's quiet for a long time. Then, just when I feel like apologizing for being so snippy, she takes a shaky breath and starts talking. "When Lucas died, I thought my life was over. I gave up. I hated everyone and everything and was angry and bitter. Nothing would ever make me happy again. I shut everyone out. Everyone. Including you, remember?"

"Yeah, I remember. No one knew what to do for you. I'm sorry."

"No, don't apologize. It wasn't anyone's fault but mine." She waves me away. "I was just so ... angry. Angry Lucas got cancer again. Angry he stopped treatments. Angry he died and left me alone." She wipes a little tear away. "A little while after he died, my mom gave me a notebook full of letters. They were all written to me and from Lucas. I've never told anyone but Carson and my mom about them, but I thought you'd like to know. What he had to say, even in his darkest days, was just what I needed to hear. Those letters changed me. I'm a better person because of them, and all that anger melted away. Then I met Carson. He changed me, as well."

I sigh. "It's not the same."

She lets out a breath and twists her engagement ring around her finger. "I know it isn't. No one ever has the same problems or the same feelings. No one knows what's going on in anyone else's head. Or life, even. We all grieve differently and process things in different ways. But I just wanted you to know what helped me. I gave those letters a chance. I could have thrown the notebook away, hating him for dying and leaving me alone. But I took a chance and read them." Her voice cracks, and I reach out and take her hand. "I was so tired of being angry. And seeing you now, knowing what you're going through, I know you are, too."

A tear slips down my cheek now and I leave it. I feel so ... alone. Even though I'm really not.

"I'm not angry," I whisper, gathering my thoughts. "I'm . . . furious. He ruined our lives. He broke our hearts. Especially my mom's. He . . ." It takes a moment to say the words, but they eventually come out. "Killed two people. And they'll never have a chance to grow old together. Have a life. It would be easier if he would have died in that accident, too. Knowing he's alive and sitting in prison is so much worse."

"Is it?" she asks, so quiet I barely hear her.

I throw up my hands in frustration. "Yes! He wants things to be normal again. That's why he wrote those. Things will never be normal again. Nothing about my life is normal. I'm not even going to see him for *years*! How can he change things if I can't even see him? How can he make up for killing someone? Does he even feel bad about it? Is there any remorse?"

She ignores my outburst and shoves a letter in front of my face. "Have you even read one of them to see what he has to say?"

I turn away. "No."

She nods, then stands and sets the stack on of letters on my lap. She doesn't look angry. Doesn't even look hurt. She just looks at me like she feels sorry for me. Which makes me even madder.

"I'm sorry," I say. "I just . . . I don't know how to deal. Obviously."

She shakes her head. "Don't be sorry."

"I still am. You're trying to help me and I'm sorry."

"Take some time to think," she says.

"I've already thought about it. I'm not reading them."

She sighs. Then reaches for my hand and gives it a squeeze. She gestures toward the letters as she lets go. "Words are remarkable things. They can shatter you into a million pieces, or have the power to put your broken pieces back in place and make you feel whole again." She pauses. "Being broken is the worst feeling in the world. Let me know when you're ready to take a chance, to put your pieces back together. I'll be here."

She squeezes my shoulder and walks inside, leaving me alone with fresh tears.

CHAPTER 31

"Till this moment I never knew myself."
—Jane Austen, *Pride and Prejudice*

I'm in my bedroom later when I hear a knock at the door.
"Lucy?" Oakley's voice is quiet. I wonder if she thinks I'm
mad at her.

I'm not.

"Come in," I say, so quiet I'm not sure if she's heard me
until she opens the door.

I stare at my phone again, flipping through the pictures
of Mira and me, and stopping on the ones of Jack. I miss
him. And her.

"You're not afraid I'll yell at you again?" I ask as she
closes the door behind her.

"You're not that scary," she says.

I look up at her and she gives me a small smile. "Why
did you come here?" I ask. "Not that I don't want you here.
I just . . . what made you come?"

"I had a feeling you needed me. I'm not sure why. And
since we were driving up the coast anyway, we decided to
make a slight detour."

"Thanks," I say. "For visiting. I've missed you."

"I missed you, too." She sits down on the bed next to me. "I just wanted to let you know we're staying the night then leaving tomorrow. Carson wants to drive up to Seattle and spend a few days there. I've never been."

"That sounds fun."

"We're going to Florida for our honeymoon, but that's still a month away. Might as well take a vacation while we can, since we don't have school right now. I guess I *am* taking an online class, but I can do that anywhere."

"Is college hard?"

"It's different, but interesting. If you work hard and enjoy your major, it's great. You're coming to the wedding still, right? Even if you're mad at me?"

"Of course. I wouldn't miss it."

She nods. "Good. It wouldn't be the same without you there."

"And I'm not mad at you."

"Good to know."

I stare at my phone again and can feel her eyes on me. "Is that Jack?"

"Yeah. How did you ...?"

"Your mom may have mentioned him. She says something happened between you two and she hasn't seen him over here for a while."

"Yeah. I really screwed this one up."

"Still not talking then?"

"No."

"What can I do to help?"

"Nothing. I can't even do anything myself."

"Have you tried talking to them?"

I shake my head. "They won't talk to me."

"You can still fix it, I'm sure. You just have to think outside the box."

"Sometimes things are too broken to fix."

"But sometimes they're not."

I shake my head. "I've thought about how to fix this so many times, but I don't know how. I don't know how to do anything anymore. Move on. Go forward. I can't even tell my friends the truth about my life."

"So, that's what happened? You lied to them?"

"I told them my dad died when I was little." I pause, not glancing over to see the look I know is on her face. "I didn't want to tell them the truth. What would they think of me? Of him? It was just easier to lie. Or I thought so anyway." I laugh, knowing how stupid this whole thing sounds. "What kind of a person does that? Pretends her dad is dead? What's wrong with me, Oakley?"

"Nothing's wrong with you. You've just been through way too much."

I close my eyes and lean back on my pillow, taking a few calming breaths. "I don't know what to do."

"Apologizing to your friends is one thing. A first step."

"They won't listen. I've tried texting."

"Talking is much better than texting."

"I know. I'm afraid to face them in person. I hate contention."

"Me too."

"But if I do talk to them, then what? What if they don't forgive me?"

"If they are truly your friends, they'll forgive you. Communication is the first step in any relationship. I learned that the hard way with Carson. I liked keeping things in. He likes to talk. I've learned a lot from him. Good things."

I put my head in my hands. "I'm such an idiot."

"Nope," she says. "You're not."

"And then there's my dad. I'm scared—terrified to read his letters. I don't know what to say to him. I don't know how to forgive."

"You know, sometimes you don't know what to say until you're in the right moment."

"It's going to be so hard for me. After all he's done. I don't understand how my mom is just fine. She doesn't seem mad at him at all anymore."

"I'm sure she's not *fine*. She can hide emotions just like you can."

"She seems like she's forgiven him though. She's happier now. Other than when she's talking to me, I guess, because I haven't made things easy for her." I glance at her. "How can I forgive someone who has hurt me so deeply?"

"Time," she says. "You don't have to forgive everything yet. But you can start *working* toward forgiveness. You may not be able to fix everything, but holding in so much anger will eventually be too much for you. Forgiveness is hard, but necessary."

I think about the other letter I haven't read. The one from the family of the couple Dad hit. Have *they* forgiven Dad? He took actual lives away from them. Could they forgive him so easily when I can't forgive him for the same thing?

And I didn't even lose anyone.

There I go. Being selfish again. Why is this so hard for me?

I sigh. "Why do you always have to be right? You should be a therapist or something."

She shrugs and scoots next to me, leaning back on my pillow. "I'm just that awesome. But I don't want to be a therapist. There are better people for that profession. I'd get too attached to people and worry about them too much."

I lay my head on her shoulder. "Worrier."

"You know it."

We both laugh.

She slips an arm around me and gives me a squeeze. "You know you'll get through this, right? That's what Nelsons do. We overcome hard things and come out better for it."

"Most of the time," I say, thinking of the most obvious Nelson. Dad. Maybe he's overcoming things in his own way. "You're better than me at that." I glance up at her. "Do you still miss him? Your brother?"

"Every day. But I know Lucas is looking out for me." She smiles. "And you too."

"He is."

CHAPTER 32

*"Life appears to me too short to be spent in nursing animosity
or registering wrongs."*
—Charlotte Bronte, *Jane Eyre*

After everyone's in bed that night, I sit on my bed, staring
at the unopened letters. More have come in the past few
weeks, all stuffed in the same drawer as I vowed not to read
them. But then I took them out and Oakley found them.

I've been staring at them for hours, it seems, trying to
be brave enough to open one. Maybe even read it.

Anger pours out of me as I blame Dad for so many
things.

Again.

But then something unexpected hits me. A realization
I know has been inside, and have acknowledged, but I've
tried to push away every time it shows itself.

I really do miss him.

It's a truth I want to ignore. But how can I not miss
him? He's been part of my life since I was born.

Dad is not an intimidating person. He never has been.
Before, he was loving, helpful, always looking for ways to
serve others, held a steady job. He had a good heart. After,

he still had a good heart, even after all he put us through. I'll never know exactly what made him turn to the drugs, since Mom doesn't talk about it, but there must have been something there, under all the smiles, eating away at him. Something he wouldn't talk about or get help for.

I suspected depression for years, since some days he'd miss work and lie in bed all day for no reason at all. But I'll never know. Not until Mom decides to tell me.

I can't keep expecting him to be who he was before.

It's not fair to me or him.

We've both changed. For better and worse. But we can still try to have some kind of relationship. He is my dad, after all. And I'm his only daughter. I can't just wish him away when I know, deep down, I still need him.

And he needs me.

Focus on the good memories. The good outweigh the bad, even if the bad are the most recent and unforgettable.

I pick up an envelope in my trembling hand. The first one he sent, weeks ago. The week we moved here.

I slide my finger under the glue to open it, then pull the folded paper into the palm of my hand.

I take a deep breath and open it, tears filling my eyes before I even see what's written. The paper shakes in my hand, but I tell myself to be brave.

I can do this.

I can be brave.

So I read.

CHAPTER 33

"Let us never underestimate the power of a well-written letter."
—Jane Austen, *Persuasion*

Lucy,

I've sat here for days, wondering what to say to you. What to write on this clean sheet of paper, knowing you may not read it. Actually, knowing you won't read it. I know you. We are similar in how we grieve, drown ourselves in anger. I'm sorry you got that trait from me. But anyhow. I know I've disappointed you in so many ways. I know I messed up. I've let you and your mother down, especially you. I'm supposed to be the example. The person you look up to. Your dad.

All I am to you is a stranger now. And I regret that so much it hurts. There are no words to express how horrible I feel. The guilt I have to live with because of those two lives I took because I was so careless. I'll never get over it. Never. And when I saw the look on your face the last time I saw you, I knew you hated me. That look haunts me when I sleep. I'll never get over that either.

I love you.

I'm sorry.

For everything.

Dad

Tears drip down my face, off the tip of my nose, dropping on the letter. I set the piece of paper down and rip open the next envelope, wanting—no, needing—to know what it says. I didn't realize how much his words would affect me. Dad has always had a way with words, just like Oakley does. I guess it's a Nelson thing. He's always been so intelligent. So why did he waste it all on his addiction?

I sniff and wipe my eyes, unfolding the next letter.

Lucy,

You haven't written back, which is what I figured would happen. It's alright. I know how you feel about me. I just want you to know I'm doing well here. It's nice to have someone to write to. Good therapy.

The food isn't great, but it's food. The accommodations aren't great, but it's a place to live. I've been working out a bit, but you know how scrawny I am. It will take a while to get muscles. I've detoxed, which was the hardest week of my life, getting off those drugs.

Please never use drugs. Being an addict is not how I imagined my life would go. I never planned it. I met the wrong people, had some mental health issues, and it all spiraled down from there. And for that, I'm sorry. I regret it all. I had a wife and daughter who loved me for me. I should have gotten help in other ways, instead of listening to my so-called friends.

Life here is okay, but boring and uneventful. I know I need to get used to it. I'll be here for a while. Which I deserve. But it's still hard not to see you every day. You probably haven't changed a whole lot, but I'm sure there have been subtle things. Maybe your hair is different. You're taller maybe? I wish I knew. I wish I could see you. Apologize.

As for me, I no longer have a beard. I'm clean shaven, hair cut short. I actually look quite handsome. In my personal opinion.

I hope you're moving forward. Thriving. Making friends. Send your mother my love, even though she won't accept it.

I love you. I'm truly sorry. I'll always be sorry.

Dad

So he did have mental health issues. I reread the letter again, looking for anything I may have missed. He could have gotten help. He could have gotten better. I shake my head, knowing one choice messed up his entire life. And mine. I wish I could go back in time and change things. But there's no way. I reach for the next letter and open it quickly.

Lucy,

I'm going to keep writing, even if you don't write back. I hope that's okay, and I hope you won't hate me more because of it. Your silence is discouraging, but I don't blame you at all. It's my own fault and I know it.

I've heard from my brother twice. He told me Oakley's getting married. That's great for her, especially all she went through with Lucas. He was a good kid. She is too. I'm happy for her and I'm sure you are, too.

I've thought about the future a lot. I have time, you know. I thought maybe when I get out of here we could maybe get together for lunch every other week.

That is, if you want to see me.

I know you won't leave your mom alone, and you may even be married with children by then. But I swear to you, I'll be different when I get out. I'll savor the time spent with family. I'll be a good example. I'll love you, and if you have a family of your own, I want to be part of their lives.

This is only wishful thinking, though. You have every right to tell me to stay away. But I want you to know I'm going to try. I don't want to miss anything else since I've already missed so much and will continue to miss everything for the next fifteen years.

That's such a long time.

I hope you're doing well. I think of you every day. I pray you'll forgive me every day. And I'll apologize every day for the rest of my life.

I love you. I'm so sorry.

Dad

Guilt crawls through my chest, making me feel horrible. He thinks I hate him. For good reasons, but still. I open the next letter.

Lucy,

I hope you are doing well. I think of you often and hope you're enjoying Oregon. I've been sick this week, so I'm not going to write much. As always, I love you. More than anything in this world. Do wonderful things. Make good choices. Don't follow in the footsteps of your old man.

I'm still sorry.

Dad

I pick up the last letter and open it. The infamous letter that Mira saw and what brought our friendship spiraling out of control. I need to talk to her. To Jack. And most of all, I need to think of a way to write Dad back. If I can put adequate words on paper. I'm not sure I can do it. Yet.

Lucy,

I'm feeling a lot better this week. Some kind of flu crud going around here. One of the guards must have brought it in, or maybe a new guy, since it's not like we can go anywhere to pick up a stomach bug.

Anyway, I heard from your mother last week. She says you've cut and colored your hair. Purple? Sounds fun! She also told me you've stopped drawing. Please don't stop doing things on account of me. I know how much you love art. I know it's something I like, too, but don't let that stop you. You have so much talent. Don't let it go to waste.

I hope you are doing well. Your mother says you're struggling a little. I'm sorry about that. It's my fault, I'm sure. Just know that things will get better. If they can get better for me, they can get better for you.

You are confident, beautiful, and strong. You can face anything. Even backlash from people knowing your dad is in prison.

Honestly, this is the best thing that could have happened to me. I'm reflecting a lot on the past, leaving it behind me and looking toward a better future. I'm going to do better. Be better. Love unconditionally. Care about my family more.

I'm sorry it had to happen this way. I'm sorry for all I've done. I miss you more than words can say and I hope to see you again. Maybe. When you're ready. If you can find it in your heart to forgive me.

I love you.
I'm sorry for everything.
Dad

I set the letter down, wiping more tears from my eyes. I pick up a pen, grab a piece of paper.

Where do I begin?

I write.

CHAPTER 34

"Heaven knows we need never be ashamed of our tears, for they are rain upon the blinding dust of earth, overlying our hard hearts. I was better after I had cried, than before—more sorry, more aware of my own ingratitude, more gentle."
—Charles Dickens, *Great Expectations*

My pen shakes in my hand as I run my fingers over the smooth paper for the tenth time. I have no idea where to start, what to say. What do I say?

I've never had a problem with words.

But words obviously have a problem with me.

They have so much power over everything.

They cause pain.

They help heal.

They bring hope.

Oakley said the right words would just come when they were supposed to.

Then why aren't they coming?

I get up and walk over to the chair at my desk and sit. I close my eyes, begging them to reveal themselves. Wishing the letter would write itself. I pray. I cry.

Then, I write one single word.

Dad.

Tears come again, spotting the paper in a few places when I'm not fast enough to catch them.

And suddenly, the words come. They flow from my brain, all of my emotions suddenly overflowing and spilling out. Nothing holds me back. I squeeze the pen tighter.

And write.

Dad,

It's taken me a long time to process things. To get my thoughts together enough to answer you without being angry. Words have been hard lately. Not knowing what to say has been my weakness in all this. I still don't know what to say. But I'll at least try.

I'm still angry.

Part of me might always be angry. But I'm trying. I know people make mistakes. Most apologize. Some are forgiven.

I think the word that describes me right now is "trying."

I'm trying to overcome everything that has happened.

Trying to move on.

I want to thank you for trying, as well.

Thank you for continuing to write to me, even though I

couldn't bring myself to write you back until now. It will take me a while to forgive you, but I'm trying. I'm trying to focus on the good times. I'm trying to remember how much you mean to me. You were always a good dad. You were always there for me and I know you loved me. And still love me.

I'm going to focus on not dwelling on the past. I'm trying to be happier, even when my world seems to be falling apart.

Things are better now. For all of us, I think.

Mom and I are struggling a little. She's been really overprotective because of things in her past. I don't know if she's told you about Susan, but I found out she was her best friend who died after high school graduation. She won't talk about her. Won't let me do anything because of her. I want her to trust me. To let me be me. I'm not sure how to make her see that I'm going to be okay.

But I'll keep trying, I guess.

For you. For her. For myself. I'm excited to visit with you soon. Mom's planning it. I hope it works out.

I miss you.

I don't want to remember the last time I saw you. I want

to lean toward the future and help you as you put your life back together.

Sometimes we all have hard lessons to learn. Me especially.

I love you, Dad. I don't hate you. I hope you know that. And I hope you're finding some peace.

Lucy

An empty envelope sits in my drawer. I pull it out and write his address on the front, stick my letter in, and lick the envelope before I change my mind.

I'll have to find a stamp in the morning, but at least I've done it.

I wrote him back.

Now to bring myself to actually mail it. After that, I can cross it off my list. I guess it's not technically forgiving him, but it's a start. And even though the list doesn't matter, not really, I feel like a weight has lifted off my shoulders. I didn't know it was there until now, holding me down, making me feel all that hate and anger.

The list helped, even though I didn't write it just for that. I wrote it to find myself again. To help me try new things and do *hard* things, even if they felt impossible.

I set the letter on the desk next to Oakley's wedding invitation.

I run my fingers over both.

I need to thank Oakley. For lots of things.

I glance at the letter again, hoping it will start mending the broken bridge between Dad and me.

Mom's face pops into my head.

It's time to fix things with her, as well. I just have to figure out how. And when.

In the meantime, I pull out my sketchbook and dust it off. It's time to start drawing again. I'm allowed to move on and do what I love. As I flip through the pages, I find an empty one and pick up the pencil again, looking around the room for a subject.

One of my favorite things.

A book.

The pencil glides back and forth over the page and I remember why I love drawing in the first place.

It's a good feeling, realizing you've found part of yourself again.

CHAPTER 35

"It's no use going back to yesterday, because I was a different person then."
—Lewis Carroll, *Alice in Wonderland*

Oakley and Carson wait for me by the door as I hurry downstairs to tell them goodbye. Carson surprises me and wraps me in a friendly hug.

"It was so nice to meet you, Lucy," he says. "I hope we'll see you at the wedding."

"Of course. I wouldn't miss it for anything."

He smiles and puts his hand on the small of Oakley's back, pushing her forward. She hugs me tight, tears flowing again.

"It was so good to see you. It's been so long."

"Thanks for coming. I needed it."

She smiles as she pulls away. "You'll be okay?" Her hair's in a long braid today and she has it pulled over her shoulder. Bright eyes, a smile on her face. It's so good to see her smile.

I sniff, knowing my eyes are still puffy from crying last night. "Yes. I'll be okay."

She nods, hugs Mom, who has a million braids in her hair, courtesy of Oakley, and they say their goodbyes.

"See you in about a month!" I yell as they get into a Jeep outside.

Oakley waves and Carson opens the door for her, planting a quick kiss on her cheek as she climbs in.

"They're adorable," Mom says. "I totally would have dated him when I was her age."

"Ew, Mom. Don't be gross."

She turns toward me, a look of innocence on her face. "What? He's hot!"

"Mom . . ." I groan. "He's like half your age."

"I said I would have dated him when I was younger, Luce. Not now. Geez." She rolls her eyes and we both laugh as we walk back inside.

I start to go upstairs again and Mom stops me.

"Wait," she says. "I know we haven't really been talking a lot the past week or so, and I know you're struggling with something. Do you need to talk about it? I'm . . . I'm sorry I freaked that night. I'm just so overwhelmed and things just kind of put me over the edge."

"It's fine, Mom. And I'm fine. I'll figure it out."

She nods. "You're sure? I'm always here, you know."

"I know." I give her a smile and hurry upstairs. I'm still not sure how to fix things with her, and I know I need to talk to her about a lot, but I need to sit on it more. Think about what she needs from me. Say the right things.

Right now, I need to apologize to my friends.

My phone's sitting on my bed. I reach for it and send a quick text to Mira. I know she may not come, but I need to talk to her. And if she still feels any kind of friendship toward me, she'll be here.

It's time to apologize and fix things.

And I'm scared out of my mind.

I wait on the porch swing for an hour before Mira shows up. She didn't drive, just walked, which is weird. She doesn't look straight at me as she walks but finally meets my eyes when she's almost to the porch.

"I'm sorry," I say as she walks up the steps.

She shakes her head. "I'm not here for your fake apologies." Her braids are up in a ponytail today and she looks just as beautiful as ever. If only it weren't for the look on her face as she folds her arms, staring me down. She's still furious with me and I don't know if I'll be able to fix it. But I have to try.

"It's not fake. I'm really sorry. About everything. I've been thinking about what you said. That everyone has something they're dealing with. We just don't know it. I should have trusted you more. I should have told you the truth. And I feel awful about it and will apologize every single day of my life if it means we can be friends again."

She looks at me but doesn't say anything.

I stand and take a step closer to her. "I'm sorry about your mom. And your brother."

"She was a good person," she says. "Her addiction didn't define her. She didn't mean to . . ." She trails off, wiping tears from her eyes. "She was a good mom. If she wouldn't have been in so much pain . . ."

"I know. I don't doubt that she was the best mom ever. I know she was a good person by the way you talk about her. She sounds like the best."

She lets out a long, slow breath. "She was sick a lot. The doctors couldn't really give her an answer about her pain or why she was sick so much. They said it was in her head . . ." Her voice breaks and she shakes her head. "When she died, my brother Aiden didn't know how to cope. He's the one who found her. She just never woke up. Then he started taking pills, too." She sniffs and wipes a tear away. "I haven't seen him in two years. Since he stole from my dad and me and he ran after dad called the police."

"I'm sorry."

"Don't. I don't want to hear that you're sorry anymore. You don't have any idea . . ." She wipes another tear.

I sigh. "I know I don't."

She takes a shaky breath and turns to leave. "I've gotta go."

"Wait," I say, "please. Just hear me out."

She hesitates but stops and turns back around, still wiping away a few tears. After a moment, she takes another breath and folds her arms. "What do you need to say? I need to be somewhere so I don't have a lot of time."

She won't look at me.

"Mira, I just wanted to apologize, for real. My dad is a good man. Was. Is." I shake my head, trying to get my jumbled thoughts out. "He became addicted to using meth a few years ago and put our family through a lot. One night, he was driving while he was high and hit another car. The couple in the car, newlyweds, they both died and he went to prison for it."

Her mouth drops open just a fraction, but she closes it again.

"I've been struggling since we came here to tell you all the truth. When the truth came out in Wyoming, I had friends who treated me different once my dad went to prison. A few parents wouldn't let their kids hang out with me because they thought I was a bad influence. Not from anything I did, but from my dad's actions." I take a shaky breath as my eyes fill with tears. "I didn't want that to happen here. I didn't want you to react like that and think I was some convict's kid who was eventually going to take after her dad. I was afraid of feeling ashamed of who I am. Where I come from and who my parents are. I don't want to feel like that. I love my parents. Even my dad. Even with the stupid things he's done. I just don't want to be judged by his actions. That's why I lied. I didn't want to be treated differently or be an outcast because of it." I wipe a few tears away. "I'm sorry."

She stands there a moment. Then, to my surprise, she closes the distance and wraps me in a hug.

She's crying and so am I.

We've both had hard things happen. We've both had people judge us from mistakes our loved ones have made. I hope and pray we can move past this now and become close friends, and I know at that moment, I'll never lie to her again.

She steps back and wipes a few stray tears away. "Thank you. For telling me the truth. And for making me come here. I don't want to lose your friendship."

"That's why I needed to tell you everything."

"I appreciate that."

I reach out and squeeze her hand. "Can you tell me about your support group you go to? I think I might need something like that in my life."

Her eyes widen. "Of course."

"Do you think they'd let me come with you?"

"Yes, I know they would. It's been good for me to see other people going through the same thing I am. You can come with me next Tuesday."

"I'd like that."

"I'm sorry I freaked out at you. I was just so upset. You're my friend. One of my best friends, actually. I just couldn't wrap my head around why you'd lie about something so important like that."

"I know. And I deserved it. It never should have happened and it won't happen again. I swear to you, it won't. No more lies."

She nods. "I'll hold you to that." She glances at her phone. "I've got to get back home. My dad needs some help with the house today."

"Okay. Can I call you later?"

She smiles. "Yes." She starts walking away but stops. "Oh. There's someone else you may want to talk to."

My heart quickens. "I know. Jack."

"Yeah. He's ..." She trails off. "He's really broken up about it. You should go talk to him."

"Will he let me?"

"He will. Don't you know him? Even if he didn't want to talk, he'd still let you. That boy is too nice."

"I know."

She walks back over and puts a hand on my arm. "Don't worry. He still has feelings for you. I know he does. And feelings don't just go away in a week. I promise. He misses you. He's been so mopey around the stables. His parents have even mentioned it. It's been so annoying."

I chuckle at that, but my stomach tenses at the thought of talking to him. Partly because I know he's mad, and partly because I can't wait to see him again. I've missed him. "Do you know where he is?"

She shrugs and gives me a look like *duh*. "Where else would he be?"

CHAPTER 36

"I have to remind myself to breathe—almost to remind
my heart to beat!"
—Emily Brontë, *Wuthering Heights*

Jack is in the stables, exactly where Mira said he'd be.

He's brushing down Sherlock in his stall and doesn't turn when I approach, though I know he hears me.

"Hey," I say, clasping my hands together. I stop a few feet away, my whole body shaking from nerves. I'm not one for apologizing. Or contention. It takes a lot out of me and my stomach is in so many knots, I feel like I'm going to be sick.

"Jack," I say, "I'm here because I want to apologize to you." He stops brushing Sherlock but doesn't face me yet. Just stands there, listening. That's all I want him to do right now. "I never should have lied to you. To anyone. I was just so . . ." I gulp, tears pricking my eyes. "I was just so embarrassed. I didn't think anyone would understand what it's like to have an addict for a father. An addict who killed someone when he was high. Even though it was an accident, it still shouldn't have happened. If he wouldn't have been high, those people would still be alive and he'd be here and my life would be normal again."

But would it? Mom and I would still be up at night worrying if he'd be home or if the police would show up to tell us he was dead.

Would it be normal?

I know it wouldn't.

No one's life is normal. Not really.

"I was just afraid . . ." I trail off and look away, wiping a traitorous tear off my cheek.

"Afraid of what?"

His voice catches me off guard. I didn't think he'd speak to me or even look at me. Not with how mad and hurt I'd seen him the last time we were together. But his dark eyes watch me now. Curious, angry, sympathetic even.

He takes a step toward me and opens the stall door, stepping out of it and closing the door behind him. He's in front of me now, his eyes searching mine. "Afraid of what, Lucy?"

I gulp and take a shaky breath. It's harder to speak now that he's looking at me.

"I was afraid I'd lose you. And Mira. What we have. Especially you." I glance up at him. "Knowing I have a felon for a dad? What does that make me? A troublemaker, according to some of my old friends' parents. They thought I would turn out just like him, so they forbid their kids to hang out with me. And I didn't even do anything wrong."

"Does it matter now, though? You're here. And I haven't heard any rumors at all."

"People will talk when they find out. That's what people do."

He folds his arms. "Then let them talk. You need to stop caring about what everyone else thinks and focus on what *you* think and believe. That's all that matters. You. Your family. Your true friends. They are all that matter. Who cares what other people say? You know the truth and you know you'll be okay no matter what they think."

"How do I think that way, though? I've tried! I was so afraid to tell you the truth because I thought you and Mira would think the same things. My new friends finding out my dad is in prison? What would you have thought if I came out and said that?"

He reaches out, slow but certain, and links my fingers through his. "Do you love your dad?"

"Yes," I whisper, not even skipping a beat.

"Even with all the crappy things he's put you through? I assume your life has been hard, with what I know."

I close my eyes. Tears stream down my cheeks as awful memories flood back in. Staying up late, worrying for days whether or not he was alive. Hearing him and Mom fight. Knowing my life was so screwed up because of him. "Yes. I still love him. Even with everything he's done."

He takes me by the shoulders, gentle but firm, and looks me straight in the eye. "Then that's all that matters. And if you would have told me that in the first place, none of this would have happened."

He's silent for a moment as I gather my thoughts. "How can you forgive me? I'm so sorry I lied to you about it. I shouldn't have, but I was so afraid of losing everyone. And I lost you anyway."

"You haven't lost me." He brushes a strand of hair from my face and wipes at my tears. "You apologized. And I understand, now, why you lied. That would be hard. And I forgive you for it. But you have to understand something: every family has issues. No one is perfect. And when you have friends who care about you? Learn to trust them. Because Mira cares. And . . ." he gulps, "I care. Too much, I think."

He pulls me toward him and into a hug. I wrap my arms around his waist, tears falling. He kisses the top of my head. "You're going to be okay."

I feel safe in his arms. "I know."

"And you can talk to me about anything, alright? No more lies."

"No more lies. Can we start over?" I ask as I pull away slightly. His arms still linger around my waist and I don't move. "I feel so stupid."

"I don't want to start over, but I do want to figure out what was real and what wasn't."

"This is real," I say. "The stuff about my dad wasn't. That's it. Everything else was me."

"Really?"

"Yes, everything else was me. The good and the bad. And the embarrassing, unfortunately."

He chuckles. "I look forward to more embarrassing moments."

"I don't." I smile. "But I'll look forward to them anyway."

He brushes another strand of hair away from my face. "Good. Because I'm not going anywhere."

He leans down and kisses me, and I swear to myself that I'll never ever lie to him again.

CHAPTER 37

"She made herself stronger by fighting with the wind."
—Frances Hodgson Burnett, *The Secret Garden*

Jack comes over the next day, and I'm so grateful I told him the truth. I can't imagine not having him as a friend. Or more. He means too much to me to lie to him again. Or anyone else, for that matter. I won't lie again. Ever.

"So, what's next on your list?" he asks as we rock slowly on the porch swing.

"What's next on yours?" I ask, challenging him. "Or did you even really make a list?"

He surprises me by pulling out a crinkled piece of paper from his pocket. He waves it in front of my face. When I try to grab it, he pulls it away and shoves it back in his pocket.

I laugh. "You really made one, and you're not gonna tell me what's on it?"

"Did you tell me everything on yours?"

"Well, I guess not." I laugh. "I can't believe you actually made one. I'm so happy right now."

"I crossed off a few this week. Including ... reading a book."

I stare at him. "No way. What did you read? Wait. You read comics at the library."

He shrugs. "Those don't count because they were short. I wanted to read a full length novel. So I chose *Jurassic Park*."

"I love that one!"

"I do love the movie, but the book was pretty awesome, too."

I wrap my arms around him. "This is the best day ever."

He laughs again. "So, how many more things do you have to do on your list?"

"Two."

"What are they?"

"Go to an outdoor concert and visit Susan's grave."

He nods. "We can look up some outdoor concerts around town. There's always something going on in the summer. And I can take you to Susan's grave whenever you want. It's just down the street. Want to go now?"

"That sounds great." I start to stand. "Actually," I hesitate, thinking of Mom. I need to talk to her. To understand. "I need to talk to someone first. Can I call you in a bit?"

He glances at the house as if reading my thoughts. "Yes." He gives me a quick kiss and I hurry inside.

Mom's in the garage, painting shutters a pretty turquoise blue. Her dark hair is pulled in a messy bun and she has paint on her cheek.

"Need help?" I ask as I come inside.

She looks surprised, but nods. "That would be awesome. Grab a brush."

I do.

I kneel next to her and start painting the shutters closest to me. "How many coats do they need?"

"Two. At least, that's what I'm planning on. It's not too hard to cover up white."

I paint a few strokes. I don't let the silence linger, though. Too much is waiting to be said. "I know about Susan."

She glances up with wide, shocked eyes. "What?"

I'm surprised she's not angry at me for bringing her up again. She's actually keeping her cool this time. "I said, I know about Susan. Your best friend from high school. I know what happened to her. I looked her up at the library."

"Why?"

"Because I knew you wouldn't talk about it and I had to find out who she was. Oh, and she's Jack's aunt. I could have asked him the whole time."

She doesn't say anything, just stares.

"She was your best friend. The one you wrote your summer list with."

She's quiet as her eyes fill with tears. "Yes."

"Do you want to talk about it?"

"Not really."

"Please, Mom. You can talk to me about anything. You can't keep holding it in. It's not healthy and I see what it does to you. You need to talk about it."

"Where did you find the list?"

I hesitate. "In your *Anne of Green Gables* book."

"Can I see it?"

I nod then hurry upstairs to get it. Once I get back downstairs, I hand it to her.

She doesn't answer for a moment, just touches the penciled handwriting with such a sad look on her face. Then she takes a shaky breath. "We wrote this list right after graduation."

"Did you do a bunch of them before . . .?"

"We did. We finished all of them, actually. We were going cliff jumping to celebrate finishing the list the day she . . ." She shakes her head. "We wanted to do something fun. Something with our friends. Susan and I had been swimming and jumping many times. She wasn't feeling great that day, said she had a headache, but I told her to come anyway. We were celebrating the beginning of our new adult lives after all, since we'd just completed our list." She smiles, then shakes her head, her eyes cast down. "At first, we just swam. We hung out with our crushes and just had fun. Then I said we should try the cliffs."

She shakes her head again.

"She still wasn't feeling well but came anyway." Another shaky breath. "I jumped first. I waited for her at the bottom and when she jumped . . ." Her voice catches. "She never came back up."

"Mom," I whisper.

"It was my fault. I made her do it. By the time we were able to get hold of the police, it was too late. I tried and tried to find her. I almost drowned myself, but her brother saved me. He tried to find her, too."

"Wait . . . her brother was there?"

She shrugs. "We were dating at the time."

Mike. She was dating Mike. I knew it.

She keeps talking and I don't interrupt. "After Susan died, though, I broke it off. Then I moved out, much to Gran's disapproval. She and I were so close and I'm the youngest, so she had a really hard time when I left. But I couldn't stay here. Not after Susan, and with all her family living all around me."

She smiles softly. "Mike came after me, but the guilt was too much. I couldn't be with him anymore. So, I told him to leave me alone and never contact me again." A tear slips down her cheek. "I had to."

I've never thought about her being with anyone but Dad. Even since the divorce I haven't thought about her finding someone else. It's just been us three. But now that Dad's gone, she deserves to be happy again.

"Mike," I say.

"Yes."

"That explains why he was so weird when I met him the first time. He's . . . actually quite handsome. For an old guy."

She chuckles, wiping away tears. "He was."

"He is. And he asked about you."

She shakes her head. "It doesn't matter."

"Does it matter that he's single?" I don't know why I say it. It's not like I've thought much about Mom dating anyone new. But seeing her happy again? Maybe with her high school sweetheart? It's like a movie. Or a love story in a book.

Really weird though.

She stares at me but says nothing.

I sigh. "Mom. I just want you to be happy. Susan didn't die because of you. She made the choice to jump. You didn't make her do anything."

"It doesn't feel that way."

"I know, but still, she's the one who jumped. Just like you jumped. It was her choice. It wasn't your fault. You have to let it go. And I know you've been overprotective with me because of her. You're allowed to worry because you're my mom. But you can't stop me from doing everything because of it. I'm almost eighteen. I need to learn to take risks. Do things without you. Find my own way. My own job that I actually want."

"I know," she whispers. "I'm sorry."

"It's okay."

She glances around. "This place. I didn't want to move back here, but since I didn't have a lot of options, I had no choice. It was so hard for me to come back. To remember everything. To think about you being the same age. I just got carried away, I think. I'll try to be better, Lucy. I promise." She closes her eyes.

"Thank you."

She nods and glances up at me. "I still haven't visited her grave."

I grab her hand. "I can go with you, if you want. When you're ready. Jack knows where it is."

She nods and gives me a small smile as she squeezes my hand.

"And I'm sorry about Dad. He's disappointed you so much. Both of us. It's not fair."

"I still love your father. The part of him I fell in love with, anyway. I tried to work things out. But sometimes people change too much and you never know if they'll ever come back. That's why I left. I couldn't change him back. He's the one who needed to choose to change."

"And he didn't."

"No," she says.

"Do you think he'll ever be the same as he once was?"

"I don't know. I just want him to be a father to you. That's all I ever wanted."

"Kind of hard if I can't even see him."

"I know. But you can do something about that."

"What?"

"Write him back. Oakley told me you read his letters. Now you just need to answer him. Start a relationship. Forgive him."

"I know." I fiddle with my paint brush. "And I did write him back. I just need to mail it."

She blinks in surprise. "Really? You did?"

"Yes."

"I'll mail it tomorrow. If you're okay with that."

I let out a breath. "Yes. I think I am." She reaches for my hand again and gives it another squeeze. "So, no dating for you then?"

She shakes her head. "No. Not now at least."

"What about me?" I smile.

"Jack?"

"Yeah."

"Is he good to you?"

"Yes. Too good."

"Then go for it."

"Maybe you and Mike can double with us one day?" I hesitate. "That would be super weird. My mom dating? Gross."

"Yes. It would." She rolls her eyes, then pulls me into a hug so fierce that I know I'll never doubt how much she loves me ever again.

CHAPTER 38

*"It's in vain to recall the past, unless it works some influence
upon the present."*
—Charles Dickens, *David Copperfield*

The cemetery is quiet as Mom, Jack, and I make our way
down the path toward Susan's grave.

Mom's quiet.

I'm thoughtful.

It's been so long since Susan died, but by the look on
Mom's face, no less difficult.

We walk up a small hill and see a person standing near
a tree, looking at a small headstone underneath. It's not
showy or extravagant, but small, clean, and cared for.

"I didn't know Mike would be here," Jack says, watching his uncle bend down and scrub something off the
headstone.

"Mike?" Mom says.

He looks up, his jaw dropping slightly as he sees us. He
sets the cloth down in the grass and stands, stepping toward
us.

"Jack, Lucy," he nods toward us, then his eyes linger on
Mom. "Ana," he says, soft, unsure.

"It's been a long time," Mom says.

He nods. "It has." He hasn't taken his eyes off her, and I swear she hasn't blinked.

I glance between both of them, since the silence is deafening. It's a little uncomfortable seeing her stare at him like that, so I pretend to clear my throat. "Um, my mom wanted to see Susan's grave. She still hasn't seen it."

He nods again and steps back, letting Mom have access to it.

She doesn't move.

"Mom," I whisper, nudging her to take a step forward.

She shakes her head, her breathing heavy. "I . . ."

I shoot a worried glance at Jack. I'm not sure what to do. I can't force her to walk over there, but I don't want her to just stand here either.

As I raise a hand to touch Mom's shoulder, Mike steps forward, holding out a hand. "It's okay, Ana. It's okay."

She stares at his hand and shakes her head. "It's not," she whispers.

He takes a step closer to her, then another, until he's standing right in front of her. "Come on. You don't have to go alone." He's so kind. So gentle. So patient. He reminds me a lot of Jack.

"Ana," he says softly. Mike holds out his elbow, and after hesitating only a moment, Mom slips her hand through it. Her knuckles are nearly white as she hangs onto his arm. Mike doesn't seem to mind, though, and leads her to the grave.

As I watch them, Jack's hand finds mine and he pulls me back a few steps, allowing them some space.

They stop. Mom lifts a hand to her mouth as she reads the headstone's inscription and lowers herself to her knees. Mike kneels down next to her, his arm still around her as her silent cry turns to a sob.

"It's okay," Mike says. "She's okay."

Mom shakes her head and Mike pulls her closer. She wraps her arms around him and sobs into his shoulder.

We back away more, letting them grieve together.

"They were both there when she died," I say, as Jack squeezes my hand. "She's had such a hard time letting it go. I can't imagine seeing my best friend die." Then I remember Jack's best friend died. I pull him into a hug, wrapping my arms around his waist and leaning my head against his chest. "I'm sorry about Ben."

He strokes my hair, his voice full of emotion when he speaks. "He's buried right over there."

"Do you want to visit him?"

He shrugs. "I've been there a lot, but yes, I'd like to show you."

I step away from him but still hold his hand as he leads me to his friend's grave.

He stops in front of one with a bunch of flowers set around it. "His family keeps up on it pretty well. There are always fresh flowers here, almost every week."

I look at the inscription. Benjamin Eric Williams. He was only sixteen.

Jack brushes a few strands of old grass from the head-stone, left there by the wind. He takes my hand and stands up again. I squeeze his hand and we turn back toward Mom and Mike.

They're sitting in the grass now, talking softly. Mom's still wiping her tears, but she's not sobbing anymore.

"He never married."

"Mike? Really?"

"He always told us the one he wanted slipped away from him. He's never looked twice at another lady. Not that I've noticed. And there have been plenty of women who have been interested. Some of the riding students' moms even." He shivers and I laugh.

"He's been in love with her this whole time," I say.

"Looks like it."

"That should go in a book. I mean, if they work out. My mom's still working things out, though. She's had to deal with a lot of hurt over the past five years."

"Well, he's waited this long, I suppose."

"Yeah." I stare at Mike, rubbing Mom's back, his expression so tender as she talks. "He has."

CHAPTER 39

*"I'm not a bit changed—not really. I'm only just pruned down
and branched out. The real ME—back here—is just the same."*
—Lucy Maud Montgomery, *Anne of Green Gables*

A letter arrives from Dad a few days later. I hurry upstairs
to open it, happy with how things are going but still a little
nervous of what the contents contain.

Lucy,

Thank you so much for writing me back. I've missed talking to
you so much. You brightened my spirits when I received your letter
and I can't count how many times I've read it. Thank you. From the
bottom of your old dad's heart. Thank you for still caring and calling
me Dad.

As for your mother. She's gone through some hard stuff.
Especially with Susan. Don't be too hard on her. She's just looking
out for you because she loves you and worries. She'll come around.

I enclosed a sketch of the Rocky Mountains. I've missed drawing and I hope you'll send me some of your work, too. My cell is pretty dull.

Oh, and I was going to ask you about your friends. Tell me all about them. I want to know everything.

I hope you're doing well. I pray for you. I love you. I miss you.

Dad.

I hang the drawing of the mountains on my wall and open my drawer to pull out my sketchbook when I notice an envelope peeking at me.

From the family. The family Dad killed.

"You still haven't read that?"

I glance at the door where Mom's leaning against the door frame. "No."

"How about we read it together?"

I nod, my stomach in knots.

She sits down on my bed and pats the space next to her. I join her and hand her the letter.

Dear Lucy,

I know you didn't know my daughter and her new husband, but I know the pain you're feeling. Your dad made a mistake and my daughter was in the wrong place at the wrong time. I know you're young. I know you're struggling with the pain of having your dad taken from you and know that I'm struggling with not seeing my daughter again. But through all this, I want you to know:

None of this is your fault.

I sought your name from your mother because of how young you are and I know how young minds think. They think everything is their fault. That the actions of their loved ones are because of something they did, or something they didn't do.

Please know I hold no ill will against your family. This was an accident. It was not malicious in any way. I forgive your father, and if you haven't done the same, you should, too. Addiction causes unbearable heartbreak for all parties involved, and I pray for you and your family that you can find healing, hope, and most of all, love.

All my love,
Cynthia Gordon

There are no words as we finish the letter.
All I can feel are the emotions of her words.
Healing, hope, and love.

CHAPTER 40

*"To love or have loved, that is enough. Ask nothing further.
There is no other pearl to be found in the dark folds of life."*
—Victor Hugo, *Les Misérables*

The waves crash onto the beach, singing their beautiful watery song. I sit in a crowd of maybe fifty, watching my dearest cousin walk down the aisle toward her true love. She's dressed in white, a fitting dress that hugs her slim curves. It's elegant and classy.

Oakley gives me a wink as she passes, and I squeeze Jack's hand. He sits next to me on one side, Mom on the other.

Her dad walks her down the aisle, and Oakley's mom sits in the front row next to a woman with long curly hair. I've forgotten how much my uncle looks like Dad. They are brothers, after all. Dad is skinnier, shorter. But they do resemble each other.

An ache forms in my chest as I think of him. He would have loved to be here today to support his brother and his niece.

"You okay?" Jack asks, leaning closer to me.

I nod.

He shifts, putting his arm around my shoulders and grabbing my hand with his other hand. He smiles, reassuring me that everything's going to be okay.

I wonder what it would be like to have Dad see me get married one day. He won't be able to, of course. I would like to be married sooner than he's out of prison. I wonder, though, what he'd say if he could be there.

I glance at Mom, who's sitting next to Mike, holding his hand. He sits up straight, no cowboy hat, which is weird, and she leans against him.

They have both been through a lot.

We all have.

I'm surprised Mom is okay with dating so soon, but Mike is growing on me more and more. He makes her happy, and I love seeing her happy. I'm okay with it.

The ceremony starts as Oakley walks down the aisle, the bottom of her white slim gown flowing around her feet from the slight ocean breeze. She's by herself; her Dad sits and watches from the front row and they have no wedding party lined up either. She's always liked things simple. She's also not one for tradition.

Carson's all smiles as she reaches him. He's dressed in a black tux. Both are barefoot in the sand.

I try to listen to the words of the bishop who marries them, but my mind keeps wandering, thinking of when and if I'll marry. If I'll want to live somewhere like this. Somewhere where the light touches the ocean and spreads its fingers, illuminating everything in its path.

Oh, how I'd love to see that every day.

I look back at Oakley, at how happy she is. She and Carson haven't taken their eyes off each other. And for good reason. They both look amazing.

As I try to pay attention to the ceremony, a guy in front of me chuckles and the girl next to him elbows him in the ribs. I recognize her, I think. Emmy. Oakley's best friend, from what I can remember. We had sleepovers together when I'd come into town to visit when we were younger.

The guy chuckles quietly as she whispers something in his ear, then he pulls her against him and kisses her temple.

Emmy wouldn't remember me, but I do remember her. She had a thing for Lucas. At least that's what Oakley told me. It looks like she's found someone new, which is a good thing. She looks happy.

There's another girl, sitting next to Emmy, whom I also recognize. From magazines, actually. She's Jaxton Scott's girlfriend. Mia, I think? He's the ex-lead singer of Blue Fire so everyone knows him. And up front with an acoustic guitar in hand is Jaxton Scott himself. He played the music as Oakley walked down the aisle.

He's even hotter in person.

I have no idea who knows him or how they managed to get him to play at Oakley's wedding, but I'm excited to hear him sing some of his songs at the reception after. He has a beautiful voice, which he revealed when he went solo. And even better? I can cross that off my list. Attend an outdoor concert. Done and done.

Since Jack counts as my official summer romance, I crossed that off a while ago. And hopefully we'll have a romance that lasts much longer than that.

My list is complete. It feels so satisfying.

Jack squeezes my hand and gives me a look as he catches me checking out Jaxton.

I just shrug and he chuckles.

"I know pronounce you husband and wife," the bishop says. "You may kiss the bride."

Carson leans down and Oakley pretty much jumps on him as they share their first kiss as a married couple. The crowd chuckles as they nearly make out in front of everyone, then they stop, Oakley putting her hands to her lips, her cheeks red.

Carson doesn't seem phased at all.

Jack kisses my cheek and I lean into him, watching the happy couple as they raise their entwined hands in the air and everyone cheers.

"This is perfect," I say as Oakley and Carson move down the aisle again, heading toward the reception area, which is further down the sand. "I may have to buy a beach house. Want to join in?"

"Now?"

"In a few years." I smile. "After we graduate, of course."

"I'll think about it."

"Yeah, I don't know if I could get you to leave your horses."

He laughs. "Probably not."

"It's okay. They're growing on me, too."

Jack kisses me and all thoughts of moving to California fly out the window.

"Hey. Cool it," Mike says. "We really don't need to see that."

"*Luce*. People are staring," Mom says. Then she winks at me and squeezes Mike's hand.

We both laugh as we join the others for the new couple's reception.

Jaxton Scott's voice echoes over the beach, and Oakley and Carson slow dance even though the music is really not a slow song. I see Jaxton's girlfriend, Mia, dancing with a girl who looks exactly like her. Her sister maybe? Mia's eyes meet Jaxton's and he winks at her.

But my eyes go back to Oakley, even as Jack takes me in his arms.

It makes my heart happy to see her so happy. To see how much she's overcome, ever since Lucas died. He'd be happy for her. And I know he's here with her tonight.

I look at Mom and know she's happy as well, even if her heart is still a little broken. Mine is too. I laugh as Mike twists Mom around on the dance floor, though. He's loved her since high school and never stopped.

As I dance with Jack, swaying slowly in his arms as a new song starts, I realize that even though things aren't perfect and my family is a little different, I still have people I care about. And those people care about me. Mom, Dad, Jack, Mira, Oakley. And so many others.

I can't be afraid to let people in. I've learned to trust those I love more, even if it's hard. It pays to be kind. You never know whose lives you'll touch with just a simple smile. Life is short. I need to remember to tell those I love that I do love them. Lucas did. And he's left such a beautiful mark on our lives because of it.

I've realized the past few months that I need to love my family no matter what. Even if my family, and my heart, is a little or a lot broken. No one's family is the same. No one's family is perfect. I never have to be ashamed of my story, no matter how hard it may be. We just need to hold on to one another when things get hard and not let go. And it's okay to be angry once in a while. But forgiveness is key.

Dad and I write every week now. Sometimes it's hard stuff we talk about, other times it's light. But what matters is we're writing. Communication, like Oakley said, is everything. We're working on our relationship, and it makes me happy to have him in my life again, no matter how far away he may be. I know he loves me and I know he cares. Things will never be the same, but we'll figure it out. We just have to keep moving forward and not dwell on the past.

Also, I'm not going to be afraid to fall in love. Even though my parents didn't work things out, there's hope for *my* future. Because I'm not *them* and I have my *own* story. My life is my life, and I can do whatever is right for me. I can dance like no one's watching, enjoy quiet nights watching the stars, cliff jump like nobody's business, read as many books as I want, ride a horse even if I can't get on myself, and most of all, love fiercely and deeply, without restraint or the thought of what others may think.

I haven't told Jack those three special words yet, but I feel like they'll be used frequently in the future.

Sooner, rather than later.

The End